The
ITALIAN
DAUGHTER

The
ITALIAN
DAUGHTER

Soraya Lane

**GRAND
CENTRAL**

New York   Boston

Copyright © 2022 by Soraya Lane

Reading group guide copyright © 2023 by Soraya Lane and Hachette Book Group, Inc.

Cover design by Leah Jacobs-Gordon. Cover images by Shutterstock. Cover copyright © 2023 by Hachette Book Group, Inc.

Grand Central Publishing
Hachette Book Group
1290 Avenue of the Americas, New York, NY 10104
grandcentralpublishing.com
twitter.com/grandcentralpub

Originally published in 2022 by Bookouture, an imprint of StoryFire Ltd.
First Grand Central Publishing edition: December 2023

Grand Central Publishing is a division of Hachette Book Group, Inc. The Grand Central Publishing name and logo is a trademark of Hachette Book Group, Inc.

The publisher is not responsible for websites (or their content) that are not owned by the publisher.

The Hachette Speakers Bureau provides a wide range of authors for speaking events. To find out more, go to hachettespeakersbureau.com or email HachetteSpeakers@hbgusa.com.

Grand Central Publishing books may be purchased in bulk for business, educational, or promotional use. For information, please contact your local bookseller or the Hachette Book Group Special Markets Department at special.markets@hbgusa.com.

Library of Congress Control Number : 2023026367

ISBN: 978-1-5387-5695-9 (trade paperback)

Printed in the United States of America

LSC-C

Printing 1, 2023

For my editor, Laura Deacon. Thank you for believing in this series from the very first moment I pitched the idea to you. I will be forever grateful for the opportunity.

AUTHOR'S NOTE

Dear Readers,

In my home country of New Zealand, we experienced some of the strictest lockdowns in the world during the pandemic, so in 2020 I found myself spending weeks at a time at home, dreaming of all the places I wanted to travel once our international borders reopened. That was when I began to dream of ideas for a series that could be set in beautiful locations around the world; I wanted my readers to remember what it was like to travel, to be around people, to fall in love . . . and so The Lost Daughters series was born!

I sat down one day with a notebook and filled it with the stories of eight women in the present day, and eight women in the past. When I stopped scribbling notes, very late that night, I knew I had created what would become an eight-book series that would take place all over the world.

This first novel in the series, *The Italian Daughter*, truly feels like the book of my heart. As I was writing it, I was right there with Lily as she fell in love, as she worked on the vineyard and discovered Italy, and my heart broke as I wrote parts of Estee's story. When I sat down to write the second novel, *The Cuban Daughter*, I felt the same all over again. Quite simply, they feel like the stories I was supposed to share, to bring love, happiness and hope to readers all around the world.

I hope you enjoy reading *The Italian Daughter* as much as I loved writing it, and that you fall in love with Lily, Estee and, of course, Italy.

With love,
Soraya x

PROLOGUE

LAKE COMO, 1946

ESTEE

Felix reached into his jacket, and Estee's breath caught in her throat.

"Estee, I bought this ring the day after I saw you on stage at La Scala, all those years ago," Felix said, holding a little red velvet box. "You're the only woman I've ever loved."

She wanted to see it so badly, wanted to drink in the sight of the diamond he'd chosen for her, but instead she reached for his hand and gently closed it over the box. *He's still engaged to another woman.*

"No," Estee whispered. "It's not the right time. I want you to propose to me when you're truly free to do so."

His eyes never left hers as he slid the box back into his pocket. "May I ask you one thing?"

She nodded. "Of course."

"If I'd asked you first, would you have said yes?"

The tears that had been missing earlier suddenly filled her eyes. "Yes, Felix. A thousand times over, *yes*. You're all I've ever wanted."

1

LONDON, PRESENT DAY

Lily pushed open the door to her flat and took a step inside, hauling her suitcase and duffel bag behind her.

"Hello?" she called, nudging the door shut with her foot as she dropped everything to the floor.

When she didn't receive a reply, she took a few more steps, looking around and realizing that nothing had changed in the four years she'd been away from home. Not the warm-white walls, the plumped-up cushions on the sofa or the gold mirror hanging above the fireplace that was a buffer to the countless photo frames crammed onto the mantel.

Lily paused to glance at them, seeing her own wide smile beaming back at her from most of them. She reached out to touch the one of her dad, tracing her thumb across his face, before moving on to the one of her mother and realizing just how much she'd missed her.

She walked through to the kitchen, knowing instinctively that her mum wasn't in the house without having to look further. She saw a note on the bench and reached for it, leaning back against the counter as her eyes ran across the words.

Can't wait to see you, darling, but I've decided to spend the next few weeks in Italy since the weather is so beautiful right now. See you there? Love, M.

Lily laughed and dropped the note. *Here I was expecting a long-awaited reunion, and she's gone to Italy!* She couldn't blame her, though; she'd had to make a life for herself without her only daughter once Lily had moved abroad, and she loved that she was happy.

She saw a pile of unopened envelopes discarded near the toaster and she reached for them, expecting them to be for her. She found a few addressed to her mother, but it was the one at the bottom of the pile that caught her eye.

To the Estate of Patricia Rhodes.

Lily turned the envelope over in her fingers, wondering why her mother wouldn't have opened something addressed to the estate of Lily's paternal grandmother. She noticed the official stamp from a law firm and slid her nail under the seal, deciding to take a look as she yawned, the jet lag from her twenty-two-hour flight starting to catch up with her. It must be almost midnight where she'd been living, so it was no wonder she was feeling tired.

To whom it may concern, in regard to the estate of Patricia Rhodes.

Your presence is requested at the offices of Williamson, Clark & Duncan in Paddington, London, on Friday, 26th August, at 9 a.m., to receive an item left to the estate. Please make contact with our offices to confirm receipt of this letter.

Kind regards,

John Williamson

Lily rubbed her eyes and reread the words. Her grandmother had passed away when Lily was a teenager, more than a decade ago, and seeing her name sent an unfamiliar shiver through her. She'd adored her grandma; she was one of the most loving, kind women she'd ever known, and she guiltily realized how long it had been since she'd truly thought about her compared to how often she thought of her dad. She smiled as she remembered going to visit her, how often they'd sit in the sun drinking tea as Lily recounted all her problems as a teenager to her.

She reached for her mobile, quickly sending an email to the solicitor to ask for more information. *They must have the wrong person. I would know if there was anything unresolved about her estate, wouldn't I?*

Lily opened her eyes. It took her a few moments to figure out where she was, the high white ceiling initially unfamiliar as she stared up, before pushing herself up onto her elbows.

She eventually swung her legs off the bed and ran her fingers through her hair as she attempted to untangle it. The room was dark, the only light filtering in from the hall where she'd obviously left the light on, and as she glanced at the clock beside her bed, she could see that she'd been asleep for hours. It was almost four a.m., which meant she'd slumbered through most of the day and night, and she didn't feel any better for it, her head even groggier than when she'd first lain down.

She wandered into the bathroom and splashed water on her face, staring at her reflection in the round mirror above the sink unit. Without makeup on, she could see that the bridge of her nose and the middle of her cheeks were smattered with light freckles, an ode to the fierce sunlight in New Zealand where she'd been living and working. She touched her fingertips to her skin and smiled, liking her new sun-kissed look. Combined with her long, dark, untamed locks, she looked more beach than city girl now, and she liked that, too. It was a more relaxed her; a version of herself that it had taken years to find, and she didn't want to give that girl up just because she'd moved back home to London.

Lily scooped her long dark hair up and twisted it into a top-knot, padding through to the kitchen to look for her phone and finding it on the counter where she'd left it. She scanned her emails and saw one from a former colleague, along with a photo of the vineyard where she'd worked, the grapes covered with netting and the grass tinged white from the frosty weather. She smiled, imagining herself back there, getting her daily coffee when the restaurant opened, staring out at the rows and rows of vines that now stretched as far as the eye could see. Lily sighed. Perhaps she should have stayed in New Zealand instead of taking the summer position in Italy, but she'd always promised herself that she needed to get as much experience from different regions as she could before settling anywhere.

She went back to her inbox, scanning for anything interesting, and saw there was a reply from the law firm.

Dear Ms. Mackenzie,

Thank you for making contact. We appreciate that the contents of our communication with you may have seemed mysterious, but we feel it would be best to discuss this with you or another member of your family in person. Please confirm that you will be able to attend the appointment on Friday, otherwise we will arrange another time to meet with you.

Kind regards,

John Williamson
on behalf of the estate of Hope Berenson

Hope Berenson? Lily's brow furrowed as she turned the name over in her mind, trying to figure out whether she'd heard it before or not. It didn't sound familiar, and she only wished her mother were there to ask. Perhaps it was someone from her grandmother's past; maybe someone had left something to her in their will, not realizing she'd long since passed away. She only hoped it wasn't some old knickknack that she was going to have to cart home with her after the appointment.

Lily set her phone down and decided to make coffee, desperately in need of caffeine to help her wake up.

* * *

"Darling! It's so good to hear your voice!"

Lily laughed, pressing her phone to her ear as she struggled to hear her mother's raspy voice later that day.

"I can't believe you just decided to go to Italy!" Lily said. "I was half expecting a welcome home party." She tried not to sound too crestfallen that she'd returned to an empty apartment—if her mother was happy, then she was happy. She hadn't met her mother's new partner yet, but they certainly seemed to have a wonderful lifestyle.

"Darling, you hate being the center of attention, I was hardly going to throw you a party."

She was right. Lily did hate it, while her mother thrived on it. She'd always wondered if her mother's extravagance had influenced her more timid, introverted nature.

"When are you here? Will we see you at Lake Como?"

"I'm arriving in a couple of weeks. It'll be so great to see you, although it might only be for a night or two."

"Wonderful! Now I have to go, darling, we're about to board a beautiful yacht for the day, but are you sure you can't change your flight and come earlier to spend more time with us?"

Lily shook her head, even though her mother couldn't see her. She was looking forward to traveling through Italy; it was somewhere she'd always wanted to visit, but she didn't want to be in the thick of tourists. She couldn't wait to soak up the culture and walk through the vineyards, inhaling the fresh air and meeting the people responsible for harvesting and making the wine. She wanted to discover little restaurants and rub shoulders with locals at quaint markets, not add to the throng of fans at Lake Como trying to get a glimpse of George Clooney. Which, funnily enough, was exactly what her mother would like to be doing.

"I have some things to do in London first, so I won't be able to change it, but I can't wait to see you," Lily said. "Oh, and before you go, does the name Hope Berenson mean anything to you?"

"No, why?"

"It's just there was a letter here, from a lawyer, addressed to Grandma's estate."

"You know what I'm like with mail, darling. I must have forgotten to open it."

"It's fine. I'll find out what it's all about and let you know."

"Ciao, bella!" her mother singsonged, before the line went dead.

Lily held the phone for a moment, imagining her mother in one of her brightly colored kaftans, dripping with jewelry as she stepped onto some beautiful boat. She was truly happy for her. She'd always been a wonderful mum, always putting her first as a child and holding everything together after Lily's father had died, focusing on them as a little family until Lily had gone off to university. And as grateful as Lily was that her mother had met someone, she was also nervous about meeting the first man who'd captured her mother's heart since her dad had died.

"Have fun," she said to the phone as she set it down, deciding to go and take a shower. She turned the tap on in the bathroom and waited for the water to run hot, steam filling the room, still turning over the name Hope Berenson in her mind as she shut her eyes and let the water run over her face and down her body.

She had two days to wait until the appointment, and the curiosity was killing her.

3

Lily sat in the waiting area of Williamson, Clark & Duncan, a magazine perched on her thigh as she pretended to read it. She glanced up when a young woman came in, watching her as she stood and spoke to the receptionist in hushed tones.

Before the woman turned, Lily quickly dropped her gaze to the magazine again, not wanting to be caught staring. But it was the oddest thing; there was only one man sitting, waiting. The rest were all women of a similar age to her, flicking through magazines as they silently sat.

She looked at her watch and shifted in her seat, at the same time as a voice caught her attention.

"Excuse me, everyone, and I apologize for addressing you all as a group, but could Lily, Georgia, Claudia, Ella, Blake and Rose please follow me."

Lily exchanged glances with some of the other women, wondering what on earth was going on.

"Do you have any idea what all this is about?" Lily whispered to a pretty blonde woman who'd fallen into step beside her.

The blonde shook her head. "No idea. I'm actually starting to wonder why I came at all."

"We're too curious not to, I suppose," another woman said, and Lily smiled as she caught her eye. "Perhaps we're here to inherit millions, or else we're about to be kidnapped. Either way, I'm secretly convinced it's a scam."

Lily laughed. She was fairly certain that they weren't going to meet a grisly end at a glass-fronted law firm with offices in Paddington, but she certainly shared her skepticism.

When they finally stepped into a large conference room, they were ushered to seats, with a well-dressed man in a gray suit positioned at the head of the table. To his left was a woman in her mid-thirties. She was impeccably dressed in a silk blouse and high-waisted black trousers, her hair pulled back into a tight ponytail, but despite her polished appearance she seemed nervous, her eyes wide.

Lily sat as the assistant who'd directed them into the room passed out sheets of paper. No one touched the pastries and coffee that had been placed in the center of the table, even when the assistant invited them to take something.

"I'd like to welcome you all and thank you for coming," the man said, standing and smiling at them. His hair was gray, a shade lighter than his suit, and he appeared younger when he addressed them. "You'll notice that there are six of you here today, and although I know it's highly unusual to be invited to an unexpected group meeting, it made sense in this case to have you all together."

Lily studied him, still none the wiser about what was going on. She cleared her throat, tempted to simply get up and walk out, but her curiosity got the better of her once again.

"I'm John Williamson, and this is my client, Mia Jones. It was her suggestion that I summon you here today, as she's following the wishes of her aunt, Hope Berenson. Our firm also represented her aunt many years ago."

Lily reached for the paper in front of her, her fingers worrying the edges as she listened.

"Mia, would you like to take over now and explain further?"

Mia nodded and stood, looking nervous, and Lily sat back in her chair to listen.

"I'd also like to thank you all for coming today, and I apologize for my red cheeks. I'm not used to speaking to so many people at once." She gave a worried-looking little smile. "I have to confess I've been nervous all morning."

Lily smiled, and it was almost as if everyone collectively exhaled, the room instantly feeling more relaxed after her admission.

"As you've just heard, my aunt's name was Hope Berenson, and for many years she ran a private home here in London called Hope's House, for unmarried mothers and their babies. She was very well known for her discretion, as well as her kindness, despite the times." Mia laughed, looking nervous as she glanced around the room. "I'm sure you're wondering why on earth I'm telling you all this, but trust me, it will make sense soon."

Lily leaned forward. What could her grandmother have had to do with this Hope's House? As far as she knew, she'd only had the one child—her father. Was there another child out there in the world, from her grandmother's younger years? Or did the connection go further back?

"The house has stood derelict for many years now, but it's scheduled to be demolished soon to make way for a new housing development, so I went back there to take one final look at the place before it came down."

Lily glanced at the other women around the table, all staring at Mia, most with their brows furrowed or eyebrows raised, as if they, too, were trying to work out their personal connection to this house she was talking about.

"What exactly does this old house have to do with us?" a young woman with chestnut hair seated across from Lily asked.

"Sorry, I should have started with that!" Mia said, looking embarrassed as she moved out from her chair and crossed the room. "My aunt had a large office there, where she kept records and such, and I remembered how much my own mother had liked the rug in that particular room. So I decided to roll it up and see if I couldn't use it somewhere instead of it being thrown out, only I saw something between two of the boards when I pulled it up. And me being me, well, I had to come back with something to pry them up and see what was down there."

A shiver ran through Lily, and she swallowed, waiting to hear the rest of the story and watching as Mia lifted a small box from the table at the back of the room.

"When I lifted the first board, I could see two dusty little boxes, and when I pulled back the second, there were more, all in a line and with matching handwritten tags. I couldn't believe what I'd discovered, but as soon as I saw there was a name on each box, I knew they weren't mine to open, no matter how badly I wanted to see what was inside." She smiled as she looked up, turning her eyes to each one of them before continuing. "I brought those boxes here with me today, to show you all. I can't believe that my curiosity has drawn you all together."

Mia carefully placed one box after the other on the table, and Lily craned her neck to see. And that's when Lily saw it, as clear as day: *Patricia Rhodes*. She looked up at Mia in disbelief as the lawyer started to speak again. *Why is my grandmother's name on one of those boxes?*

"When Mia found these, she brought them to me, and we went through all the old records in her aunt's office. Her documentation was meticulous, and although those records should have stayed private, in this case we chose to search for the names on the boxes, to see if we couldn't reunite them with their rightful owners. I felt an obligation to do what I could."

"Did you open any of them?" Lily asked, meeting Mia's gaze.

"No." Mia's voice dropped, softer now than before. "That's why I asked you all to be here today, so you could each choose whether to open them or not." Her eyes filled with tears, and Lily watched as she quickly brushed them away. "To keep them hidden all these years, they must have held such importance to my aunt, but what I don't understand is why she never reunited the boxes with their rightful owners during her lifetime. I felt that it was my duty to at least try, and now it's up to each one of you whether they remain sealed or not."

Lily had the most overwhelming urge to stand up and hug Mia, but as she watched her, she saw her back straighten, her moment of vulnerability over.

"What we don't know," the lawyer said, planting his hands on the table as he slowly lifted from his chair, "is whether there were other boxes that were given out over the years. Either Hope chose not to give these seven out for some reason, or they weren't claimed."

"Or she decided, again for reasons of her own, that they were better kept hidden," Mia finished for him. "In which case, I may have uncovered something that was supposed to stay buried."

The lawyer cleared his throat. "Yes. But whatever the reason, my duty is to pass them on to their rightful owners, or in this case, to the estates of their rightful owners."

"And you have no idea what's inside any of them?" another woman asked from across the room.

"No, we don't," Mia replied.

"Well, as interesting as all this sounds, I have to get back to work," said a beautiful dark-haired woman seated farthest away from everyone else. "If you could pass me the box labeled Cara Montano, I'll be on my way."

Lily was surprised at how disinterested the woman seemed; she herself was itching to open her grandmother's box to see what it contained.

"Thank you for coming," the lawyer said. "If you have any questions, please don't hesitate to contact me."

The woman nodded, but from the expression on her face Lily doubted she had any intention of staying in touch. No one else

moved as she signed a piece of paper and showed her photo iden-
tification, dropping the small box into her oversized handbag and
striding out of the room. Lily saw that her name was Georgia.

The lawyer cleared his throat. "If you could state your names
one at a time and sign the documentation in front of you, I'll be
able to hand out the remaining boxes. I appreciate that others of
you may have places to be."

Lily stayed seated as she scanned the paper in front of her,
smiling at Mia when she passed her a pen. "Thank you." She
signed and then looked up. "This is all rather mysterious, isn't it?"

Mia smiled, and Lily noticed how pretty she was when her
face softened. It was like she'd been held together with a mask,
feigning confidence perhaps to speak to them all.

"I know it's strange, this whole situation, but when I saw how
carefully my aunt had labeled each box, I was compelled to find
their rightful owners. I couldn't have lived with myself if they'd
been in the house when it was demolished."

Lily nodded. "It's such a shame they were hidden for so many
years."

Mia took Lily's papers for her and passed them along to the
lawyer, before giving her the little box. It was made of wood, with
string tied tightly around it, a card name tag distinctly identifying
the recipient. Lily traced her eyes over her grandmother's name,
the letters all linked together in the most perfect style of writing,
as on all of the labels. Clearly the same person had labeled each
box.

She was tempted to pull the string and untie it right there and
then, but instead she ran her thumb across the surface, letting her
imagination run wild, wondering what could be inside.

"I have nothing further to discuss, so unless there are any
questions . . ." the lawyer's voice trailed off.

Lily shook her head, finally looking up and catching Mia's eye
again. There was something about her that struck Lily, perhaps a

loneliness, and as the meeting was adjourned, she found herself leaning toward her.

"I'm tempted to open mine right now," Lily said. "I've never been good with surprises."

"Before you open it, just make sure you actually *want* to uncover the past. Once you know, it might change things, things about your family, or about what you thought you knew about your grandmother. Some secrets are supposed to stay hidden, which was my only fear in finding you all."

Lily nodded. "I understand. If I'm honest, it is a bit of a shock knowing that my grandmother is somehow connected with all this."

Mia nodded. "Trust me, I know. I knew so little about any of this until recently, but my aunt kept a diary and I found it hidden with the boxes. I've actually been reading through it these past few weeks. Dozens of women passed through that house, some women who wanted to be rid of their babies, and others who were heartbroken over giving up their child." She paused.

"But if so many women gave birth there, wouldn't there have been more boxes?" Lily asked.

"Perhaps," Mia replied. "But maybe those boxes were already claimed. Perhaps your grandmothers are the ones who never came looking for answers?"

"Oh, did someone forget that?" Lily asked, gesturing toward a leftover box as she put her own safely in her handbag.

"No, this seventh one is unclaimed," Mia said. "I don't know why I even brought it, to be honest, because we couldn't find any contact details, but it didn't seem right to leave it behind."

Lily stared at it, reading the unfamiliar name on the tag and wondering who it might belong to. The fact that the rest of them had arrived to claim theirs was incredulous in itself, but then she guessed the other women had all been as curious as she had.

"Thanks again, for doing all this," Lily said.

"I hope the box doesn't contain too many surprises," Mia said, holding her hand up in a wave.

Lily waved back and left, smiling at another woman who was walking out at the same time as her. A few hours earlier, she'd been homesick for a country that wasn't actually her home, missing the people she'd spent the past four years with and half tempted to get on a plane and go back. But suddenly she felt like London was exactly the place she was supposed to be. And if she hadn't come home, she would never have been given the strange little box bearing her grandmother's name.

She'd never believed in fate before, but maybe there was something to it after all.

4

ITALY, 1937

She would never forget the first time she saw him.

Estee stood on the stage, her heart beating so fast that she worried it might actually leap from her chest. The crowd was clapping and smiling as she faced them, bowing deep into a curtsy before rising on her toes again and carefully walking off the stage. She kept her back straight, her arms extended, gritting her teeth through her smile, even as her back, arms and feet ached.

"Well done," her mother murmured when she emerged, her arms open as she enveloped Estee in a hug, dramatically kissing each of her cheeks, still within eyesight of the gathered crowd. "They loved you."

She knew what that meant. Her mother wanted everyone to see, everyone who meant something, that is, and today had been about showing all the affluent families in Piedmont and farther afield just how talented the girl in their midst was. She'd seen someone press money into her mother's hand earlier, too, so she knew her family was being paid for her performance. And the only reason she was receiving affection from her mother was because they were still on display. She tried not to hold her body so rigidly, pretending it was normal to receive such warmth from her.

Estee loved to dance; her mother often told the story of the little girl who'd danced before she could walk, although she knew that story was more than a little embellished. But the truth was, she had danced since she was small, and it hadn't taken long for someone to see her talent once she'd started ballet lessons.

As her mother began to greet families as they rose to leave, Estee stood to the side, her posture flawless as she wiggled her fingers in a perfect little wave. She fixed her smile, her head dipped slightly, trying to appear demure, lest she do something wrong and be chastised for it later.

She was to be the one to change her family's fortunes. The weight of her family's world was resting on her shoulders, and at times it made her stomach churn, the pains easily as sharp as the other ones she felt in her stomach at night, her body desperately crying out for more food. She trained all day yet was given mere morsels of sustenance compared to what her siblings received.

You are to be tiny, like a little bird, Estee. Nobody would like a fat little dancer, would they?

She glanced down at her legs, knowing how much her mother already fretted about every inch of weight she put on, even though she was barely twelve. Her calf muscles were getting bigger by the month, a result of her dancing and something her ballet teacher told her to be proud of. But sometimes she wondered if her mother confused muscle for fat, and the more hours she danced each day, the more developed her muscles became. *And the less food I'm allowed.*

A boy approached then, standing slightly away from his parents and siblings, and when he caught her eye, Estee suddenly forgot all about her stomach. This boy, his eyes were bright, and there was something different about his smile; where everyone else looked as if they were forcing smiles simply to be polite, his smile lit up his face. He grinned at her, and she found herself grinning back, her perfectly held composure cracking in response to his attention.

As his family spoke to those around them, and with her mother deep in conversation with another woman, Estee edged closer to the boy, wondering who he was. She didn't attend school anymore, and they hadn't been living in Piedmont for long; it had been a recent move for her father's work, so she didn't know any of the local children. Not that her mother would have let her mix with them, anyway. She wasn't allowed to do anything that might distract her from her ballet.

When the boy inclined his head and gave her a little wave to come with him, Estee found she couldn't resist, following his dark head with her eyes as he disappeared through the crowd. Where was he going? And why did he want her to come?

Estee glanced at her mother again and found her so involved in conversation still, she doubted she'd even notice her little ballerina had gone, and so she slowly stepped forward, through the gathered crowd, smiling politely to everyone she passed. And the more steps she took, the braver she felt, until eventually she'd managed to disappear. A shiver ran through her, the chill of the autumn air on her bare shoulders as she stepped outside and looked for the boy who was impossible to ignore.

There he is.

She glanced over her shoulder before approaching him, half expecting her mother to have suddenly noticed her absence already and come after her. But there was no one behind her. She swallowed, hesitating, second-guessing her decision to follow him. If she was seen alone with a boy, she could only imagine what would be said. Sometimes she felt every inch a little girl still, but she knew how she looked; on the cusp of womanhood and easily able to turn a man's head when she walked by, which meant she shouldn't be alone with anyone, man *or* boy. Yet still she found herself walking toward him.

"Hello," he called out, sitting on the grass, throwing stones out into a small pond.

"Hello," she replied, carefully dropping to her knees, not

wanting to sit too close and trying desperately to preserve her modesty in her tutu.

They sat for a minute in silence, and she watched as he absently plucked grass between his fingers, before taking something out of his pocket. She found she was curious as to what he was reaching for and she looked on as he placed a cigarette between his lips, striking a match and lighting it, before taking a puff. He coughed a little, which made them both laugh, and offered the cigarette to her. For a moment he'd looked so grown-up, but now she could see that he was just a boy, pretending to be older; just as she was a girl, playing at being a woman. She knew he was trying to impress her and wondered if he'd stolen the cigarette from his father.

Estee hesitated, her fingers clenching as she fought against her better judgment. *Just take it.*

She could hear her mother's voice in her head, knew she shouldn't do it, but there was something about this boy, and she was so tired of always doing what her mother told her to do. He was smiling at her, but he was different somehow. She was used to men whispering and nudging each other, making her feel uncomfortable with their praise and innuendo, and she knew all about boys acting full of bravado and talking so much it was as if they liked the sound of their own voice. But not him. He just had a curiosity about him, a quietness that she was drawn to.

Estee held out her hand and he shuffled a little closer, carefully passing her the cigarette, their fingers brushing together as she tried to hold it like he had. She'd seen movie stars on the screen smoking and making it look so elegant, and rich women with their friends at ballet concerts and parties using fancy holders that made them look even more glamorous as they smoked, and she tried to look grown-up as she did the same. Only her first puff resulted in the smoke curling and catching in her throat, which sent her into a coughing fit—not exactly the glamorous look she'd been trying to achieve.

The boy smiled, but he didn't laugh at her naivety. Instead, he came and sat closer to her, taking off his jacket and draping it over her shoulders as he gave her a couple of pats on the back. She snuggled back into his jacket, grateful when the cold wind stopped biting against her bare skin and embarrassed at how easily he'd leaned across to touch her.

"Why does everyone like these so much?" she asked, passing it back to him. "They're awful."

He shrugged, taking another puff and blowing out the smoke. "You just need to take little puffs to start with. You get used to it."

But she wasn't convinced he liked it either, or that it was something he did often, because as soon as she showed her displeasure, he dropped it and squished it beneath his shoe. Either that, or he was being polite. In any case, the cigarette was gone.

"I'm Felix," he said, holding out his hand.

"Estee," she said, clasping it and giving it a little shake.

They both laughed awkwardly as they dropped their hands and stared out at the pond. If they'd been adults, they'd have kissed cheeks, but they were stuck somewhere in between, and it seemed that neither of them was very good at playing make-believe.

"Do you like dancing?" he asked, giving her a sideways look, accompanied by a shy smile.

"I love dancing," she said, knowing her response to be both deeply true and yet also a lie. She had once loved dancing, but she wasn't sure if she loved it quite as much anymore.

"Then why did you look sad before?"

She felt her eyebrows leap upward in surprise. "When? I wasn't sad."

"I think you're just good at pretending to be happy," he said. "Your eyes looked sad even though you were smiling."

She made a mental note to change the way she held herself, the way she looked, the way she blinked. She needed to appear happy all the time, not just when she was dancing, but when she was meeting people, too. She dug her nails into her palms, anger rising inside her. If a boy had noticed, then how did she expect to fool anyone else?

If I'm not perfect, I'll never make it. There's no time for smoking cigarettes and talking to boys. What am I even doing here?

"Why are you doing that?" he asked, reaching for her hand as she pushed her nails so hard into her skin that it took all her willpower not to cry out. "Why do you want to hurt yourself?"

She snatched her hand away, mortified that she'd been caught.

"I'm not doing anything."

Estee quickly shrugged out of his jacket, but he caught it before it hit the grass. She should have stayed inside—what had she been thinking?

"I shouldn't be here," she said, her fingers worrying the edge of her pink tutu as she looked down at him.

"Aren't you allowed to have fun?" he asked, not putting his jacket on, holding it out instead as if he thought she might want it back.

"No," she said, unable to disguise the sadness in her eyes this time, no matter how hard she tried. "I'm never allowed to have fun. I'm only allowed to dance."

"Tell me where you live," he said. "I sneak out at night sometimes and run down to the river. You could come if you'd like?"

She shook her head, not about to give some boy her address. She knew better than to sneak around at nighttime with anyone, and he had to be, what, thirteen? Perhaps even fourteen? It wouldn't be right. If someone saw them, her reputation could be damaged forever. He should know better than that.

"I have to go," she said, tempted to sit back down despite her words. She knew all the reasons she should go, but her mind was still trying to convince her to stay just a little longer.

Felix stood and gently put his jacket around her shoulders again. "If you change your mind, come and find me," he said.

"You'll be safe with me, I promise. Sometimes I go out at night on my own, sometimes with friends."

She looked into his eyes, so warm and dark and innocent, and knew in that instant that he was telling the truth. There was nothing nefarious shining from his gaze, and she found herself drawn to him in a way she'd never felt before. Her entire life had always been about dancing, to the point where she'd ended up alone most of the time. She was either at school or she was dancing, and there hadn't been time for friends or boys. Once, she'd danced for the love of it, but that time had long since passed. And now even school had been taken from her.

Felix came closer to her then, and something changed between them. She saw the way his eyes dropped to her lips, the way those kind eyes darted back to hers as if to ask if it was all right. When he looked back down, she caught him by his shirt, holding the fabric in a ball in her hand as she gently tugged him forward and pressed her lips to his, as she imagined a grown-up version of herself might do. Their teeth knocked and their mouths moved awkwardly, but for a second, just one blissful second, their lips parted and moved at the exact same time. And for the first time, something other than dancing sent a jolt of anticipation through her body.

"Estee!" came a call in the distance.

"I have to go," she whispered as she let go of Felix, his cheeks red as she smiled up at him.

"Just throw a pebble," he said, stumbling over his words as she backed away. "If you ever want to see me again, just throw a pebble at my window. Our house is the big residence with the terracotta roof at the end of town. I'm the upstairs bedroom closest to the peach tree."

She knew his house, had walked past it countless times on the way to her dance lessons, and it was easily the largest house in the area, so it was impossible to miss. But no matter how badly she wanted to kiss him again, she wasn't going to make promises.

Estee grinned as she spun around, clutching his jacket to her shoulders as she ran to find her mother. She should have given him his jacket back, but keeping it gave her a reason to go looking for him.

"Estee!" he called after her.

She turned back, her eyes meeting his.

"I hope I get to see you dance again."

She grinned, giving him a quick wave before spinning back around and hurrying off, careful not to slip in case she hurt her ankles.

And although her mind was a jumble, there was one thing clear as day: she was most definitely going to be throwing a pebble—she just needed to figure out how to sneak out of her own room first.

"Estee!"

"Coming, Mamma!" she called.

She was breathless when she found her mother.

"What's wrong?" her mother asked the moment she stopped in front of her, dropping her gaze in the hope that her mother wouldn't see her face. She almost expected her to know just from looking at her that she'd been kissed, that her lips might look bee-stung or her cheeks too pink.

Her mother roughly took hold of her chin and turned her head from side to side, narrowing her gaze. "You're flushed. Are you sick?" She placed her hand over Estee's forehead. "You feel hot. Where were you before? I couldn't see you anywhere."

And that was when Estee remembered the jacket, and bile rose in her throat as she stared back at her mother. She should have taken it off before she walked back inside. Her mother was going to find out.

"Who does this belong to?" her mother demanded, flicking her nail at the shoulder of the jacket.

Estee possessively wrapped the jacket further around herself.

"I went out for fresh air, I wasn't feeling well and a, a nice boy lent it to me. He could see I was cold."

Her mother made a *tsk*ing sound she knew all too well. "What boy?"

"His name was Felix," she replied, not about to lie to her mother.

"Felix Barbieri?" she asked.

Estee shrugged, surprised her mother knew who he was, and received a sharp slap from her mother across the hand for her insolence. Her mother didn't tolerate any behavior that didn't show the utmost respect. Her skin stung, but she kept her chin jutted high, refusing to let her know how much it had hurt.

"Were you alone with him?"

Estee dropped her gaze then, her eyes downcast as she nodded, knowing better than to defy her mother. If she'd kept her chin high, she'd have received a slap across the face instead of the hand.

"Do you have any idea what people would say about us, if they saw you unchaperoned with a boy?" she hissed. "Boys only want one thing from girls like you, Estee. Do you hear me? What kind of future do you think you'd have if someone started saying that the pretty little ballet dancer spends time with boys? That you are up to no good?"

She swallowed as her shoulders, her hands, her knees, began to tremble.

"Do you understand what I'm saying?"

"Yes, Mamma," she replied, as the jacket was torn from her shoulders, cold the moment she was bare again. She had no idea what boys might want from her, not really, but if it was a kiss, then she was the one to blame for that, not Felix.

"When everyone has gone, I want you back up there again, practicing. I want your timings to be perfect." Her mother sighed. "You could have done better today, Estee. You can *always* do better."

Estee's dance had been perfect. She knew the routine like the back of her hand; could and *did* dance it in her sleep. But nothing was ever good enough for her mother.

"Yes, Mamma," she replied, knowing better than to argue about her performance. It was easier simply to do what was asked of her.

But when her mother turned her back and strode off, she quickly darted forward and retrieved Felix's jacket, folding it into a ball and rushing over to her bag. Estee lifted it to her nose and inhaled the smell, rewarded with fresh cigarette smoke from their little puff and something else, perhaps the soap he used, citrusy and fresh. *The same smell that filled my nostrils when I pulled him toward me.*

She pressed the jacket into her bag and zipped it up, walking up onto the stage to begin her dance all over again. Only this time, there was no one there to watch her.

I want to kiss that boy again, and nothing's going to stop me.

PRESENT DAY

Lily ran the last few steps back to her apartment after her meeting with the lawyer as rain sent heavy drops falling from the sky.

She took the steps two at a time, out of breath as she flung open her door and shut it behind her. The little wooden box seemed to be burning a hole in her bag, begging to be opened, and she flung her handbag down on the table and immediately rifled through it.

Lily held the box in her hand, staring at it and wondering what it would contain. Mia had mentioned it was likely to hold some sort of clue to the past, but the trouble was, she hadn't even known there was a past to be discovered, and she couldn't stop thinking about what she'd said. *Will I regret opening it and discovering something about my heritage that's been a secret all these years?*

She ran her fingers over the little card bearing her grandmother's name and tugged at the string that held the box tightly shut. The knot was taut, though, and she ended up having to find scissors when her fingernails failed her. She sliced through and let the string drop, wondering how long it had remained in place, imagining this mysterious woman named Hope securing whatever lay inside before cutting a length of string to wind around it.

Maybe this Hope never saw what was inside. Perhaps all she did was write the name and hide the box for safekeeping?

Lily lifted the lid, expecting a letter folded tightly into a square, or perhaps a birth certificate, but instead she found a piece of paper with typed words on it. She could see that it had been torn from a larger sheet, perhaps something official, and all she could make out were the words *Teatro alla Scala* in the corner. The rest was in a foreign language. She fumbled for her phone and opened Google, inputting the name and instantly seeing results. The La Scala appeared to be a prominent theater in Italy, famous in Milan.

Later, she would try to translate it online, but she set the paper aside to look back in the box. There was another piece of paper, but this one was softer, as if it had come from a writing set perhaps, and the ink was put there by hand and much more faded than the printed text.

She stared at the words, once again not sure what she was looking at, although it appeared to be a recipe of some kind from what she could tell. She set that paper aside, too, annoyed that she'd been so looking forward to discovering what was in the box, only to find nothing she could even read.

Lily lifted the box and carefully inspected it, turning it over as if expecting to find something else hidden there, a secret bottom compartment perhaps, but there was nothing else.

"Italian, huh?" she murmured to herself as she reached for the pieces of paper and carefully folded them back up again.

Did this mean her grandmother had been Italian? Is that where her own ink-dark hair had come from, and her father's handsome features? Did her family have Italian ancestors they hadn't even known existed? She thought back, trying to remember whether her grandmother had said or done anything, whether there was something she might have missed. Had her grandmother known and kept it a secret, embarrassed somehow about her past?

Lily suddenly laughed as she put the papers back into the box and slipped it into her bag. *Dad, you always wondered why your mother had such a fiery temper!*

Her phone pinged then, and she reached for it, scrolling through her emails to see who'd sent her a message. Lily's eyes widened when she saw the name Roberto Martinelli—the wine-grower in the Como region where she was heading in just over a week.

Lily,

Ciao, bella! I hope this email finds you well. The grapes are maturing faster than expected this season, so I need you here earlier than we'd planned. If you can make it work, please change your flight to this Monday and I will reimburse you.

Sorry for the short notice.

R. M.

Lily grinned. Perhaps she wouldn't need Google Translate after all. If she was going to be in Italy on Monday, she could just ask one of her new work colleagues to translate for her.

She quickly replied to Roberto and then hurried into her bed-room, eyeing the enormous pile of washing on the floor. She had less than forty-eight hours to prepare and pack, and if everything went as planned, she'd be there for at least the next few months, so she needed to think carefully about what she should take.

But clothes were the last thing on her mind. She couldn't stop thinking about Milan and this La Scala Theatre, and just what connection her grandmother could possibly have had to such a famous place.

6

Lily took a deep breath of the warm, humid air as she stepped out into the sunshine. *Italy.* Finally. The flight had felt short to her after her recent long-haul trip; it was only just over two hours from London to Malpensa Airport near Milan, although now she had to travel by train to Como. She glanced around, wishing she had time to explore Milan. It was a city she'd always dreamed of visiting.

She stood for a moment outside the airport, turning on her phone and checking which terminal she was supposed to catch her train from. She waited to see if any messages came through and looked around her, happy she'd worn her flowing maxi dress as the warmth of the day embraced her. The back of her neck was slightly damp, and she lifted her long hair with one hand, wishing she'd thought to tie it up.

Her phone pinged then, and she let go of her hair, quickly scrolling through her messages. There was one from her mum, and she touched on it, surprised she'd even sent a text. They were going to have lunch and Lily would stay with her overnight before heading to the vineyard in the morning, and as she glanced at the time, she realized it was going to be almost impossible to get there on schedule.

She saw a taxi go past, not far from where she was standing, and groaned. She doubted it would take more than forty-five minutes to get to Como if she went by taxi, but it would be ridiculously expensive.

Lily slipped her phone into her bag, glancing at the box she'd packed safely beside her purse. She'd found it hard not to think about it since she'd opened it, but she still hadn't been able to glean anything useful, other than a few Google hits on the La Scala Theatre.

I could skip lunch and go for a look, just to see it for myself. She shook her head, internally scolding herself for even thinking that; she hadn't seen her mother in forever. Besides, how would physically going there help her? All she had was part of an old program, and she couldn't exactly go up to just anyone there and ask if they could assist—she didn't even know what she needed help with, and she didn't speak Italian!

She put her bag back over her shoulder and walked in the opposite direction to the train station. Suddenly the idea of a fast trip with the entire back seat to herself felt like exactly what she needed, even if it was going to cost a small fortune.

Lily waved for a taxi, which didn't stop for her, but another did, and she leaned down to speak to the driver through the window.

"Lake Como?" she asked.

"Si," he said with a wide smile, his dark eyes giving her a quick once-over and making her blush. Italian men seemed to have a way of appreciating women with their eyes, and Lily found she didn't mind it at all.

Within seconds he was out of the car and taking her bags for her as she climbed into the back seat, staring out at the people crossing the street and the bustle of cars bringing people to and from the airport. When the driver was back behind the wheel, she saw him glance at her in the rearview mirror, and she smiled back at him.

"Do you speak English?" she asked.

He nodded. "A little."

"More than my Italian, I'm sure."

She stared out the window, wondering exactly where the theater was from where they were now.

"How long have you lived in Milan?" she asked.

"All my life," he said, his eyes darting between the road and the rearview mirror.

"Do you know much about the La Scala Theatre?" she asked, realizing the moment she said it how stupid her question was. He no doubt took passengers to the iconic theater every day!

"It is beautiful, would you like to go there first?"

She shook her head. "No, no I don't want to go there, I just, I'm wanting to find out more about it." She didn't really know what she was even trying to ask him. "I think my grandmother, or perhaps my great-grandmother, had a connection to it. I'm not sure what it was, though, or when, but maybe after the war."

He smiled at her, and she presumed she'd lost him, that his English perhaps wasn't good enough to follow her ramblings.

"Perhaps she was a performer there, a dancer or singer?" he suddenly said.

Lily looked up, surprised. "Perhaps," she agreed.

"Was your grandmother Italian?" he asked. "You are very beautiful. You have Italian blood, no?"

She laughed. "I don't think so, but thank you. It's very flattering."

Italian! Ha! She laughed to herself at his words. She was definitely not Italian, although it had crossed her mind more than once these past few days. *But I would know, wouldn't I, if I was?*

* * *

Lily straightened as the car slowed, staring out of the window and taking everything in. Como was different to what she'd expected, more bustling than quaint.

"It's so busy," she said.

"Si." The taxi driver sighed, sounding sad. "We need the tourists for their money, but we hate them for it, too."

She understood exactly what he was saying, because she could see it for herself. It was heaving with people, and it wasn't even the middle of summer.

"They started buying houses here, and they never stopped."

Lily could only imagine what it must be like for the locals, with all the new money pouring into their little slice of paradise. As testament to her thoughts, she watched as speedboats raced along the river, and when she opened her door, she could hear the deafening roar of engines.

"*Santa Maria*," the taxi driver cursed, and she groaned along with him, feeling his pain.

Lily paid him before stepping out into the day, finding it slightly more humid than it had been an hour earlier, as the driver took the bags out for her. The temperature was perfect, though, and she basked in the warmth and enjoyed the sunshine on her shoulders. She was about to eat the best food of her life, drink stunning wine and be surrounded by beautiful people. New Zealand had been great, but Italy was going to be something else.

"Grazie," she said, waving to the driver as he blew a kiss to her. She pretended to catch it and touched her palm to her cheek, which made him laugh.

It turned out that Italy made her a flirt, too. Who would have known a country could change her usually shy demeanor so easily?

Within minutes she was standing at the entrance to Villa

d'Este, the hotel her mother was staying at, and where she'd insisted Lily join her. She was thankful her mum was paying for it because the cost was eye-watering, but the hotel was as beautiful as she'd imagined it would be. She'd read about it on the plane and knew it was one of those undiscovered family-run places that oozed old charm and even older money, and she wasn't surprised when she stepped inside and saw ornate chandeliers hanging from the high ceilings.

It was nothing short of magical.

"Darling!"

Before the concierge had time to take her bags, Lily was swept up in a colorful hug as her mother's bright kaftan engulfed her, her perfume as consuming as her presence.

"It's good to see you, too," Lily said, smiling as her mother stepped back, before hugging her tightly again.

"Look at you! You look fabulous."

Lily glanced down at herself. "Really? I think you're exaggerating."

"Not your clothes, but you, just look at you." Her mum was shaking her head. "Your skin looks amazing, your hair!" She reached out and fluffed Lily's hair. "Promise me you won't cut it? It looks incredible, long like that. *You* look incredible like that."

Lily instinctively raised a hand to her hair, feeling like a little girl again as she lapped up her mother's praise. But her attention quickly turned to the man her mum was waving over, who up until then had obviously been watching the reunion from a chair, a newspaper folded over his knee. She immediately recognized him—Alan had often said hello on video calls when she'd been chatting to her mother from abroad.

"Alan! Come and meet Lily!" Her mother beamed.

"It's lovely to meet you properly, Lily," Alan said as he came closer.

"I feel the same, it's so lovely to meet you, too," she replied, immediately warming to him as he put an arm around her mother.

They seemed happy, and as much as she would have liked to spend some time alone with her mum, all she'd ever truly wanted was for her to find someone to enjoy the rest of her life with.

"Let's get those bags up to the room, shall we?" her mother asked. "Then we can go out for lunch and enjoy this beautiful weather. I just *love* feeling like a local."

Lily stifled a laugh. *A local?* She doubted an Italian woman would be seen dead in her mum's bright, louder-than-loud outfit. But she certainly wasn't going to be the one to break it to her.

"Have you got a favorite place to have lunch?" she asked as her mother took her arm and Alan instructed the concierge to take her bag.

"Well," her mum said, leaning in close. "There's this little place that Leonardo DiCaprio apparently *loves,* and I thought if we went there, well, we might end up rubbing shoulders with some Hollywood royalty."

Lily laughed. Her mother was whispering to her in such a conspiratorial way, it was like she was telling her national secrets.

"I'm sure it'll be fabulous," she replied.

"Now tell me, are there any young men in your life? Did you break any hearts in New Zealand?"

Lily sighed. "No, there are no men, Mum. I promise I'd have told you if there were."

"I know you've found it hard to get close to anyone since your father passed, but I just don't want you to wake up one day and wish you'd been open to love, that's all."

What she didn't tell her mum was that there had been plenty of lovely men in her life these past few years, but she'd ended up gathering friends, not lovers. Most of the time it was her own fault; as much as she'd have liked to have someone warming her bed at night, she was her own worst enemy at keeping men at arm's length. Her work had always been the most important thing in her life, honoring her father's memory; and the idea of falling in love and then not following her dreams because she was in a relationship wasn't something she wanted to consider. Which meant as soon as things even looked like they could become serious or her feelings too strong, she used her tried-and-tested "I think we're better as friends" line.

"Just promise me something, Lily."

She turned when her mum stopped walking, worried by the serious look on her face.

"Of course. What is it?"

"That while you're in Italy, you'll at least find someone to have great sex with, won't you? You'll regret not making the most of that beautiful young body while you had the chance. Trust me."

"Mum!"

"Oh, don't be a prude, you know I'm right! If you don't want to settle down, at least have some fun."

With her mouth gaping open and her cheeks on fire, Lily stood as her mother strode off in a whisk of silk and perfume.

Why didn't I just go straight to the vineyard?

Lily glanced out of a picturesque window onto an even more picturesque view, and imagined the acres being covered in grapes instead of grass.

"Come on, darling, we're going to be late for lunch!"

She dragged her eyes from the view and walked toward a grand staircase that wouldn't have been out of place in a palace.

It was hours later that Lily finally managed to get her mum alone. They sat together as the sun began to fade, the activities on the river having dwindled, to be replaced with a hum of people coming and going from the restaurant. They were seated at an outside table, sipping negronis and watching the world go by. Lily was so relaxed after their late lunch and drinks, melting into the chair as she chatted with her mother, that she doubted she could move even if she wanted to.

It was then Lily realized she hadn't mentioned the clues.

"Mum, did Dad ever say anything about Grandma being adopted?" she asked. "Was there anything ever mentioned?"

"Never! Is this to do with the letter that was sent to her estate?" Her mother shook her head. "If your grandmother were adopted, your father would have said."

"It's just, well, the lawyer had her birth certificate and some adoption records there. The law firm had formerly handled all adoptions and paperwork for a place called Hope's House. It seems they took in unmarried mothers until they gave birth, and then arranged for adoptions in London."

Her mother took a sip of her drink before settling back into her chair. "I can't believe it. You actually think Grandma was born there?"

"I do. And there's more," Lily said, reaching down into her bag and taking out the little wooden box. "Some of the mothers were apparently encouraged to leave something behind, in case their child ever came looking for answers, I suppose. And this was left for Grandma by her birth mother."

She'd never seen her mother appear slack-jawed before, but this news had her mouth hanging open. "And you're quite certain this is true? That it's not some sort of—"

"Hoax?" Lily smiled. "Trust me, that's exactly what I was thinking in the beginning, but it's not. In fact, the niece of Hope, the woman who ran the place, was there to meet us all. She was the one who uncovered the boxes, and all she wanted was to return them to their rightful owners, or rather their descendants."

"Well, you couldn't have surprised me more if you'd tried." Her mum took a larger gulp of her drink this time. "So, what's in the box?"

Lily sighed. "That's the trouble, I can't really make head or tail of it," she said, carefully taking the two pieces of paper out. "There's this piece of a program from the La Scala Theatre in Milan, and what appears to be a recipe that someone has handwritten."

She watched as her mum turned the papers over in her hands and studied both, her brow creasing as she looked from one to the other and back again.

"Fascinating. Absolutely fascinating." She sighed. "If only your father were here to see all this."

Even as Lily's fingers itched to take the papers back and fold them into the box again, she found herself saying: "Would you like to keep them?"

She received a firm shake of the head in response. "No, you keep them, Lily, they're yours. Perhaps you can ask around while you're here, see if anything makes sense, once you've been here for a while. I'd love to know more, but I like the idea of you trying to piece it all together. I think Grandma would like it, too."

They both looked at one another.

"And your father," her mum said. "I think he'd love the fact that you're doing this."

"It's a strange coincidence, don't you think?" Lily asked, blinking away tears that always welled up when they spoke of her father.

Her mother raised her eyebrows in question.

"Just that I'm here, less than an hour's drive from the famous theater that's stamped on the program," she said. "What were the chances?"

Her mum touched her hand, her fingers lacing with Lily's. "Even more reason for you to follow whatever path those clues take you on," she said. "Perhaps there's a reason they were given to you now."

Lily squeezed her mum's fingers in response. "You really believe that?" she asked.

Her mum leaned forward, their eyes meeting. "I do." She smiled. "And, Lily, your father would be so proud of the woman you've become. *I'm* so proud of you."

She smiled back as tears filled her eyes, holding her mum's hand tightly as they settled in their chairs to look out at the view.

7

ITALY, 1937

Estee had never disobeyed her mother before; nothing had ever been worth it. *Until now.*

She stood in the shadow of the big tree, knowing that the moment she stepped away from the cover of its canopy, she'd be illuminated by the moonlight. She wore a dark cape with a large hood, and she pulled it over her head to help disguise herself as she finally found the nerve to move.

Her fingers worried the small stones in her palm, clammy despite the cool of the night air. But she knew that if she lost her nerve tonight, she'd never come back, and if her mother found out she'd been gone, she might never get the chance again, either.

Estee bravely walked to the thick patch of lavender and hoped she'd understood Felix correctly as she threw a pebble as high as she could. It hit the lower part of the roof, the noise sounding as loud as thunder to her in the silence of the night, the pebble tumbling all the way down to the ground. She glanced at her hand and saw she had three pebbles remaining. ·

I need to throw it higher.

The second pebble almost reached the window, but once again trickled down the roof. She took a step closer and threw the next one with all her might, holding her breath when it connected with the window. Nothing. There was no sound, no movement, *nothing*.

She tried again, wondering if perhaps he hadn't heard it, and once again it connected with the glass. She stood for a moment, hoping to see something, anything, to show that he was up there, but still nothing happened.

Estee turned then, feeling foolish in her hooded cape, standing there on the manicured lawn of the Barbieris' property. Perhaps he hadn't even been serious about her throwing a pebble if she decided to find him? But just as she was scuttling away to the cover of the trees again, she heard a noise that made her turn, followed by someone whispering her name.

"Estee? Estee, is that you?"

She dropped her hood as Felix appeared in the window, the glass pushed up so he could lean out. Suddenly all thoughts of feeling foolish disappeared. A shiver ran through her, realizing just how much trouble she'd be in if anyone found out, if her mother found out, and what it might mean. But seeing Felix, his hair rumpled from bed and smiling down at her from the second floor of his house, told her that she'd risk it all over again if she had the chance.

He didn't say anything else, disappearing from sight as she stood, starting to get warm beneath her cape as she waited for him. She backed away a few steps, nervously, as if someone might see her standing there, might think her an intruder, but just as she'd started to fret all over again, Felix reappeared, climbing out of his window and scrambling down the roof. She found herself holding her breath as he got to the lower part, as he crouched down and somehow reached out far enough to the tree, swinging perilously before landing on a thicker bough that allowed him to climb down. Her heart leapt into her throat as she watched, and now suddenly he was running toward her, and her heart was racing all over again.

"That was quite some escape," she said.

"I've had a lot of practice," he replied, running his fingers through his tousled hair. "If my parents found out, my punishment would be swift."

She stared at him, eyes wide as he looked back at her. "Would they *physically* punish you?"

"Of course not!"

"Oh, of course, I was only teasing." She tried to smile, holding back her words, not about to confess what would happen to her if she was found out.

"Wouldn't yours?" he said. "Just tell you off, I mean. Not actually hurt you?"

She nodded, hoping he didn't see the flare of her nostrils or hear the rapid beat of her heart at the mention of her mother. Her sisters seemed to avoid their mother's rage, but she wasn't so lucky. She worked the hardest, practiced as if her life depended on it, but still she was the only one to suffer her mother's wrath.

"Where are we going?" she asked.

"How about I take you to my favorite place?" he asked. "When I'm with my friends, we go to the lake, but I have a feeling you might not want to go so far. Without anyone to chaperone us, I mean."

She nodded. She had no idea where she wanted to go; she'd just felt the most surprising pull toward him, knowing she needed to see him again.

"I think you'll love it," he said.

They walked in silence for a while, and she wondered if he didn't know what to say any more than she did. Estee glanced at him, pleased the moon was giving them so much light to see each other by. She wanted to ask him about his friends, about why he'd wanted to meet her the other day after her performance, about his family, but instead she held her tongue, hoping he'd start the conversation.

But when his hand bumped against hers, she reached her

fingers out a little, just enough that they stayed touching for a while, until Felix's little finger caught hers. And so they walked, in silence, neither seeming to know what to say, with their fingers looped together in the most innocent of holds.

They could have been children, just friends holding hands, but she knew they weren't. There was something different about Felix; and when he looked over at her, she knew that he felt the same. It made her breath quicken, her heart skip a beat, her feet move just that little bit faster—it wasn't something she'd ever experienced before, and she wasn't entirely sure what it meant.

"It's in here," he said, breaking the quiet moment between them as he tugged her down a little hill toward a large outbuilding. She could see flowers in pots hanging outside, the yard perfectly swept with immaculate cobblestones leading to the building, but it took her a moment to realize where they were. Until a dark nose appeared over a half-door. They were horse stables.

She hesitated when another head appeared, a light gray one this time, and Felix's hand fell away from hers as he walked confidently over to them, lifting his hand to stroke first one large equine face and then the other, the second horse nuzzling him as if they were long-lost friends.

"Don't be scared, come closer," he said.

Estee inched closer, jumping when the horse made a snorting sound. It seemed absurdly loud in the otherwise dead silence of the night. Felix seemed to sense how nervous she was and reached back for her hand again. It should have been strange even thinking about holding hands with a boy she didn't know, but there was somehow nothing strange about being with Felix. Or perhaps she was simply so desperate for contact with someone her own age that she would have felt the same with anyone.

I'm lying. I've never felt this interested in being with anyone before.

"You're making *them* nervous," Felix said. "If your heart races, then theirs will start to race, too."

Her eyes widened and she tentatively took another step, trying to slow her breath and calm her fast-beating heart. It was her reaching for his hand then, his fingers closing around hers once she bravely stepped forward. And as soon as she was within touching distance, he lifted her hand and placed it to the horse's cheek, holding it there, pressing her palm to the soft hair.

And just like that, her heart stopped pounding. Nothing had ever made her feel so calm before, so at peace, and she knew then she'd done the right thing in sneaking out to see him.

"He's beautiful," she whispered.

"*She's* beautiful," he corrected.

Estee laughed. "I've never actually been near a horse before," she admitted. "I've always been scared of them."

"They're the most peaceful animals on the planet," he said. "I come and hide down here all the time when I want to be alone."

She could understand why he liked it; if she had somewhere like this, she'd hide down here, too, to get away from the world.

"Felix, why did you want to meet me that day?" Estee asked.

He shrugged, dropping his hand from hers as he scuffed his boot into the cobblestones. When he finally looked up, she knew what he couldn't say, and she almost wished she hadn't asked the question. *Almost.*

But it felt nice knowing that someone liked her.

"Do you ever have this feeling as if your entire life has been decided for you?" he asked.

"Yes," she said as her eyes suddenly filled with tears. She quickly blinked, hoping he didn't see.

Felix started to walk, and she followed him as he ducked into an open stable, where two wooden boxes were already overturned. He sat down and she did, too, sitting across from him, unused to the smell around them that she guessed was a combination of horse manure and perhaps the straw beneath her feet, which prickled her ankles.

"I think you and I are very alike," he said. "My parents have planned my entire life, including who I'm to marry. I'm expected to take over my father's business, to marry the right girl from the right family, and you . . ."

"I'm to be the best dancer Italy has ever seen," she whispered. "I am to live and breathe dance, whether I like it or not."

"But don't you love to dance? Don't you *want* to be the best dancer Italy has ever seen?"

"I want," she started, clearing her throat and clenching her fists. Felix saw and held out his hands, as if he knew it was the only way to stop her from hurting herself, as if remembering what she'd done last time. Taking a deep breath, she let him prize her fingers away from digging into her palms and gently hold her hands in his, the first person to ever notice, or perhaps care, what she was doing to herself. "I want to dance, but I also want to laugh and have friends and . . ." She took a big breath. It was the first time she'd ever said these things out loud before. "I just want to be a girl sometimes."

They sat quietly for a moment before he suddenly laughed. "You do realize that you're already a girl, don't you? That part might not be so hard to achieve."

She laughed, too, because it sounded so absurd when he repeated her words. But the way he smiled at her, she knew he understood, despite the teasing.

"Who are you going to marry?" she suddenly asked. She shouldn't have been surprised; it wasn't exactly uncommon for marriages to be arranged, especially amongst prominent families, but it still came as a surprise to her.

"Her name is Emilie," he said. "We were friends as young children, but I don't see her often."

"I'm sure she's very nice," Estee said, even as a flutter of jealousy rose inside her.

"We don't come from old money," Felix said, his voice lower now, as if he were worried someone might overhear them. "I think it's why my parents are so determined for me to make the right marriage, for us to live in the right house. They want to do everything possible to make sure they fit in with the people they admire."

"It's the same reason my mother pushes me," Estee said. "They want it to be different for us. They want our lives to change for the better."

There was no point in arguing about it, they both knew that. Their fate, their future, was already decided by their families, and there was little either of them could do to change it.

Her stomach rumbled then, as if there were a storm brewing inside her, and it made the corner of Felix's mouth kick up into a smile.

"You're hungry."

"I'm always hungry." She couldn't see the point in lying to him.

"Why?"

She held her breath for a moment, knowing she couldn't take back the truth once she said it. But he just waited, and she realized how much she liked his patience.

"Because I have to stay tiny," she said. "My mother counts every morsel I eat."

"Do you know what my family does?" Felix asked.

She nodded. "You own bakeries," she said.

"Next time I see you, I'm going to bring you food." He smiled and she found herself smiling straight back at him. "We make the best *saccottini al cioccolato* you've ever tasted."

She flushed and looked away, embarrassed that he could tell how ravenous she was, and because she could only imagine how good his family's food was.

"Estee, you have tasted one before, haven't you?" he asked.

When she didn't say anything, he leaned closer.

"How about a *cornetto*?"

She slowly shook her head. "I'm not allowed anything like that. My sisters, I'm sure they have, but . . ."

"Can you come back tomorrow night?" he asked. "Or the night after?"

"I don't know. If my mamma finds out . . ."

He nodded, seeming to understand the risk she'd taken. Just speaking of her mother made her nervous, and she knew that every moment longer she stayed with Felix made it more likely her mother could discover her deception. She'd already been too long, risked too much in staying out so late.

"I have to go now," she said, standing and stumbling away, suddenly wishing she hadn't come. It had only shown her what she didn't have, what she was missing out on.

The same horse she'd petted earlier was still standing with her head over the stable door, and she lifted her palm, bravely letting her nuzzle it. She closed her eyes, stepping even closer, leaning forward a little until her face was almost touching the horse's.

Felix stood silently beside her, until she finally moved away. They walked together to the tree by his house, standing awkwardly for a moment until she turned, not sure what to say to the boy she'd just spent an hour with, yet felt like she'd known her entire life.

"Estee," he murmured.

She turned; hopeful, waiting.

He reached for her hand, holding it a moment, before slowly letting her go. And all she could think was that he wasn't going to kiss her because it wasn't worth it, because he was already promised to someone else, even though he was barely fourteen.

She walked away, disappointed, bitterly cold despite her cape as she hurried back to her house. She had to sneak in without anyone hearing her, and she fretted the entire way back, not brave enough to ever risk climbing out of her window in case she fell and couldn't dance again.

Estee touched the door handle, gently turning it and then pushing the door open and sliding in, careful not to make a noise. She half expected her mother to be sitting at the dining table, her eyes narrowed, a wooden spoon waiting to smack her in places no one would ever see the bruises, but instead she was greeted with darkness. And silence.

She tiptoed up to her room, graceful as the dancer she was, and undressed quickly and slipped into bed. She pulled the covers up to her chin, trying to still the beat of her racing heart as she willed herself to find sleep, knowing how tired she'd be, come morning.

But the very next afternoon she knew it had been worth the deception and fatigue. Because sitting on her bed, somehow, as if by a miracle, was a brown paper bag. And when she opened it, careful to make sure she was alone first, she found something inside that made her heart sing.

It was the *saccottini al cioccolato* Felix had promised, and the smell alone was enough to make her fall in love.

Not just with the pastry, but with Felix, too. He'd somehow sneaked into her room without being discovered, leaving something for her that couldn't be from anyone else.

She only wished she could eat one every day.

Estee lay on her bed, savoring every flaky bite and licking her fingers until there wasn't so much as a taste of pastry left. She closed her eyes, her belly fuller than it had been in years, and thought of him. Had he somehow shimmied onto her roof and climbed in a window, or had he brazenly sneaked in through a door?

She smiled as she thought of him; of his hair casually pushed back off his forehead, his bright eyes, the slightly crooked upturn of his mouth when he grinned at her. Estee sighed and carefully bunched up the paper bag that had contained the pastry, hiding it under her bed and then standing to stare out of the window, hoping her room didn't smell of the forbidden treat she'd just consumed.

"Estee!" her mother yelled.

She closed her eyes and took a deep breath as another yell echoed up the stairs and into her room.

"Estee!"

"Coming, Mamma," she called back, wrapping her arms around herself for a moment as she imagined a different life, a different family, a different set of expectations.

But wishing for something she couldn't have was dangerous, she knew that well enough. Felix was her friend, but there was no point in dreaming of more. One day she'd be a famous ballet dancer, and he'd be married to his Emilie, a brood of children filling their enormous house.

Their lives were taking them on different paths, but she was happy to have him as her friend. She smiled to herself as she hurried down the stairs, her fingers tracing along the narrow banister.

My friend who leaves treats worthy of the gods on my bed.

8

PRESENT DAY

Lily stepped out of the hotel, wistful as she looked back, half expecting her mum to be standing at the bottom of the ornate staircase, waving goodbye. But alas, the staircase was empty, and she smiled as she thought of her upstairs, getting ready for the day.

"Lily?"

She spun back round to find a man with eyes as dark as cocoa, his skin tanned golden, calling out to her from the steps below.

"Si," she replied. "You must be—"

"Antonio," he said, holding out his hand. She expected him to shake it, but instead he used it to pull her closer, kissing first one cheek and then the other. "Welcome."

His eyes were warm, his smile even warmer, and she found herself blushing as he looked up at her. It seemed she easily fell for the charms of Italian men.

"May I take your bags?"

She nodded, lifting the smaller one herself as he took her larger case. He carried it down a few steps before nodding in the direction of his car.

"Over here," he said, indicating toward a 4x4 vehicle that looked as if it had seen better days. She loved it. It was so different to the expensive European cars she'd seen since she arrived, and with a handsome Italian man standing beside it, his shirtsleeves rolled up to his elbows and his jeans faded from years of wear, it told her she was heading in exactly the right direction.

She put her bag in the back seat as he hefted her case up and settled into the passenger seat at the same time as he opened the driver's door.

"How long is the drive?" she asked.

He started the engine, muttering something under his breath when he had to turn the key twice to get it going. "A little under an hour," he said. "Just the perfect amount of time to get to know you."

His wink made her laugh straight back at him. If only her mum could have seen Antonio—she'd have heartily approved.

"So, tell me," she said as he pulled away from the hotel and out onto the road. "What do you do on the vineyard?"

"What don't I do?" he replied, glancing over at her as he drove. She ran her eyes over his masculine jawline, black hair pushed back from his face, once his eyes were back on the road.

"You've worked there a long time?"

"My parents are Roberto and Francesca Martinelli," he said, one hand on the wheel now as he settled back into the seat. "They started me working there as a boy, and I do everything from fixing machinery to harvesting the grapes. It's the way we do things on a family vineyard, although technically I'm the viticulturist."

She cleared her throat, embarrassed that she hadn't realized he was Roberto's son.

"I'm so sorry, I just didn't think—"

"That they'd send me to collect you?" His smile was infectious.

"I was expecting some lowly employee," she admitted.

"Ahh, bella, but that's exactly what they sent."

They both laughed then, the feeling easy between them even if Lily was more than slightly intimidated by the handsome man seated across from her.

"I hear you've been working abroad?" he asked.

She nodded, turning slightly in her seat so she was facing him. "I have. I spent time in California, then I went to New Zealand to better understand their sparkling wine production."

"Ahh, and now you want to know the secrets to our Franciacorta production?"

"Exactly. And I'm told, no, I *know* that your family makes some of the best sparkling wine in the region."

"According to my father," he teased.

"According to many of the best winemakers in the world, actually," she replied. "Although I won't tell your father that if you don't want me to."

"*Penso già che tu mi piaccia.*"

"What does that mean?" she asked.

"I said, I think I like you already." He laughed. "And I have a feeling my father is going to love you."

They drove in companionable silence for a while, with Lily staring out the window at the changing landscape, absorbing as much of the view as she could. Her favorite part of her job as a winemaker was traveling to different countries; she loved holding the soil of another country in her hands, meeting the people, watching the ways they worked. And her favorite vineyards were always the family ones, because they had traditions that descended through the generations. There was nowhere better to learn, and nowhere she'd rather be, even if it did make her think of her father often, and what she'd lost.

When her father had died, she'd become single-minded in following her dreams, on doing the things they'd always talked of together, things he'd wanted to do one day but hadn't been able to when a heart attack had stolen him from her. She'd wanted to be a winemaker from the moment she'd trailed around after him between the vines as a girl, as he explained to her how to tell if the grapes were ready, how to touch them, how to pick them by hand. As a teenager she'd watched him swill wine, describing to her what notes he could taste, before spitting it out, and she'd do the same, trying not to wrinkle her nose at the taste as she desperately tried to detect the hints of oak or citrus he described.

And then one day he was simply gone, with no warning whatsoever before that fatal moment. She'd cried for days, then decided she never wanted to set foot on a vineyard again, but eventually she'd given in and followed her heart back to what she loved. She could still hear his calm, deep voice when she tasted wine to this day, almost as if he was sharing it with her, telling her the notes or agreeing with her on whether it was a good year or not.

"Did you always want to work on the vineyard?" she asked Antonio, pushing away her thoughts of her father as she focused on the man beside her.

"It's our way of life," Antonio said with a shrug. "I was expected to work with my family, and luckily for me I wouldn't have it any other way. My brother, he feels the same, and so does my sister."

She didn't tell him that she had read extensively about his family; it was one of the reasons she should have known who he was. She racked her brain, remembering Marco and Vittoria, and . . . *Ant*. That's why she hadn't recognized it immediately.

"Do you prefer Antonio to Ant?" she asked.

He looked surprised. "Ahh, so she *has* done her research," he said with a grin. "Everyone who's known me since I was a child calls me Ant, but in truth, I hate it. I was the smallest boy at school, my legs were as skinny as could be and my brother was a giant beside me. So, they teased me and called me Ant, one of the downsides of learning the English language so young."

Her eyes quickly ran the length of his body. He was certainly no "ant" now. She guessed he was at least six foot one, maybe taller, and he easily filled out his shirt and his jeans.

"I don't think you have to worry about the nickname any longer," she said, blushing when he caught her staring at him.

"I didn't grow until I was sixteen, and now I'm taller than everyone in my family. But the name . . ." He shrugged. "It never left me."

He slowed down then, and she turned to look out the window, noticing that the landscape had changed yet again. It was beautiful, with vines suddenly stretching across the hillside as far as the eye could see, under a canopy of clear blue sky.

"Welcome home," he said as he turned into a driveway lined with trees on each side, their leaves waving lazily in the breeze. "I promise you, it's paradise."

As they made their way slowly up the drive, she saw a woman on a horse, her long dark hair flowing out behind her, hand raised as she waved to them.

"That's my mother," Antonio said.

Lily shouldn't have been so surprised, but the idea that the beautiful woman on the horse was mother to three grown-up children seemed impossible. She'd thought the picture on the family's website had been outdated, but it seemed it wasn't only the men in the family who were gorgeous.

"I have a feeling I'm going to love it here," she whispered.

Antonio's hand unexpectedly brushed hers as the drive stretched up a gentle hill, toward a sprawling home with a terra-cotta roof and plastered walls dotted with high windows. "So do I."

Lily had a feeling he wasn't just talking about the grapes, and as much as she'd always refused to mix business with pleasure, her mother's parting words were still ringing in her ears.

Have fun, Lily. You're only thirty once, and you need to let your hair down and let yourself fall in love. Or at the very least, fall into a gorgeous man's bed.

It turned out Antonio had taken her directly to the family home, which was perched on a hill overlooking their hectares of grapes, and with a view that stretched much farther than their own land-holding. Apparently, his parents had insisted that she be wel-comed informally by the family before they moved on to business.

"Ciao, Lily!" The loud, friendly voice that carried from an outdoor table framed by a vine-covered pergola struck her as being an older version of Antonio's. And the man it belonged to looked like a more stately, mature version of his son, albeit with silver hair.

"Mr. Martinelli, it's so wonderful to meet you."

"The pleasure is, how do you say, all mine," he said, rising and coming over to greet her, holding out his hands to clasp hers and then kissing her on each cheek. "Please join us, and call me Roberto. Have you had breakfast?"

"No, I actually didn't have time to eat anything before your son arrived."

"I hope he was on good behavior, si?"

His English was much more heavily accented than Antonio's, and she was immediately drawn to how welcoming he was. Her boss in New Zealand had promised her that she'd love being with the Martinelli family, when he'd recommend her for the job, and she had a feeling his instincts had been right.

"Si," she replied, looking over at Antonio and receiving a wink in reply. "He was very well behaved."

"Coffee?" Roberto asked, holding a pot. "And we have fresh bread rolls, just out of the oven."

Antonio sat down at the table and reached for one of the rolls, which he promptly covered in butter and jam. Her stomach growled in response, but just as she was about to sit down and take Roberto up on his offer of breakfast, they were joined by the woman they'd seen horse-riding—Antonio's mother, Francesca. And she looked as beautiful up close as she had from a distance, with faint lines fanning from her eyes the only hint at her age.

"Ciao, Lily! It's so good to have you here." She was dressed in jodhpurs, tall black boots and a slim-fitting, sleeveless shirt; a picture of elegance as she strode forward and kissed Lily on each cheek.

"Thank you, it's wonderful to meet you, too," Lily replied. "Your home is so beautiful, but I didn't expect to be invited here."

"Why not? You are to be as family while you are with us. We only ever invite one assistant winemaker each season, sometimes none at all, so you are very special to us."

She walked past Lily, and Lily saw that Roberto was already holding out a cup of coffee to his wife.

"Lily?" Antonio asked, indicating toward the empty cup on the table.

"Please, I'd love one," she said, taking a seat as the family began eating a late breakfast, Antonio and his father immediately starting to speak in rapid Italian that Lily hadn't a hope of deciphering.

"Excuse them," Francesca said, leaning toward her. "They disagree on at least one thing every morning, it's exhausting." She laughed. "It's also why I usually take my horse out early, so by the time I come home, I can sit out here in peace. *Alone.*"

They both grinned, and Lily looked around her as she took a bite of her bread, still warm from the oven as Roberto had promised.

"It's even worse when both my boys are here. And with you"—she sighed—"they would be like a pair of roosters, trying to outdo one another."

She watched Antonio as he threw his hands in the air before raking his fingers through his hair, his conversation with his father clearly heated.

"What are they talking about, if you don't mind me asking?"

"The same thing as every other morning," Francesca said with a sigh. "Antonio has new ideas, things he wants to change, and my husband wants to do the same things his father did before him. The older generations do not like change."

"I think that's why I was so drawn to this region, actually,"

Lily said. "I'm fascinated by the history and the generations-old rules around your production of Franciacorta. So much has changed around the world when it comes to grape production and methods, but here you are, so pure, so dedicated to preserving the way it has always been."

Antonio groaned, and she realized it wasn't just his mother who was listening to her.

"I fear you won't be the breath of fresh air I was hoping for," he grumbled.

"And I have a feeling she is exactly what we needed here," his father disagreed. "To remind us why we have to uphold tradition."

"I'm sorry, I had no intention of wading into a family argument."

"You've done nothing of the sort. Now finish your breakfast—you can bring your coffee with you for the tour," Francesca said. "I want to show you some of the property, before you walk the vines. This is a very special time of year, and you'll want to inspect the grapes. We've been keeping a very close eye on them. The conditions have to be just right, as you well know."

"And you still pick by hand?" she asked.

The men stopped talking again then, and it was Antonio who answered.

"That is one part of the tradition that must never change," he said as he relaxed back into his chair, nursing his coffee cup in one hand. "Every grape is picked by hand—it is the only way to harvest. There are no machines, it is not permitted, and we carefully transport each basket when it is full. We strictly follow the traditional method."

"I have a feeling you would follow the traditional method even if it wasn't required."

"One day in Italy, and she knows all our secrets," Antonio teased.

"We honor the past with each production, with every single

grape, and we pay homage to our ancestors," Roberto said. "Nothing is more important to me than the tender handling of each grape and seeing my family work shoulder to shoulder."

"Enough work talk. Come," Francesca said, dismissing the men. "Can you ride?"

Lily's last mouthful of bread went dry in her throat, and she quickly took a sip of coffee to wash it down. "I do, but it's been a very long time."

So long, in fact, that she felt an unfamiliar flutter of butterflies in her stomach, although she tried not to look as terrified as she felt.

"Good, then we shall ride, and I will show you every inch of this property before you get to work. Ant?"

He nodded. "Yes, Mamma, I will saddle a horse for Lily."

Lily sat back and finished her coffee, watching Antonio rise and kiss his mother's cheek before disappearing through an open door into the house. It was the kind of traditional, elegant home that was usually reserved for the pages of a magazine, steeped in history yet somehow still modern at the same time. It appeared cool, as if it would be comfortable even on the hottest summer day, and she loved the way it opened to the large alfresco area where they were sitting.

"He's a good boy, my Antonio," Francesca said. "Restless at times, but with the heart of a lion."

Lily thought of the way he'd so willingly obeyed his mother and kissed her, his attitude seeming so different to that of an Englishman. She could see that Francesca was most definitely at the helm of this family.

"It must be nice to have him close. Does he live here, too?" Lily hoped she wasn't being too nosy, but she was trying to fit all the pieces of the puzzle together.

"He has a house a few minutes' drive away, on our family land, but he always joins us for meals. It was perfect for him before, when he was . . ."

Lily leaned forward, wanting to know what Francesca had been about to say.

"Anyway, he likes being close almost as much as we like it," Francesca continued. "Although his brother is something else entirely. He prefers to keep an apartment in Milan, running the business side of things there for us."

Lily nodded, still curious about Antonio and wondering how long she'd have to bide her time to find out more. She knew how everyone talked, though, how quickly she'd fall in with the other workers, especially here with everyone encouraged to work so closely together. There were bound to be loose tongues after the first week or so.

"Come, let's find some boots for you, and we'll head down to the stables. There's so much to see."

Lily followed, and with the sun brushing her shoulders and the wind dancing against her cheeks she thought, and not for the first time that day, that there was nowhere she'd rather be.

Italy was good for the soul: it was a slogan she'd read on the plane that had stayed with her, and she had to say she whole-heartedly agreed.

9

"You've certainly chosen the perfect time of year to visit," Francesca said as they rode quietly along the rows of grapes, with Lily becoming so engrossed in what she was seeing she almost forgot she was on horseback. "We're one, maybe two weeks away from harvest, according to my husband."

"It's absolutely beautiful here," Lily said, wishing she were on foot. She wanted to linger over different rows and inspect the grapes, although she knew there would be plenty of time for that later.

"I can see the passion in your eyes," Francesca said with a laugh. "It's as if you're looking at a lover."

Lily grinned. "My only true love affair in years has been with grapes, so you're not wrong."

They rode in silence a while longer, until Francesca halted, staring out into the distance. "My husband's father was as passionate about grapes as most men are about fast cars and beautiful women," she said. "He had everything he could want at his fingertips, and yet he still wanted more. And that something more was a vineyard that could produce a sparkling wine to rival the best champagne in France."

"Well, he certainly achieved it," Lily said, admiring the view. Grapes stretched as far as the eye could see.

"But a feud has divided this family in recent times. It's why my husband gets so frustrated when Antonio wants to make changes. He hasn't spoken to his brother in years."

"I've read extensively about your husband's family, especially his father," Lily admitted. "He was the inspiration for the entire movement, for winegrowers in this region adopting the traditional method?"

"He was. He helped to make our Franciacorta as famous as Prosecco."

She wondered what the family had feuded about, recalling that Roberto's brother had once been involved with the vineyard, but she didn't like to ask more.

Francesca nudged her horse on, and Lily followed, surprised by how at ease she felt back in the saddle. She'd learned to ride as a child, on holidays at her aunt's country house, but her last experience had involved being thrown from the saddle over a prickly hedge, and she'd never ridden since.

"Tell me, how does the sparkling wine in New Zealand compare?"

"The vineyard I spent the most time at, it was family-owned, with siblings running the entire production. They had fresh ideas, but also a passion to remain true to the past, which just so happens to be my favorite kind of vineyard to spend time on," Lily explained. "I loved the way they still gathered some of their grapes by hand, as an ode to their father, who'd developed his sparkling wine for his late wife, and insisted on collecting all the grapes himself in the early stages. He was, like you, passionate about his family's involvement."

"Ahh, a beautiful story that I'd love to hear more of, but here is my son, come to take you away from me."

Antonio appeared on a bay gelding, riding up between them and looking as effortless as he could be in the saddle. She imagined he'd been on horseback since he was a child, not to mention toddling amongst the vines and getting lost in the greenery. She smiled at the thought.

"Sorry to interrupt you, but it's time to get to work."

Lily nodded at Francesca. "Thank you for a wonderful introduction to your property."

"I'll see you soon," the older woman replied. "I have a feeling you and I are going to enjoy one another's company."

With that, she was off, trotting and then breaking into a graceful canter as she disappeared in the opposite direction. Lily tightened her own reins, stiffening up as she panicked her horse might try to follow, but he appeared more interested in snoozing in the warm rays of sunshine than galloping away.

"You look tense," Antonio said. "She's not going to throw you, my mother put you on our sweetest mare."

Lily ignored him, making a conscious effort to lower her shoulders and appear more at ease. She knew he was right, but she still didn't like being told she was doing something wrong.

"What's our first order of business?" she asked.

He nudged his horse into a walk, and she did the same. "I introduce you to everyone, and we inspect the grapes. My father likes us to walk the vines daily and keep meticulous records heading into the harvest, as do I."

She nodded. "Of course."

"And then we walk you through our production, before settling you into your accommodation."

"Wonderful. But please put me to work straightaway. I like working a full day, I'm used to very long hours."

"You forget, you're in Italy now." His chuckle was belly-deep. "We have long lunches and *riposo*, our afternoon rest."

"I see." The Italians must follow what most Mediterranean cultures did—rest at the hottest part of the day. In New Zealand, they'd barely stopped for a lunch break. "But when it comes to the harvest?"

"We don't stop," he said. "Until the very last grape is picked."

A shiver ran down her spine. That was exactly what she wanted to hear. She'd been a workaholic all her life, which was precisely why she'd chosen to travel to Europe and do two harvests back to back.

She thought of her mum then, and wondered what she would be doing, smiling as she pictured her and Alan strolling along the lake or enjoying another late, long lunch together. If only she'd arranged for her mother to travel to the Martinelli family vineyard before she returned to London.

Perhaps I should; she would love it here.

"Everyone, this is Lily," Antonio introduced her an hour or so later. "Our new assistant winemaker."

Everyone looked up, and as Antonio gave a little clap, they all joined in, looking at her curiously. She held up her hand in a wave, smiling back at them all and hoping at least a handful of the workers spoke English.

"Ciao," she called out. "I look forward to getting to know you all."

Antonio touched her arm and steered her away from everyone, toward what she soon realized was the vineyard's restaurant. They stepped into a room that resembled a tunnel with its curved ceiling, a counter along one side and low tables throughout the rest of the space. It was simple but elegant, with stone features and glass doors framing the end of the room, looking out over the acreage.

But they didn't stop there, going through the restaurant and into the kitchen, which was a bustle of sizzling pans and moving bodies, steam billowing up into the air. He was certainly taking her on a whirlwind tour.

"Vittoria!" Antonio called out, waving at the air as smoke curled toward them. "Come and meet Lily!"

A chef set down her frying pan halfway across the kitchen and made her way toward them, her eyes the same dark shade as Antonio's, her smile even wider.

"Ahh, so you're the one my brother thinks will change Papà's mind."

They shook hands as Lily turned slowly to face Antonio, eyebrows raised in surprise. "That's what you think I'm here to do?"

He shrugged. "Let's just say I was hoping you'd help me to convince him to make some changes," he said. "After all, you've worked all over the world, you must have some new ideas for us."

Lily laughed, shaking her head. "Not a chance. I'm here because I want to know the traditional ways and work alongside one of the best."

Vittoria threw her hands up into the air as if to say, "What do I know?" before waving and hurrying back to her station. "I have lunch to cook. See you later, Lily." But then she laughed, walking backward for a few steps. "But be warned, you don't want to know what happened to the last assistant winemaker."

"What happened to the last assistant winemaker?" Lily asked.

Antonio turned and started to head away from the kitchen, muttering something under his breath, and Lily didn't know whether to be annoyed or flattered about what his sister had said, although she was trying to convince herself of the latter. But she was so fixated on why she'd been employed, that she forgot entirely about her final comment.

"Antonio, why would you think I'd—"

Antonio turned to her. "My friend, at the vineyard in New Zealand, he told me you were one of the best young winemakers he'd ever met." He blew out a breath. "I thought perhaps in bringing you here, that maybe—"

"I'd be the one to convince your father to change his ways?" It was almost comical. "Your father is renowned for his work, he's, well, I don't think I even need to explain. He's the reason I wanted to come here, the reason I thought I'd have no chance in securing the job in the first place because of all the other young winemakers vying to spend time with him."

"He is, but I fear our competitors are getting an edge on us," Antonio said. "He sees the past, but I want to make sure we have a future, and a long one at that."

It wasn't that Lily didn't understand what he was saying, because she did, but she just couldn't believe there was anything she could teach Roberto Martinelli. She'd come to learn from *him*.

"You're the reason I was offered the job, aren't you?" she whispered. "I thought it was your father. When they said Mr. Martinelli wanted to offer me a short-term position as assistant winemaker, I thought . . ."

"We invite a winemaker from another region to join us every few years, but yes, it was me." Antonio shrugged. "I made sure he was aware of you, because my father is much better if he thinks an idea is all his. I just pointed him in the right direction."

She should have been even more flattered, but for some reason she felt duped. Or perhaps it was simply her ego being dented.

"Well, thank you," she said. "I'm honored to be here, regardless of which Mr. Martinelli actually chose me."

They kept walking, this time through rows of enormous stainless steel vats, so contemporary-looking amidst the old-world feel of the rest of the property, and suddenly she thought of the little box she'd been given, and the clues it held. And she wondered, not for the first time, how she'd ended up in the same country her grandmother had such mysterious links to.

"Come, I want to show you our cellars," Antonio said, striding ahead. "We have a meeting in half an hour, but we have just enough time for me to give you the final part of the tour."

Lily ducked her head as they went through an arched doorway, and stepped back in time once again, the stainless-steel vats seeming to belong to another time and place as they headed for the cellars. It was getting darker, but her eyes slowly adjusted, and within minutes she was seeing row after row of previous years' vintages.

"Oh my," she whispered, lifting her hand to trace the precious bottles.

"Three years," he murmured. "That's how long we wait for our Franciacorta to mature."

"So long? I thought it would be two."

Lights hanging above barely lit the space through which they walked, but she found she could see just fine, and could easily make out Antonio's features as he leaned closer to her.

"Good things take time," he said, smiling down at her. "And our Franciacorta takes much longer than the rest. It's one of our secrets. We don't rush anything here."

She held her breath as he looked down at her before moving on. It was verging on workplace harassment the way his eyes simmered at her, his body far too close to hers for comfort, but she found that there was nothing about his behavior that made her want to complain.

Lily cleared her throat, reminding herself why she always kept her distance, why she never mixed business with pleasure. It had been a long time since she'd had her heart broken, so close to sacrificing her own dreams to follow someone else, and she'd vowed never to make that mistake again. It was one of the reasons she'd left London to travel in the first place.

She just had to make sure that if she ever *did* cross that line, it was for pleasure and nothing else. No falling in love; just enjoying a holiday fling.

Antonio smiled back at her as he beckoned for her to follow.

Promise me, if a gorgeous Italian man wants to take you to bed, you'll say yes.

She smiled back at him. Perhaps she needed to follow her mother's advice for once in her life.

She was in a beautiful country, on the vineyard of her dreams, with a handsome man showing her the ropes—it was as simple as that. But there was always that little voice, that reminder in her head that told her to stay focused, to not let anything slow her down from what she'd set out to achieve.

Which was how she'd ended up moving overseas after graduating from Plumpton. She'd done her time in the UK first after graduating, before emailing through her dad's contacts, then buying a ticket to take her across the world, first to California and then Marlborough, in New Zealand's South Island. Which was when she'd known it was the right thing to do, to make her father's dreams her own. She'd slowly healed as she held earth in her hands, inspecting soil, as she'd walked with some of the best winemakers in the region, picked grapes by hand, swilled and tasted, learning the craft and eventually becoming assistant winemaker. He'd somehow been with her every step of the way and being in Italy was one of his last dreams that she had to fulfill. *Of our dreams.*

She remembered him saying that most of his peers had dreamed of going to the Champagne region in France, but he'd been convinced that Italy was the place to go, to see the traditional method being practiced in a place that wasn't France. After that, he'd talked of them developing their own sparkling wine in England and leaving his job as head winemaker of a renowned vineyard in Oxfordshire, wanting her to go abroad to learn about growing grapes in frost-prone New Zealand and the methods used there, and then to Italy to learn how to create the best sparkling wine from Chardonnay and Pinot Noir grapes. In light of what she'd recently discovered, she wondered if he'd had a deeper connection to Italy than he'd realized.

"Are you coming?" Antonio called from up ahead.

She hurried along, pushing her memories away and smiling when she caught up with him.

"This," he said, "is where we keep our vintage bottles. We always celebrate by drinking one if we've had a good harvest."

"Well, let's hope this year's a good one, because I very much want to taste it."

Antonio glanced at his wristwatch, clapping his hands together when he saw how late it was.

"Time to go," he told her, indicating that she should turn and go back the way they'd come in. "My father is a stickler for punctuality."

So am I, she thought with a smile. *No wonder I liked him so much.*

As they walked out, through a different building, she stopped, seeing glass doors that led to yet another space. "You still use oak barrels here?" she asked, surprised. It wasn't common, not anymore, and as she lingered, she could almost smell the wooded, oaky scent that she knew would surround her if she stepped through the door.

"Another ode to the past," Antonio said with a chuckle.

"One day you'll look back and be grateful your father was so loyal to the ways of old. And let's not forget, your grandfather was one of the first winemakers in the region to make sparkling wine, so maybe he's more forward-thinking than you give him credit for."

"Ahh, well, perhaps you're right. Although moving him from a typewriter to a computer doesn't seem so unreasonable, does it?"

Lily laughed. "You're not serious."

"Si, bella," he said, sadly shaking his head. "But I am."

10

ITALY, 1938

It had been months since the day Estee had first met Felix, and from then on, they'd seen each other at least once a week. Now it was summer, they'd started sneaking out more often, sometimes during the afternoons when she was able to pretend that her dance lessons were taking longer than scheduled. It was a friendship that should never have happened, but it was almost as if they'd been destined to meet, their paths crossing that day to bring them together. She often wondered how different her life in Piedmont would have been without him, how desperately boring the past months would have been if he hadn't asked her outside that day after her recital.

Today, they sat in the sun, his trousers rolled up to his knees, and her skirt skimming her thighs as they dangled their legs in the water. It was the perfect kind of day, with a whisper of wind to cool their skin as the sun shone high above.

"You're awfully quiet today," he said, leaning back on his elbows as he watched her. "Are you worried about something?"

She knew what he was referring to; even she, with her lack of schooling, knew that the world was changing around them. Neither she nor her sisters were allowed to engage in political talk at the dinner table—their father would have exploded if they'd even tried to discuss what was happening—but she'd heard the rumors and whispers about a war. But it wasn't the world her mind was on today; she had something to tell Felix, and she had no idea how to even broach the subject.

The time she spent with him had come to mean so much to her—it was her lifeline, the only thing in her life that wasn't dance or family. The thought that it might be coming to an end was enough to break her heart.

"I've been invited to audition at La Scala Theatre ballet academy," she said, keeping her eyes down as she spoke, not wanting to meet his eye as the words tumbled from her mouth.

"In Milan?" he asked. "You're going to *Milan?*"

She blew out a breath. "Yes."

"Estee, this is wonderful news!" he said, his face broadening into a wide smile. "You must be thrilled!" He sat up when she didn't respond, leaning forward and flicking some water at her.

"Stop it," she said.

He cupped his hand the next time and splashed her dress.

"Felix!"

"Admit that it's good news and I'll stop," he said, grinning as he leaned forward again. "You look like someone's just died!"

"I should push you in," she muttered.

"*Estee,*" he warned, dangling his fingers in the water, his expression suggesting he might actually soak her this time.

"Fine," she admitted. "It *is* good news."

"So, why are you so sad? What is it?"

Estee looked out across the water, not wanting to meet his gaze. She bit down on her lower lip, hating how emotional she was, how much it hurt to think about leaving. She'd perfected the art of not showing her sadness, her tears, her frustrations; and then Felix had come along and turned her life upside down. She'd never have let her mother see how she was feeling, nor her younger sisters, but with Felix she couldn't seem to hide anything.

"Estee?"

"Fine," she blurted out, hurling the words at him as if it were all his fault. "It's because I won't be able to see you again. This, whatever this is, it'll be over."

He went silent then, and she finally found the courage to turn and look at him, her eyes slowly finding his.

"It's what you've been training for," he said, but she could see the recognition on his face, too. It wasn't only she who'd enjoyed the time they'd spent together. "This is what you wanted, isn't it? To become a famous dancer, to have the chance to perform at La Scala?"

"We both know that what either of us wants in this life is inconsequential," she said. But he was right; it was what she wanted with every fiber of her being. She just didn't want to give him up at the same time, and knowing that she could only have one if she turned her back on the other was almost impossible to digest.

"I'm going to be so hungry all the time without you," she said, laughing even as tears fell down her cheeks.

"I always knew it was all about the food with you. If I didn't bring you pastries, I bet you wouldn't even make time to see me," he said, bumping shoulders with her. But she could see tears in his eyes now, too.

"I'm going to miss you so much," Estee whispered, gasping back emotion, hating that he was seeing her like this. She didn't like to be vulnerable, not for anyone, not even him.

Felix shuffled closer to her, and they sat together, leaning back on their elbows again. Her shoulder and arm were pressed to his, and she didn't dare move, needing his touch more than ever. They'd never kissed again since that very first day; it hadn't seemed right, or perhaps neither of them had been sure what to do, or perhaps it was the fact that they both knew that whatever existed between them was ill-fated. He was promised to someone else, and she was never going to be good enough for his family, even if he didn't already have a marriage arrangement.

"I'll never forget you, Felix," she forced herself to say.

"Don't say that. It makes it sound like we're never going to see one another again."

Maybe we won't ever see one another again.

Estee didn't answer, because she didn't trust her own voice, but when Felix cleared his throat and pushed up slightly on one elbow, she bravely met his gaze as he looked at her mouth.

"Estee," he murmured.

She smiled up at him, somehow knowing what he was going to say, what he was going to ask her before he even said the words. "*Yes*," she whispered in reply.

Felix bent lower and she stayed deathly still, not wanting to ruin the moment. And as the sun beat down on them, the summer-scented air curling between them, his mouth gently touched hers in a kiss that told her this was most definitely goodbye, no matter how much he wanted to pretend that they would see one another again. Because how would they ever cross paths again if her audition was successful?

His kiss deepened, lips moving over hers, no inexperienced clashing of teeth like last time. But eventually Felix pulled back, touching her hair as he hovered above her, stroking it as if it were silk, touching her so tenderly it almost broke her heart all over again.

"They're going to love you, Estee," he murmured. "You'll be the most beautiful dancer at La Scala one day, I just know it."

She very much doubted she'd be the most beautiful, but in Felix's eyes, she suddenly saw herself as he saw her; could tell from the way he was gazing at her that he truly meant what he'd said. For the first time, she understood that he loved her as much as she loved him, even if their love for one another could never mean anything. Even if they'd never be brave enough to tell one another.

"I wish things could be different. I wish—"

"Let's not," she said, shaking her head as fresh tears filled her eyes. "We can't change our families or our destiny, so can't we just enjoy today? Can't we just pretend, as if this isn't the last time?"

Even if I were staying, we could never have been together. And if I'm not successful in my audition, my mother won't let me leave the house anyway.

Felix's smile matched hers when she reached for him and pulled him down, giggling when he wrapped her in his arms. She leaned forward a little, finding his mouth again and sighing against him when his lips parted and made way for hers.

Tomorrow, she would be traveling to Milan, perhaps never to return to Piedmont, and she wanted to stamp Felix into her brain so that when she was long gone and he was married, she'd always be able to remember his warm kisses under the sun beside the lake.

They might need to last me a lifetime.

* * *

The following day passed by in a blur. Milan wasn't all that far away, but Estee had no idea how long she might end up staying there. She had an aunt, her father's sister, who lived there and had offered to take her in if she was selected, and as she stood in the center of her bedroom, she wondered if she'd ever set foot inside it again. Would she ever live in this house again, or would her life take her farther and farther away from Piedmont? Before Felix, it was what she dreamed of; getting away, finally being able to step out from the shadow of her overbearing mother. But everything she'd truly wanted before Felix seemed like a distant memory now, because suddenly all she wanted was to stay and have more stolen moments with him.

It was silly, because she'd most definitely be coming back at some point, even if she was chosen, but as she stood and turned around, taking it all in, she still felt nostalgic. Her two sisters had to share a room, and although they were treated far better than she was by their mother, she'd been given her own room to ensure she had adequate time to rest without being disturbed. And when she wasn't dancing, she was studying music in her room; her mother wanted to make sure she was accomplished at all things relating to dance, and music was one of those things.

Estee crossed the room and stared out of the window, wishing she could see all the way to the river or to Felix's house. She couldn't, but it didn't stop her closing her eyes and imagining it, picturing herself in the almost dark, scurrying along the road to his house for one of their secret rendezvous. If she left now, she knew just how many steps it would take to get to her gate, how many minutes it would take to get to his house once she ducked out onto the road.

"Estee?"

Her mother's voice was softer than usual, but she still felt her body instinctively straighten, prepared for the blow that might come or the sharp command. Surprisingly, it never came, but it did make her abandon any thoughts of leaving the house.

"Daydreaming?" her mother asked.

"No, Mamma," she replied. "I was going through the recital in my mind." She hated how easily the lie rolled from her tongue, but when it came to her mother, she'd learned how to avoid her temper—most of the time.

"Good," she replied, and Estee watched as she stood over her narrow bed, examining the things her daughter had folded but was yet to pack. She found herself holding her breath without even realizing she was doing it.

"I don't have to remind you what an opportunity this is, for our whole family, do I?" her mother asked as she turned back to face her. "This might be your only chance to impress, your only chance to join the academy. You must be *brilliant*."

"I know, Mamma," Estee replied, keeping her voice soft,

making sure her gaze wasn't too direct. She knew what her mother wanted to hear, understood exactly how to tiptoe around her. "I will dance as if my life, as if *all* of our lives depend upon it."

"Good." Her mother turned and waved her hand in the air. "Now hurry up. I want you packed before dinner and then well rested. We have a big day tomorrow."

Estee knew she wouldn't sleep a wink. How could she? She was going to be auditioning with the best young dancers in Europe, and if she didn't impress them, she might never get a second chance. Even if she didn't get one of the highly coveted positions, she needed to ensure they remembered her. *I have to be unforgettable.*

To get away from here, from this house, from Mamma. This is my chance.

I have to forget Felix. Once I'm there, I can't ever look back.

Sometimes she hated what she'd become, the pressure of ballet, the life she'd been forced to give up for her dance, her childhood. But then she'd remember that it was the only way she was ever going to break free. And for that, she'd do anything. Her mother thought she was doing it for them, for her family, but in truth she was doing it for herself.

Estee carefully put her things in the suitcase, and then placed it on the floor, before lying on top of her bed and squeezing her eyes shut. She just wished she could stop thinking about Felix, because it would have made leaving so much easier.

Because no matter how much she kept telling herself to forget him, it was impossible.

11

PRESENT DAY

"So tell us, Lily," Francesca said as they sat in their chairs around the alfresco table, fairy lights twinkling around them as someone brought coffee and a small bowl of chocolates after dinner. "How does this compare to the last vineyard you worked on?"

She smiled as she reached for a chocolate. "I thought it would seem more similar, being another family-owned estate, but it's actually quite different. Italy is truly like nowhere else in the world."

Antonio raised his eyebrows at her from across the table.

"Honestly, the earth smells different here, the people, *you*, are all so different. The way you all sit together at each meal, and the way you look at the grapes, it's more passionate. New Zealanders are more reserved perhaps, although they couldn't have been more welcoming to me, and they certainly take their wine *very* seriously."

"You'll find our winemakers like to be very involved in the entire process in this region, particularly on the old family estates."

"I'm well used to that, although I heard a rumor that you all join in on the first day of picking. Even the winemaker."

Roberto laughed, a big, belly-deep rumble. "It's more than a rumor," he said. "I personally pick the first grapes on the first day of harvest, and I start every day out amongst the vines, making sure they're picked to my satisfaction, before going inside as the first harvest arrives in for inspection. I check everything myself before it goes into the press."

Lily listened intently, surprised only by the fact that he was involved in some of the handpicking himself.

"My father is like a lion. We call him the king of the jungle as we near harvest, prowling the rows and deciding when picking will begin," Antonio said.

"And do they all obey you?" Lily asked Roberto with a grin.

"It is the one time I let him boss me around," Francesca interrupted, blowing her husband a kiss. "We do as he says, because harvest is his time to shine. Although he is very bossy."

"Your father," Roberto said, taking the attention away from himself. "His reputation precedes you, Lily. The skills a winemaker needs are instinctual, they can be refined, but you either have the gift or you don't." His smile was warm as he studied her over his wine glass. "I'm told you have the same instincts he had."

"I was hanging from his coattails my entire childhood, so everything I truly know, I learned from him." Lily cleared her throat as her memories resurfaced for the second time that day, not expecting him to come up in conversation but flattered all the same that someone remembered how talented her father was, especially after all this time. "But I hope that I can prove myself without needing to use his name these days."

"I understand he trained in California?" Roberto asked.

"Yes, although he always told me not to spend too much time there, that he wished he'd traveled right here to this very region, and to New Zealand. He felt the winter climate there was particularly interesting, that it would have parallels with the conditions in England."

"Your father passed away?" Antonio asked, his voice softer now.

"He did," she replied. "Just shy of my nineteenth birthday."

"I'm so sorry," he said, his eyebrows creased together as he looked at her.

She shrugged, as if it were nothing, when, in fact, the pain was still so deep sometimes that it cut right to the bone.

"The pain never goes away," Francesca said, leaning closer and placing her hand over Lily's. "I still have tears in my eyes when I think of my mother, God rest her soul."

Lily didn't move her fingers, finding she liked the comforting weight of the other woman's hand there. It seemed like forever since she'd had a moment of physical contact with anyone, even though she'd only been with her mother the day before. Other than that, it *had* been a while.

"Was your mother a winemaker, too?" Lily asked Francesca.

"No! And I am merely a winemaker's wife, I have no formal training," Francesca clarified. "I'm very useful when it comes to harvest, and I have been known to make some good suggestions, but my husband is the winemaker."

"And your son," Antonio growled, making his mother, and himself, laugh. "Don't forget the viticulturist."

"How could I possibly forget my darling eldest son?" Francesca said with a grin. "My mother was actually a seamstress, and she spent much of her life making beautiful costumes for ballet dancers in Milan, where we lived, so my childhood was far removed from the life I live now."

Lily was about to reach for her coffee, but instead she turned back to Antonio's mother, her words making her pause.

"Was there a specific theater or academy she worked for?" Lily asked, her breath catching as she thought of the clue she'd been left. Surely it would be too much of a coincidence for the Martinellis to have a connection to the same theater?

"Why, yes, she worked in many theaters, but her most memorable years were with the La Scala ballet academy. She was there until she retired."

Lily suddenly wished she had the torn piece of paper with her, to show Francesca. "I know this sounds like a coincidence, but I've recently discovered that my great-grandmother may have had a connection to La Scala," Lily said. "I was actually hoping to uncover some clues while I'm here in Italy."

"Well, let me see if I can think of anyone you could contact. What information do you have? How can I help?"

Lily shook her head sadly. "I feel that I'm fumbling at loose ends, to be honest. I don't have much to go on."

"Still, I will see what old contacts she might have that could help. If you'd like?"

"I'd like that very much, thank you." Lily picked up her coffee cup and found her hand was shaking this time, and when she looked up, she also saw that it hadn't gone unnoticed by Antonio. But bless him, he never said a word, and she sipped her coffee and pretended everything was fine, even though her mind was racing and her heart pounding.

The clues were like little bundles of knowledge burning a hole in her bag, insisting that she pull them out and put them to use. But with or without Francesca's assistance, it still seemed like a long shot that she would ever find the connection to her great-grandmother, although perhaps sharing them with every Italian she met might help her at least get closer.

She finished her coffee and took one last glance around her at the idyllic surroundings before excusing herself.

"Thank you all so much for an amazing day and night, but I think it's time for me to turn in," she said, still not sure where exactly she was sleeping after a long day that had resulted in them finishing work and heading straight outside for dinner. "I'm exhausted."

"Antonio, show Lily to her room, would you?" his mother asked. "Your bags have already been taken there for you."

He folded his starched white napkin and left it on the table, rising and indicating that she should go inside.

"Where are the workers' quarters?" she asked, expecting to be housed elsewhere on the property. She'd seen some quaint little cottages dotted away from the production area.

"You're staying here," Antonio said. "It seems my mother took one look at you and decided you were to have the guest suite."

Lily studied him, half expecting him to laugh and say he was joking with her. But from the way he pushed one hand into his pocket and sauntered forward, leading her down the high-ceilinged hallway to the other end of the house, it was obvious he didn't even think anything of it.

"I thought I'd be—"

"This is you," he said, nudging open the door to one of the most luxurious rooms she'd ever seen. An enormous, four-poster canopy bed took pride of place in the center of the room, with double doors leading out to a small courtyard, fairy lights draped around the pergola; a mini version of the large alfresco area where they'd eaten dinner.

Antonio pulled the curtains shut, even though she had every intention of pushing them open again as soon as she was alone.

"You have a private bathroom through there." He gestured to the other side of the room. "My mother wants you to feel at home, so please, anything you want, just let one of us know. You're to treat our home as yours."

If only this were my home. It's the most beautiful place I've ever set foot in.

"Thank you, Antonio, it's perfect."

She half expected him to kiss her cheeks or wink before he left, but instead all she received was a brief smile before he disappeared, calling good night as he strode away.

"Oh, before you leave," she called after him.

Antonio stood, braced by the door as his eyes found hers.

"What did happen to the last assistant winemaker?" she said, realizing she'd never asked him after his sister had mentioned it.

Antonio frowned. "You're looking at him."

She went to open her mouth again, but his expression stopped her. He wasn't joking.

"Buona notte, Lily."

She smiled. *Good night.* That was one phrase she'd managed to learn in the few Italian language podcasts she'd listened to before her flight. "Buona notte," she replied, realizing that whatever had happened between him and his father was most definitely a story for another night.

As soon as she was alone, Lily walked to the doors and flung the curtains open again, just as she'd planned, looking out at the gently twinkling fairy lights that reminded her of stars, and wondering if her dad was looking down on her.

It's just as wonderful here as you always said it would be, Dad. I only wish you were here with me.

Lily wiped her cheeks and then turned, kicking off her shoes and peeling off her clothes, before putting on her silk pajamas and climbing beneath the crisp white sheets, her head dropping to the plump, feather-filled pillow.

But she was only in bed a moment before she remembered the clues, and she crawled out of bed to retrieve them, turning them over and over in her hands as she studied them, still not seeing how she was ever going to make head or tail of them.

And as she settled back again into the pillows, the papers resting in her fingertips on top of the duvet, she wondered whether her great-grandmother had really wanted to be found one day, or if the clues were ever going to bring her closer to finding out her grandmother's heritage. Or her father's.

How was it that something she'd never known about, never known was even a mystery before now, suddenly felt so important that she could feel the weight of it in her bones? There was nothing she could do to change what had happened, or even ever know whether her grandmother was aware of her adoption, but it meant something for *her* to know. To honor the woman who'd meant so much to her as a child.

With that, she closed her eyes, her fingertips still holding the papers as she gave in to the soft, luxurious feathers beneath her and drifted off to sleep.

12

ITALY, 1938

Estee stood, holding her body at the most perfect of angles, her chin tipped up, her back as straight as could be. She could feel sweat curling at the back of her neck, her arms on the verge of trembling as she held them high, taking frantic little sips of air, even though she felt like gasping to fill her lungs.

Almost all of the ballerinas had been chosen, and she wasn't one of them. She held her smile, well versed at what she was supposed to do, at how to impress, at how to appear serene even when she was crumbling inside, but the dancers here were different. The other ballerinas here made her feel incompetent, made her wonder if she even deserved a place at the audition, whether she would ever have a chance against them. But one thing Estee wasn't was a quitter. If she failed, then she would accept her fate, but until then, she knew better than to concede before the final place was given. It was one thing she would give her mother credit for.

She saw the panel of four leaning inward, discussing something, and she closed her eyes for just a moment, seeing Felix in her mind, seeing their special place by the lake, the sun brushing her shoulders as she dipped her toes into the water.

When she opened her eyes, everything changed, everything somehow seemed brighter. And when she was invited to dance one more time, Estee kept the lake in her mind, refusing to give up, knowing this was her last chance to show them what she was capable of. All she needed was the chance.

You'll be the most beautiful dancer at La Scala, Estee.

She heard Felix's words in her mind as she rose higher, reached higher, pushing herself to her limits as she truly danced like she'd never danced before, her assemblé perfect as she landed on two feet with barely a sound, finishing with a grand jeté jump that was longer than she'd ever managed on stage before.

When she stood again, her breath fast as she held herself perfectly still, the oldest of the women watching, judging her, nodded. The woman didn't smile, but she didn't frown, either.

"Please come forward," she said, her voice as rigid as Estee's back.

Estee did as she was asked, making sure each step was graceful, purposeful, as if it were part of her performance. She had a part to play, and she was staying faithfully in character until the day was over.

They were all still talking, saying something she couldn't hear, but she saw the way the two men and two women looked her up and down, as if they were considering her body. It was part of being a ballerina, the scrutiny, although it was something she might never get used to, and she only wished she could hear what they were saying.

"How old are you?"

"I'm thirteen," she said, her voice carrying more bravely than she'd expected. In truth she wasn't thirteen for a few more weeks, but her mother had told her to lie lest they think her too young.

The critical appraisal began again, eyes sweeping the length of her body, and suddenly she wished she hadn't eaten all the pastries Felix had brought her. Had she been so distracted by him that she was no longer thin enough? Had she indulged one too many times? Was her mother right about her needing to be as tiny as a bird?

"Your bone structure is heavier than the other girls. But your face . . ."

She breathed. It was all she could do. The tiny, frantic sips started again. She was the youngest, which meant she wasn't supposed to be the heaviest. It took all her strength, all her willpower, to keep her hands soft and not make them into tight fists so she could press her nails into her skin.

"You face is exquisite, though," the other woman said. "Come closer, please."

Estee did as she was asked, lowering her eyes demurely as she moved, knowing that she was so close to being sent home. *Or perhaps my face might save me. Perhaps my face will change their minds.*

She'd parted her raven-dark hair down the center that morning, careful to make sure it couldn't escape. Her lashes were black, her lips painted a soft pink that was so at odds with her otherwise dark features, her high cheekbones illuminated by the pink blush her mother had carefully applied for her. She knew there was something about her appearance, something about the way she looked that made her appealing, but to hear that her face was exquisite? It gave her the confidence she needed, and she imagined herself in ten years' time, saw herself on the stage, imagined the life she would have if she succeeded.

You're light as a feather. You are the best dancer La Scala will ever see.

She summoned her body, her limbs graceful, refusing to be intimidated by the way they were whispering to one another. If she'd strained her ears she might have heard, but she didn't need to hear. Whether she heard what they were saying or not, it didn't matter. The only thing she could do was try to make them fall in love with her.

Estee resisted the urge to look behind her, to the other

hopeful ballerinas who would all be praying she failed, holding their breath as they waited for her to be sent away. She softly cleared her throat as the small panel looked up, wanting to break the silence and tell them why she deserved to be chosen; but she knew speaking wasn't part of the audition, and she could ruin her chances entirely if she spoke at all. They didn't care what she had to say, they only cared about the way her body looked and moved on stage.

"Our final ballerina," one of the men announced, loudly enough for everyone gathered on stage to hear as he nodded at her.

She gasped. *Me?*

Me!

It was as if she'd said the word aloud, because the younger of the women sitting on the panel gave her a little smile, as if to confirm the news, the first expression of warmth from any of the adults who'd been studying her.

"Thank you," she said, with a little nod and smile, desperately trying to retain her composure. "Thank you for this incredible opportunity."

I'm in. I made it!

Estee almost collapsed to the ground, the exhaustion of such a long day dancing and the emotion of waiting to hear the final choices almost too much to bear; but she forced herself to turn and walk gracefully off the stage. Her mother hadn't been allowed in, and she was grateful to have the moment to herself, to absorb the news.

Another girl passed her, her shoulder painfully hitting hers as she purposely walked into her, and Estee stepped back, seeing the sneer on the other girl's face. It was obvious they'd both been vying for that final position.

Estee went to open her mouth but decided to nurse her bruised shoulder in silence. It wasn't worth it. She was in, and that was all that mattered.

"Ignore her," came a confident voice from behind Estee. "Once they're all gone, it'll be better."

She turned and came face to face with a pretty blonde ballerina. She recognized her immediately as the first dancer chosen; her limbs were long and lithe, her body as perfect as a ballet dancer's could be. Estee immediately felt intimidated, knowing she was in the company of someone great.

"You danced beautifully today," the girl said. "I knew you'd be chosen."

"I'd started to lose hope," Estee admitted, surprised at how freely she'd spoken the truth. "I didn't think I stood a chance at the end."

The other girl shrugged. "Perhaps they were going to choose you all along," she said. "Don't think about it again. It doesn't matter which order we were chosen in, what matters is that we *were* chosen. We're all in this together now. No one will ever remember who was first or last."

Estee hadn't thought about it like that. Perhaps the pretty blonde was right; the only thing that mattered now was whether you'd been picked or not, although she doubted anyone would ever forget being the very first to be chosen.

"I'm Estee," she said.

"Sophia," she replied, holding out a dainty hand that was warm and soft against Estee's.

"Come on, they're going to give us all our information about when we start and what's expected of us," Sophia said, keeping hold of her as she started to walk, their palms pressed firmly together.

Estee couldn't hide her smile. The other girls parted as they walked through, Sophia straight-backed and regal ahead of her, and just like that, she felt her worries sliding away as she let herself become excited about the future. Her new friend had to be at least fifteen, but it didn't matter. She'd taken her under her wing and Estee had never felt so confident as she trailed in her wake.

I'm in Milan. I'm going to dance at La Scala one day. I've officially been accepted into the most prestigious dance academy in all of Italy.

Her heart would always ache for Felix and what could have been, but it was time for her to live her life now. It was time to leave the ironclad grip of her mother, of her girlhood, behind. It was time for her to become a woman.

Sophia glanced over her shoulder at her, dazzling her with her smile.

Everything's going to be fine. The next few years are going to be the most amazing years of my life; there's no time to look back and wonder what could have been.

She'd never stop wondering about him: about how pretty his one-day wife was, about what his family would have thought of her if they'd ever met, or whether they could have stayed friends. But her life was ballet. There wasn't time for distractions any longer. She was going to have to dance like her life actually depended upon it now, because it did.

"I can see us on the stage together at La Scala," Sophia whispered into her ear as she walked them to the front of the small group. "Can't you?"

Estee squeezed her eyes shut as a smile danced across her lips.

"I can, too," she whispered back, the image taking her breath away as she saw herself there. "I can, too."

13

PRESENT DAY

The conditions were perfect. Everyone was humming with anticipation, the feeling on the vineyard so different now to the day
Lily had first arrived. And she'd seen that lion side of Roberto
now for herself—the grim set of his mouth as he barked orders,
the intensity of his gaze as he studied the grapes each morning—
quite another person to the relaxed man she'd met on her arrival.

"Walk with me," he said, seven days after she'd arrived.

Lily set down the notebook she'd been writing in, tucking her
pencil against it and following Roberto. She fell into an easy step
beside him, not worried at all about the change in his demeanor.
She'd seen the same change in her father each year when he'd
been waiting for the grapes to reach perfection, and instead of
making her anxious, it only filled her with anticipation. This, *this*
was what every winemaker lived for, that moment when everyone looked to them to make that final decision that would send
everyone into a flurry of excitement.

"I asked you to join me, Lily, because I want to know what
you think," he said. "You've checked the grapes daily with me,
and tasted them, but today . . ." He frowned, then looked up at the
sky, and she wished she knew what he was thinking.

"You think they're ready, don't you?" she asked.

"I knew in my bones it was going to be earlier this year," he said. "It's why I asked you to arrive sooner. It's been hotter than usual this season."

They kept walking, up the incline, and Lily found her pulse starting to race, but still she was thankful they were on foot. When he finally stopped, she watched as he sank to his haunches and took a small handful of earth into his dark-tanned hands, closing his palm for a moment before letting it run between his fingers.

"I know everything there is to know about this land," he said. "The way it should feel, smell, taste . . ." He brushed his hands on his trouser legs and took a few more steps forward, carefully taking two grapes into his hand, inspecting the flesh, bringing it to his nose and then finally tasting it. She could almost imagine she were walking the grapes with her own father; Roberto was as warm as he was knowledgeable.

Lily followed Roberto's lead, going through the motions, the very same steps she'd taken each season she'd worked as a winemaker. But just as she was tasting a fruity Chardonnay grape, a figure caught her eye. She'd barely seen Antonio to speak to properly since the night he'd shown her to her room, and she smiled as he approached. He lifted a hand, his mouth held in a tight line as his eyes searched for his father, as if he hadn't even seen her. She took the opportunity to study him, wishing she were walking the grapes with him instead of his father.

Roberto looked at his son, moving farther along and taking another grape, and she realized that theirs was an unspoken language, that son was watching father, knowing a decision was imminent.

But the nod she was expecting from Roberto didn't come. She found instead that he was turning to her, and as her mouth became dry, his eyes found hers.

"Lily?"

Antonio started to pace nearby, a different person to the relaxed, quick-to-smile man who'd picked her up from her hotel.

Instead of replying, she walked away, down the row, pausing to study another bunch of grapes, taking one to taste and closing her eyes as she recalled what Roberto had already told her and the notes she'd made.

"Tomorrow," she said.

Roberto nodded. "I agree."

She glanced up at the sky. "And the conditions?"

Before Roberto could answer, Antonio threw his hands into the air and muttered something that could only have been a curse, for his father gave him a sharp look. But Antonio didn't see it as he strode away, heading back to the buildings.

"He's—" she started.

"He will ready everyone for the morning," Roberto said. "He's like this every year, pay him no heed. He thought today was going to be the day. He's impatient at the best of times."

She held her tongue as they walked back down the hill, but she couldn't help wondering if it was something to do with her being there as assistant winemaker that was irritating Antonio.

"Your instincts are good, Lily," Roberto said as they parted ways. "We'll drive over to check the other grapes after lunch. I think it's going to be a busy week."

"Thank you," she replied, but internally she was already questioning whether it should have been today. Something about the flash of Antonio's eyes told her that he felt today was the day, which meant she'd already stepped on his toes.

You weren't asked to come here to tell everyone what they wanted to hear. It was as if her father were beside her, his shoulders slightly stooped as he leaned toward her and looked out over the land. *Follow your instincts, they've never failed you yet.*

He was right, they hadn't, or at least not when it came to her job. She shut her eyes a moment, the breeze caressing her cheeks, considering her decision. It had been the right one. Today would have been fine, but tomorrow would be better.

"Lily!"

She turned and saw Antonio's sister coming out of the back door of the restaurant, a cigarette casually perched between her lips and a glass in her hand. Lily waved and walked over, happy to have the company rather than second-guessing her decision and replaying the morning in her mind.

"You look like you need this more than I do," Vittoria joked, holding out her cigarette.

Lily laughed. "I don't smoke, but I could do with a drink."

They both laughed and sat down on the steps that ran alongside the back of the restaurant.

"Busy day?" Lily asked.

"It's always busy in the kitchen. How about you? Are we any closer to harvest?"

Lily nodded. "Tomorrow. Although your brother didn't seem to agree with me."

"He said that?"

"Well, not in as many words, but he gave me a look."

"Oh, I know the look." Vittoria laughed. "Don't take it to heart, it's just the way he is, prowling around waiting for everything to begin. You wait, as soon as the first grape is picked, his smile will return, and his shoulders will relax. You'll see."

Lily watched as Vittoria smoked, making it look glamorous somehow, even though Lily abhorred cigarettes. She tried not to cough when the smoke curled toward her.

"He said something the other night, that he was the last assistant winemaker."

Vittoria smiled, and Lily waited, hoping she might tell her the story.

"It was ill-fated," Vittoria eventually said. "Papà has his ways, and Ant, too, but what he is good at is caring for the vines all year, doing the harvest, working the machines."

"And your father?"

"Deserves his reputation as the best winemaker in the region," Vittoria said, and it was impossible not to hear how proud she was of him. "My brother could work anywhere in the world, he just needed to realize what he's best at."

"I see."

"He's a good man, my brother, but life has been difficult for him these past few years."

Lily's breath caught in her throat. This was what she'd wanted to hear, the story of what his mother had alluded to, but just as Vittoria's mouth opened, dropping her cigarette and crushing it beneath her boot, a loud, cheerful and thickly accented voice called out.

"And here's the other brother," Vittoria murmured.

"Who do we have here?" he called out, opening his arms to his sister and giving her a big hug and kissing her cheeks, before holding out a hand to Lily, his eyes full of question.

"You must be the infamous Marco," Lily said, starting to get used to the flamboyant Italian welcomes and embracing his exuberant kissing of both her cheeks. There was no mistaking he was Antonio's brother; he was every bit as handsome.

"This is Lily," Vittoria said. "She's the assistant winemaker."

"Ahh, the assistant," he said, trading glances with his sister. "Why did nobody tell me how beautiful she was? I'd have left Milan sooner!"

She laughed at the compliment as Vittoria rolled her eyes. "I need to get back to the kitchen. Nice talking to you, Lily. Good luck tomorrow."

"So it's happening tomorrow?" Marco asked.

"It is," Lily replied. "And I'd best get back to work. There's a lot to prepare for."

"See you tomorrow, Lily."

She waved to Marco and walked away, even though it would have been tempting to sit in the sunshine for longer and get to know the younger Martinelli brother. She had a feeling he took life a lot less seriously than his older sibling.

It had been a busy week, learning everything there was to know, and she wished she'd had longer. Her only hope was that perhaps she'd get invited back next year if all went well, so she could have many more months on the beautiful property.

Her phone pinged in the back pocket of her jeans, and she pulled it out, glancing at the screen and seeing it was a text from her mother. Clearly, she'd finally worked out how to use her phone; it was the second text she'd received that week.

Thinking of you. Hope you're finding time for fun.

Lily smiled, starting to text her back, her head down.
Thump.

Lily looked up and into a very familiar broad chest. She'd been so busy staring at her phone, she'd managed to walk smack bang into Antonio. His white shirt had barely any buttons done up, his bronzed chest impossible not to notice.

"Sorry," he muttered.

"I was looking at my phone," she apologized. "What's your excuse?"

He grunted. "I was too busy looking up at the sky."

"The weather?" she asked with a smile.

"The weather," he repeated. "The winemaker decides the perfect time to pick, and I'm left to worry about the weather, and whether it will hold for the harvest. I've barely slept these past few nights."

"I've missed seeing you around," she found herself saying, regretting the words the moment they came out of her mouth.

"Tomorrow, we will be side by side," he said with a warm smile. "I'll be waiting for my father to change his mind, which he's done before when I had all the workers ready to start. When he picks that first grape at dawn, my smile will return for the rest of the year."

She didn't tell him that she was enjoying that very handsome smile right now; it might have been on a break, but it was most certainly back again.

"I've just met your brother."

"Commiserations."

Now it was her smiling. His ability to converse and joke with her in English was quite something, and she realized how much she'd been looking forward to spending time with him again.

"Antonio, I have to ask, you're certain you're okay with me being here? That I'm not stepping on your toes? I mean—"

He reached out and touched her shoulder, so at ease with his fingers brushing against her, as if it were the most natural thing in the world.

"Lily, don't forget that I wanted you here. My role is to look after the grapes. My father's, and *yours*, is to make the wine." His hand fell away as he turned and started to walk backward. "We'll make a great team, just you wait and see."

She watched him for a moment before continuing on, quickly replying to her mother before putting her phone back in her pocket and going to find Roberto. They had a big day ahead of them and she wanted to know the plan.

14

"It's time."

Two words changed everything. Lily had been standing beside Roberto since she'd risen at five a.m. to join him, barely able to sleep in anticipation of the day ahead.

She nodded and tried to contain her smile, which was impossible, looking up with thanks at the hot sun above them, which was giving them the perfect conditions to harvest beneath. Roberto stepped forward and took a pair of sharp shears, cutting the first bunch of grapes and placing them carefully in a basket, which led to applause from all gathered.

"*Andare!*" Antonio called out, his eyes meeting hers for a moment before waving his hands in the air and beckoning for everyone to follow. The look on his face was pure adulation when she glimpsed it; or perhaps it was simply relief for the beautiful day they'd been given. It was like a gift for their harvest day, as was the lightest of breezes promising to keep everyone comfortable, just enough to lift the wisps of hair touching her forehead. "It's time to harvest!"

Lily smiled as Roberto handed her the shears. "It's your turn," he said. "Please, do the honor."

She took them from him and stepped forward, happily cutting the bunches of grapes and placing them in the same basket as he had. The very act of cutting, of being part of such a special day, filled her with joy, and she found herself aching to follow the others.

"Let us walk the rows and watch," Roberto said, as if he'd read her mind. "Until the first baskets are taken in, we will make sure they're being careful with our beautiful grapes before they go in the press."

Francesca came to stand with her husband, a small basket over her arm, and it warmed Lily to know that even his wife was prepared to roll up her sleeves and help. At the bigger estates, and even here with some of the other grapes, it was a machine that stripped the fruit from the vines, but there was something so intimate about picking by hand, about everyone being involved.

Lily would have preferred to pitch in herself and help for the first couple of hours at least, joining the workers, especially when she saw Vittoria laughing alongside Antonio as they picked together, but she knew her place. She was to stand alongside the patriarch of the family, overseeing the harvest and then ensuring every step thereafter was completed to perfection.

It was almost an hour later that the first load was carefully transported down to the production plant, and Lily and Roberto had already walked down to receive it.

"My father would shake his head at our fancy presses," Roberto said as Antonio lifted his hand, waving at them as he descended the hill toward them. "His favorite part of harvest was to have his whole family with him, laughing and smiling, pressing the grapes by foot."

Lily could almost see it; all of the women with their dresses held high, the men with trousers rolled up to their knees, squishing the grapes beneath the sun as they talked and laughed, celebrating the season. What she would have given to go back in time and be part of it, even just for one day.

"It must have been quite an experience."

"Si, bella, it was," he said with a sigh. "I've held on to almost everything else, but that is one thing that had to go."

"It's time," she said as Antonio stopped the small truck, jumping out and beginning to cart the large baskets.

"You look happy," she said to Antonio as he passed her.

"Very happy," he replied, grinning at her as he went back for more. "Today is perfect, as it should be. Today is the day we all live for."

He was wearing shorts and a linen shirt, the sleeves rolled back to expose tanned, muscled forearms, and she found her eyes following him. He looked as she felt—exhilarated by the work. Only Antonio was working on his own family vineyard, his experience steeped in history, part of something that would continue to be passed on to future generations.

She blinked away unexpected tears as she thought of her father and the legacy he would have loved to leave behind. Sometimes her dream to own her own land, to produce her own wine using her father's name on the label, seemed like a fantasy, but at times like this, she yearned to have something to pass on herself.

If she hadn't lost her father, she doubted she'd have understood just how important heritage truly was.

"Lily."

She turned, the lump in her throat disappearing as she saw the passion in Roberto's eyes.

"Come with me."

And just like that, she was back under the spell of the older Martinelli, listening to his every word as they watched the pressing process begin.

It's my time to shine, she told herself. This was the moment she'd been living for.

It's just you and me, kiddo. We're going to make the best wine in the world one day, just you wait and see.

And with her father's words filling her mind, she inhaled the acidic, unmistakable citrus fragrance of the fruit passing through the machines and prepared to do the only thing in the world she truly loved. It was going to be a long day, with many long days still to come, but she wouldn't have it any other way.

"This is going to be a good year," Roberto said, kissing a small gold cross on a chain that hung around his neck. "I can feel it in my bones."

"I think every year here is a good year," Lily replied, smiling as they watched the slow, steady press of each bunch of grapes.

Roberto caught her eye and they smiled at one another, his shoulders softened now, his demeanor relaxed, and in that second, she relaxed, too. *I know what I'm doing. I'm good at what I do.*

She wondered if Roberto had ever doubted himself, and if she'd been braver, she would have asked.

* * *

That night, so weary Lily could barely keep her eyes open, she headed toward the house. It had been a long day for everyone, their work starting and ending in the dark, but as tired as she was, she was also exhilarated, and she knew that if she fell straight into bed, she'd probably end up lying there awake, unable to sleep.

What she needed was a relaxing bath, followed by a drink out on the little private courtyard, where she could slowly come down from the high of her day.

"Lily!" came a call as she entered the house.

She paused, tempted to keep on walking and pretending she hadn't heard, but the moment the thought passed through her mind, she felt guilty. The Martinellis were treating her like family, and she would never do that to family.

Francesca appeared in the entrance then, her hands full with two glasses of red wine. She held one out, one brow raised in question.

"Care for a glass? If you're anything like my husband, you won't be able to sleep yet, despite your exhaustion."

Lily found herself smiling and instinctively reaching for the glass. "That's exactly how I feel," she admitted. "It's like I can feel the exhaustion deep in my bones, but my brain is another thing entirely. It seems to ignore how my body feels."

"Come," she said. "Sit for a moment with us all. Roberto came in just a few minutes ahead of you." Francesca gestured for her to follow, leading her not into the alfresco area this time but to the kitchen, with its huge wooden table, large enough to fit ten. The Martinelli men were all seated, looking as tired and windswept as she felt, as well as Vittoria, who was in between her brothers.

"I really should freshen up first," Lily heard herself saying.

"Nonsense," Francesca said, taking her arm and directing her to the table. "We're all in need of a shower, but we can have one after. Sit with us, please."

She felt a sense of privilege again, to be with the family and treated as one of their own. Her own family had always been small, "the three musketeers," as her father had called them. But when he'd passed away and it had just been her and her mother, their family had felt more like a partnership, which meant that sitting with the Martinellis was even more special to her. They were like the large family she'd always dreamed of having, and even as a grown woman, she'd sometimes wondered if she should have been more focused on creating the family she wanted than the career she desired.

"Lily?"

She blinked and realized Antonio was speaking to her, and the rest of the table had fallen silent.

"Sorry, it's been—"

"A long day?" he said for her.

"Exactly." She exhaled and sat down across from him, taking a sip of the smooth, silky Pinot Noir she'd been given.

The conversation resumed around them, and Lily found

herself mesmerized by the sound of the different family members' conversations, but it was Antonio who caught her eye. It seemed he always did.

"Did you enjoy yourself today?" he asked. "Or is enjoy the wrong word?"

"Enjoy is exactly the right word," she said, taking a plate as Francesca nudged a large platter in her direction, mouthing the word "*Eat!*" Lily took a piece of bread and a few slices of cold meat, as well as some olives and cheese, and her stomach growled in response.

"Today was a good day," he said, sitting back and nursing his oversized wine glass. "And tomorrow will be just as good."

"I hope so," she said, before taking a bite of her cheese, not having realized just how hungry she was until she started eating. Antonio turned to his brother while she ate, and it was his mother who caught her attention this time as she reached for more bread.

"Lily, I've been thinking a lot about those clues of yours, the ones you told me about on your first night here."

She swallowed and turned. "I've been so busy, I've barely thought about them these past few days."

"Well, I got in touch with a few people, and it seems that an old acquaintance might be able to help you," Francesca said. "It would be easier if we knew the date of the program you have, but she said she'd take a look to see if she can help. She owes me a favor."

"You're certain it's not an imposition?" Lily asked. "I know I'm probably searching for something that's not there, but—"

"Nonsense! It's my pleasure. I have to confess, though," Francesca said. "I'd love to see what you have. If you don't mind, of course."

"You're talking about Lily's family clues?" Antonio asked.

She hadn't noticed him rise and walk around to them, and he pulled out the chair beside her and sat down.

"I would love to see them, too. Perhaps we could travel to

Milan for a day? You will have time before the second fermentation, no?"

She nodded. "In theory, yes, but . . ."

Antonio smiled. "Even the winemaker can take a day off after harvest," he said. "Because I know that's what you're worried about."

She shrugged, not about to deny it. "What can I say? I take my work very seriously."

Roberto's hands were suddenly on her shoulders then, and he kissed the top of her head in a fatherly gesture. "It's why she's here, Antonio. Don't go leading her astray."

"Half a day then," Antonio said. "An hour's drive, an hour at the theater asking questions, and then an hour home."

Roberto had walked off, and Francesca had turned to speak to her daughter, so Lily suddenly found herself in a private conversation with Antonio. His eyes were bright, his smile easy, much more like the first day she'd arrived. He slung his arm over the back of his chair, his legs spread, somehow making just sitting look sexy.

"Half a day then," she finally agreed, holding out her hand. "But you have to promise we'll be back in three hours."

He took her hand and started to shake it. "Four."

His voice was so seductive she almost fell for it, but as his fingers slid around hers, she shook her head.

"Three and a half," she said, hating that her voice had dropped to a whisper when she was so determined to hold her own against him.

He just grinned and shook her hand, before pushing back in his chair and standing. "I'll see you in the morning, bella."

Lily reached for her wine glass for something to do and took a long, slow sip, thinking how easy it would be to fall under Antonio's spell. But then perhaps he was like that with all the women in his life, a flirt and nothing more, which meant she'd just be a notch on his belt.

"He's impossible, isn't he?" Vittoria murmured in her ear, squeezing her shoulder as she passed.

"You could say that," Lily replied, tilting her head back. "You're leaving already?"

"I'm ready to fall into bed," Vittoria said with a yawn. "See you tomorrow."

Lily was weary, too, but perhaps still not ready for sleep. Although by the time she'd walked to her room and had a long, hot shower, she might feel different. She stood and started to clear some of the plates, but Francesca stopped her.

"Please, leave everything. You're our guest."

"But—"

"No buts. Now, let me walk you to your room and you can show me what clues you have. Unless you'd rather wait until another time?"

"Now is perfect," Lily said, setting down the plate she'd had in her hand. "And thank you again for your incredible hospitality."

They passed Antonio, who was with his brother, who gave Lily a wink and received a smack around the back of the head from Antonio. She just smiled, once again thinking how easy it was to be in the middle of such a close-knit family.

"My boys," Francesca muttered. "They're the cause of every gray hair on my head."

Lily glanced sideways, not convinced the older woman had any gray hairs! She opened the bedroom door when they reached her room, and she hurried over to her bag, taking out the little wooden box. Francesca sat on the end of the bed and Lily joined her, passing it to her to open.

"This is how you received it?" Francesca asked.

Lily nodded. "Yes. But with my grandmother's name attached to a tag. It seems it was left for her the day her birth mother gave her up for adoption, if I'm to believe what I've been told."

"And do you?" Francesca asked, seeming to study her face, she was looking at her so intently. "Believe what you've been told?"

Lily considered her question for a moment, but she knew in her heart what the truth was. "Yes, I do," she said. "I mean, it was difficult to comprehend in the beginning, but I see no reason for it not to be true. Why go through this whole process of tracking down the estates of these women for nothing?" She'd also immediately warmed to Mia, and she had no doubt of the other woman's intentions.

"May I?"

"Of course." Lily stared at the box as Francesca opened it, as if expecting something else to be in there. But alas, it was only the two pieces of paper. Although Francesca held them with as much care as she might have precious jewels.

"You're right, this piece of program is old—many decades old, in fact."

"It seems such an unusual clue, though, don't you think?" Lily asked. "I mean, how would anyone find a person from just that? And the next one is a recipe of some description."

Francesca seemed to study them both for what felt like an age, turning them over in her hand before folding them both back together. "Lily," she said, facing her, "I think it's not about finding someone from one of the clues, it's about what they mean when pieced together."

"You're saying that I need to find someone who can see the link between them?" she asked.

"I'm saying that for some reason, this recipe is connected to that theater, and what you need to do is figure out why. I think they very much need to be considered together, and the right person might see that connection more easily than we ever could." Francesca opened the recipe again, her dark brows pulled together. "You know, this sounds like something my own mother used to talk about. A special treat made from hazelnut and chocolate that became famous in parts of Italy."

Lily's heart started to beat just a little bit faster. "You think you might recognize it?"

"Let me think about it, ask some older friends some questions," Francesca said, putting the papers back in the box and handing it to her. "For now, you need to take a shower and then sleep. Tomorrow will be another long day."

Lily nodded, even though what she wanted was to talk more about the recipe, about the treat she might have been referring to.

Francesca leaned across and kissed both of her cheeks before rising. "Sweet dreams, Lily. And don't worry about your clues, I promise we'll find that missing link somehow."

They said good night and Lily eventually rose, stripping out of her dirty, dusty work clothes and walking naked into the bathroom, turning on the tap and waiting until it ran hot. She had a long shower, although not as long as she'd have liked, her legs suddenly aching for bed, but it was a knock at the door that made her wrap her towel around herself and step out of the steam and into her room.

She opened the door and found not a person but a glass, with a splash of dark amber liquid in it. She reached for it and looked down the hall at the same time, seeing Antonio walking away, his large frame and dark, almost too-long hair impossible to mistake.

"To help you get to sleep," he called out over his shoulder.

She held the glass to her chest and watched him disappear, wishing he'd handed her the glass of liqueur himself rather than simply leaving it at her door. She'd have liked to be the subject of his smile just one more time before the day ended.

15

ITALY, 1938

She knew she shouldn't have gone, but it was as if her feet had a mind of their own, walking her closer and closer to the Barbieri family bakery.

It was the first time in her life her mother had pressed money into her palm and told her to buy a treat for the family; it seemed Estee's recent success had changed her attitude toward her. She wasn't naive; she knew that her parents had pinned their hopes on her, that they wanted her to become famous for their own selfish reasons, but none of that mattered as she hurried down the cobbled street with her cape drawn around herself.

She entered the bakery and pulled the hood of her cape down, her breath coming in fast little pants from her light-footed run from home. It took a moment to get her bearings as she looked at the glass front that stretched from one side to the other, an array of sweet treats on display, with loaves of bread placed along the far wall. The smell filled her nostrils, making her salivate, but it was Felix she looked for; it was Felix who made her breathless as she stood and stared.

She clasped the money in her palm, nervous as she stood, waiting her turn. Estee edged forward, seeing the *saccottini al cioccolato* that Felix had so often brought for her and knowing that it was the treat she would buy for her family. It would be strange, eating it in company instead of savoring it in secret.

The two women who'd stood in front of her finally left, their orders fulfilled, and Estee found herself standing in front of the counter, frozen as she stared at the person asking what she wanted.

"Estee?"

Felix. She looked across and saw him standing there, and despite her years of practice at holding her expression on stage, she couldn't help the smile that crossed her face.

"Felix!"

She forgot all about the man waiting to take her order as Felix moved toward her, beckoning for her to follow him to the door. They moved outside, his hand skimming her back as he gestured for her to go first. There were two little tables outside the bakery, and they sat, their knees nudging together, hands on the table, not quite touching. Estee whispered her fingers forward until they finally brushed his, and Felix didn't need any encouragement. His fingers covered hers as he searched her eyes.

"What are you doing here?" he asked. "I didn't think I'd see you again."

Estee smiled. "I made it," she whispered. "I was the last dancer chosen, but I made it. I'm officially a member of the La Scala dance academy."

His smile was wide as his fingers squeezed hers. "You were always going to be chosen, Estee. I'm so proud of you."

"Would you believe, my mother is so happy she asked me to come to town and buy something to celebrate?"

"Ahh, so she's finally happy with her little bird, is she?"

Estee laughed, sensing the heat in her cheeks as they smiled at one another, the feeling between them so easy but also fueled with something that never failed to make her skin tingle with anticipation.

"I'm only home for a few days, but I had to—"

"Felix?" said a gruff voice.

She pulled her hands back so fast she hit her elbows on the chair behind her, and Felix did the same, leaning back in his chair as a man with a bushy mustache stepped onto the street. It was Felix's father.

"Felix?" the man repeated.

Estee looked down, embarrassed at being caught, even though they hadn't done anything wrong.

"Father, this is Estee, she's an old friend of mine," he said, standing and running his fingers through his hair. "Estee is soon to leave for Milan."

His father gave her a quick nod and a smile, but as he was about to turn away, he paused, as if perhaps he recognized her. She dropped her gaze, folding her hands tightly into her lap.

"Estee is a ballet dancer, soon to dance for La Scala," Felix said, and when she glanced back up, his eyes met hers.

"Congratulations, that's quite an accomplishment," his father said, before turning to his son and gesturing for him to follow.

She stood, swallowing, looking into Felix's eyes for what felt like the longest moment, but was probably only a few seconds.

He edged closer as soon as his father disappeared, slowly reaching out and catching her little finger in his. Her breath caught in her throat, and she hated the tears that filled her eyes.

"You're going to have an amazing life, Estee," Felix whispered. "One day the whole world will know your name."

She lifted her chin and smiled up at him, refusing to be sad. They'd already said their goodbyes before her audition; she needed to savor this extra moment in time.

"Goodbye, Felix," she said.

"Goodbye, Estee." His words whispered against her skin as he leaned forward and brushed an unexpected kiss against her cheek. She inhaled the smell of him, his familiar cologne replaced today by the scent of freshly baked bread, looking into his dark, mesmerizing eyes one last time.

When his little finger pulled away from hers, she had the most overwhelming sensation of being alone, but she held herself tall despite her sadness, transformed back into the dancer she was and would always be.

Estee turned and began to walk away, tears streaming down her cheeks as she thought of Felix, of never seeing him again, of the life he would live without her.

It wasn't until she was halfway home that she realized she'd left without buying the *saccottini al cioccolato*.

16

PRESENT DAY

It would have been so much easier to stay in bed. Lily was so tired it had taken every inch of willpower to kick off the covers and drag herself to the shower, but now that she'd washed her hair, applied some makeup and put on her favorite summer dress, she was almost ready to go.

She glanced at her watch and saw it was almost time, ignoring the rumble of her stomach as she dropped her phone into her bag, checked she had the little wooden box and went out to find Antonio. It only took a moment to find him, standing in the big kitchen, his hands splayed out on the huge wooden countertop. She always marveled at how stunning the kitchen was, with its curved, exposed-brick ceilings, brass pans hanging from the wall above the stove, but today it was the man standing in it that caught her eye. He was dressed in a white T-shirt and jeans, and he had a pot of coffee sitting in front of him.

He greeted her with a smile. "How are you feeling this morning?"

She slid onto one of the fabric-covered, tall bar-style chairs that stood against the counter. "Better than I was an hour ago," she confessed. "But I'm still exhausted."

"That's exactly why you deserve the day off," he said. "We've all been working so hard."

It was the same every harvest, no matter where in the world she was—the entire year led up to the moment when the grapes were picked and pressed—but she didn't think she'd ever get used to it. And he was right, she did need a day off. It was only a few months ago that she'd been through the same rigorous process in New Zealand.

"We're only going for half the day, though, right?" she asked. "Just like we agreed."

He just smiled and opened a cupboard, taking out two reusable coffee cups and pouring the inky-black liquid into each one. "Sugar? Cream?"

Lily nodded. "Both." She reached out for hers the second he'd pressed the lid on, inhaling the aroma. "This smells heavenly."

"Would you like a freshly baked bread roll?"

Her stomach answered him, and Antonio laughed. "It's an hour's drive, and we won't be stopping for lunch for a while," he said, turning to get one of the bread rolls that was sitting on a cooling rack. "Jam?"

She nodded again. "I could get used to this kind of service."

"Very funny," he said, his eyebrows raised into points. "Just *don't* get used to it. You're only lucky that I was hungry and needed breakfast as much as you."

Lily sipped her coffee and felt herself relaxing, her shoulders dropping slightly as she sat and watched him spread butter, then jam. She stretched out her back and neck, feeling all bunched up and taut after the hours she'd been working.

"Let's go," he said, licking jam from his finger and indicating the bread in front of him.

She reached for the bigger of the two, grinning at him when he shook his head.

"Thanks for breakfast," she murmured.

"My pleasure."

The house was quiet, and Lily wondered if anyone else was up, or whether they were already long gone. Francesca might have been out enjoying the morning on her horse, Roberto either in his room asleep still or perhaps out walking the land, as she'd often seen him do at this time of day, slowly moving between the vines.

Antonio went slightly ahead of her then, and when he looked back at her, she felt an unfamiliar flutter in her stomach, finding it impossible not to smile back at him. Her phone buzzed in her bag, and she held her bread between her teeth as she reached in for it, glancing at the screen. It was her mum.

I hope you're making the most of Italy. Any news?

She slipped the phone back in her bag as she followed Antonio outside, smiling to herself as she thought of her mother, and slid into the passenger seat of his vehicle, where she texted a reply. *I'm definitely making the most of Italy today, Mum, you'd be proud. Promise I'll call soon.*

"Settle in and enjoy," Antonio said as he fired up the engine, his arm already finding its way to the window as he held the wheel with one hand. "We'll be in Milan in no time."

* * *

"Oh, my goodness, it's incredible." Lily stood and stared in disbelief at the enormous theater.

"Wait till you see inside," Antonio said, taking her arm and guiding her left toward the entrance.

"We can just walk straight in?" she asked, looking all around her as he gently nudged her forward.

"We're lucky it's not the middle of summer. This place is so full of tourists then that you have to make a booking just to see the theater and museum."

Lily let him lead her, trying to stop her jaw from hanging open like probably every other tourist who'd come before her. There were plenty of people milling around, with early autumn still a popular time of year for visitors, but she was thankful they still had space to enjoy it without bumping into anyone else.

They walked inside, and a smile spread across her lips as she took it all in. The foyer was magnificent.

"May I help you?" an impeccably dressed man in a dark suit asked in Italian, stepping forward.

"Yes, we're here to see Signora Rossi," Antonio replied. "She's expecting us."

"Antonio Martinelli?" the man asked, appearing much warmer and less formal when he realized they were expected.

"Si."

"Come this way. Signora Rossi is currently in rehearsal, but she said you can go in. She'll come to you when she's ready."

Antonio spoke a few more words in Italian that she didn't even attempt to understand, more consumed with taking in the scene around her, until his hand unexpectedly slipped into hers.

"Come on," he murmured. "You're going to love it in there."

She walked quickly beside him, pausing only for the large door to the interior of the theater to be opened for them. The doors moved with a swishing noise, and suddenly they were standing in the largest, most incredible theater she'd ever seen in her life.

"Oh my God," she whispered, shuffling closer to Antonio in the half-light as he squeezed her fingers against his. "I've never seen anything like it. It's, it's . . ."

"Magical," he finished for her. "I know, I felt the same when I came here as a boy and sat right up there with my parents, seeing it all for the very first time." He pointed up, the ceiling seeming miles away as she craned her neck and looked up at all the boxes. "I don't think I slept at all that night. I couldn't stop thinking about the magic of it all."

They were whispering to one another, in a world of their own, until Antonio moved her slightly in front of him, placing his hands on her shoulders as he squared her. That was when she gasped, as the lights crossed the stage and a ballerina appeared, her body swanlike as she moved with such grace, it took Lily's breath away.

"It's like our own private show," he murmured in her ear.

Lily leaned back a little into him, transfixed by the stage and his warm hands against her shoulders, although she quickly shifted her weight forward when she realized just how close they were. He cleared his throat and started to walk past her, slowly, and she noticed he didn't reach for her hand this time, and wished he had. They walked down the aisle until they were in one of the front seats, behind the orchestra, and Lily sat beside him.

She stifled a groan when the lights changed and someone barked an order, the ballerina they'd been watching following as she gracefully walked off stage. Lily thought it was all over, that their private little show had ended, but then the ballerina reemerged, starting her sequence all over again, joined by other dancers as she neared the end.

And then it was over as quickly as it had all begun, with the lights going up completely and the ballerinas gathering in small huddles to talk, while the main dancer sat down and stretched out one of her legs. But it was the formidable woman who walked toward them from the stage who commanded Lily's attention now. She had a slight limp, but her back was ramrod straight and Lily knew, instinctively, that she must have been a dancer herself many years earlier.

She held out a hand and someone immediately rushed to help her off the stage so she could walk toward them. Lily had the most overwhelming feeling of what a privilege it was to even be standing in the ornate, decades-old theater, and she also guessed that this woman didn't take time to talk to just anyone during a rehearsal of such importance. Francesca Martinelli had clearly thrown her weight around to make this meeting happen.

"You must be Antonio," the woman said as she approached.

Antonio sprang forward, reaching out to grasp the woman's hands before gently kissing her on each cheek.

"Thank you for taking the time to see us today. I know how busy you are."

"Well, your mother can be very persuasive, and she has given generously to our ballet company over the years, so . . ." She shrugged. "What could I say?"

"Signora Rossi, my name is Lily. I'm the reason Francesca Martinelli got in touch with you."

She nodded and held out her hand, comfortably switching to English as if it were second nature to her. "Let me see it, this program of yours. Francesca tells me it's very old and that you're searching for information?"

Signora Rossi appeared to be at least seventy, her voice husky and her skin lined, which was at odds with her trim figure that someone thirty years younger would have envied. When she held out her hand, Lily was surprised to see a slight shake—it didn't match her straight back and square shoulders, or the strength of her voice.

"She told me that it had something to do with your great-grandmother?"

"I believe so, yes," Lily said. "Unfortunately, I don't know what the connection is at this stage, which is why I'm here."

She watched as Signora Rossi studied the piece of paper, taking glasses from her pocket and turning it over in her hands. She glanced at Antonio, who just gave her a small shrug when their eyes met, as if to say: "I don't know any more than she does."

"Does it mean anything to you?" Lily asked, unable to wait in silence any longer. "Do you recognize it at all? Or perhaps what it could relate to?"

The other woman didn't respond for a moment, but she did appear to be studying the piece of program intently.

"This is from 1946," she said, her eyes full of light as she finally looked up.

"Would you have any idea what this means? If that year holds any special significance?"

"Well, I recognize it because it's when La Scala reopened after the war. It has very special significance to the theater, but there were many people involved in the reopening. Although I can date it, I don't know if I can be of any further help."

Lily let out a breath she hadn't even known she was holding. It wasn't a lot to go by, but she had a year now, which meant she was at least a step closer than she had been—*1946, a year after the war ended.*

"And you have no other clues?" Signora Rossi asked. "This is all you have to go by?"

"I have a recipe," Lily said, unfolding it and handing it to her, just in case she could make sense of it. "But I have nothing to link the two."

"I think I know this," Signora Rossi said, smiling as she looked over it. "It was a famous, how do you say in English, *treat?* During the war and after, it was something delicious you could get from a bakery a few hours' drive from here, in fact, and if I remember correctly, they eventually sold it in a jar, as a type of sweet spread. I think they still do." She sighed. "And before you ask, no, I'm not that old, but my mother loved it when she was younger, and she used to make something similar for us at home. She often told stories of the chocolate shortage during the war, and how this became the perfect replacement."

Lily's pulse had started to race. "Do you have any idea what the link could be? Why these two clues would be given to me together?" Francesca had also thought the recipe might be from that era, so she was starting to think both the women might be onto something. But although it gave her a link, it didn't help point her in any particular direction.

Signora Rossi folded the papers and gave them back to her, glancing at her watch. "I'm sorry, I have to get back to the rehearsal. But if it were me, I'd go to Piedmont, from memory I think it may have been the town of Alba, and find out if there are any links to the bakery that used to make this," she said. "Perhaps they will be able to help you with your connection. Many of those businesses are family-owned and have remained so through the generations, so your search may well be easier than you expect."

"Thank you," Lily said. "I'm so grateful for your time, thank you so much." Signora Rossi smiled and kissed Antonio goodbye, asking him to pay her respects to his mother, before turning in a move so graceful that Lily glimpsed what she must have been like when she was a dancer.

"If you had to guess, after seeing the program," Antonio asked, catching the older woman just before she walked away, "who would you think we're looking for? Who could Lily's great-grandmother have been?"

Signora Rossi smiled. "A ballet dancer or someone connected with the La Scala Theatre ballet academy in 1946. The ballet company's return to the stage that year was something no one could forget. It was spectacular." She sighed. "But then perhaps I'm biased. Someone else might say it was the opera or the orchestra that made the theater famous again once it reopened."

She left them then, and Antonio turned, his hand held out for Lily as they walked back down the aisle toward the exit. It was a surreal feeling, being in the theater when it was empty, and she could only imagine the atmosphere when it was full, a captivated audience of beautifully dressed men and women gasping in delight at the ballerinas on stage.

Lily looked back one last time, inhaling the history and elegance of the theater before they were out in the foyer once again. It took her a moment to gather her thoughts, and it wasn't until

Antonio let go of her hand, his fingers brushing hers as he let her palm go, that she spoke to him.

"I can't believe it," she said, shaking her head. "I thought I'd never be able to make sense of the clues, but suddenly I have a year and a place to visit, although I still can't see how I'll ever find the answers I'm searching for."

"Can we have lunch now?" Antonio asked. "All this searching for clues has made me hungry."

"Yes," she said, grinning as he proffered his arm, slipping her hand through it. "We can definitely go for lunch. And while we wait, you can show me on Google Maps exactly how we get to this village Signora Rossi mentioned. I think it's the closest I've had to a real clue."

"*We?*" he asked. "You're inviting me on this next adventure with you?"

She didn't blush when he looked down at her this time, bravely staring back into his eyes. "If you'll come with me?"

"Of course I'll come with you. But be warned, this village isn't an hour's drive from home. We'll be gone at least a night if we go there."

"Which means waiting a few weeks, maybe longer, before we can go," she said, trying not to feel disappointed. They had far too much work to do on the vineyard for her to go disappearing for days—she'd felt guilty even taking half a day off to come to the theater.

"Your mystery has been waiting decades to be solved, Lily," Antonio said, brushing her hair from her face with the backs of his knuckles. "A few weeks or even months isn't going to change anything. The village will still be there, the family will still be there. You don't need to hurry. You have all the time in the world."

"Thank you," she said as they stopped walking and stood, looking at one another. There was something simmering between them, it was undeniable, and it was a feeling Lily had tried to avoid for longer than she could remember. Only with Antonio, it seemed unavoidable.

"For what?" he asked, his voice husky now.

"For convincing me to come to La Scala in the first place," she said. "It means a lot to me, that you're here with me. That you brought me here."

He smiled down at her, his eyes moving to her lips, but his body didn't move. Antonio glanced back up and she swallowed, moving just a little closer to him as his palm cupped her cheek. It would have been so easy to turn her face away, to step backward, but she didn't. Couldn't. He waited, as if giving her one last chance to change her mind, before closing the distance between them and touching his mouth to hers.

"It was my pleasure," he murmured after the kiss, brushing her lips one more time before straightening and looping his arm around her waist. "Now, let's find this restaurant, I'm ready for something delicious to eat."

Lily tucked herself against him, resisting the urge to touch her fingertips to her lips. All these years of refusing to mix business with pleasure, but then no one had ever kissed her like that before. No one had even come close to Antonio Martinelli, and she had no idea how they'd gone from work colleagues to something more so quickly.

"Are you okay?" he asked, his lips touching the top of her head as they walked.

She nodded and tucked in closer to his side, so she didn't have to answer. The only thing she knew for sure was that she was definitely *not* okay.

17

MILAN, 1946

Estee took a long, slow breath. It had been a long time since she'd performed for an audience, and never before had she felt the anxiety she was feeling now, not even the first time she'd stepped onto the stage at La Scala as a teenager. Her stomach curled into a knot, threatening to make her sick, even though she had nothing in her stomach to bring up.

She closed her eyes and said a silent prayer, before opening them and fixing her face into the mask she wanted the world to see, the mask she'd spent her entire life perfecting.

It was the grand reopening of La Scala, and she was to be the very first ballerina on the stage.

The principal ballerina. She let a faint smile hover before resuming control of her face, and as the curtain went up, Estee showed the Italians gathered to see her exactly what they'd been waiting for all these years. The crowd was silent; she could have heard a pin drop until the orchestra began and she took her cue.

I'm back where I belong.

Despite everything that's happened, this is precisely where I'm supposed to be.

* * *

Two hours later, Estee sat in her dressing room, staring at her reflection in the round mirror. She couldn't help but glance at the space beside her, at the empty chair where Sophia should have been. They'd been worthy of their own dressing room, Sophia well before her, but her friend had always insisted on being together over the years, reveling in one another's successes and refusing to be pitted against one another despite the fierce competition amongst the rest of the ballet company.

Estee steeled herself against the pain, the loss of her best friend. For years, they'd vied for the best roles, rivaled one another at every turn, pushed each other to be the very best they could be, but their friendship had withstood it all. Off stage they left any professional rivalry behind. From the very first day they'd met, no one and nothing had been able to come between them. But now, Sophia was gone, and Estee was alone in her dressing room. Everyone had lost someone they loved during the war, but that knowledge didn't make her loss any easier.

The silence was deafening.

Together, they'd often sat in silence, not needing to say anything. But Sophia's presence had been larger than life; she'd filled the space beside Estee with such enthusiasm and talent. Now, without her, life seemed merely a shadow of what it had been. Estee had always known she was talented, but Sophia had been something else.

A knock took Estee by surprise, and she reached for her robe, pulling it over her shoulders and drawing it gently together at her chest. On stage, she never once thought of her modesty, but alone in her dressing room, she was acutely aware of how bare she was.

"Come in," she called.

A young ballerina appeared, holding a large bouquet of flowers.

"These were left for you," the girl said, her face turning a deep shade of pink as she stood, her eyes wide.

Estee rose and smiled at the young girl. It had been some time since she'd received flowers—it had been a long time since she'd had the chance to perform—and she admired the bunch as she took them.

She knew how she looked to the child; it wasn't so long ago that she'd have been just as wide-eyed at meeting the principal dancer at La Scala herself—and after inhaling the scent of the roses, she took out one long stem and passed it to the girl.

"This is for you," she said, touching her gently on the head and stroking her hair. "Thank you for bringing them to me."

The girl blushed all over again before darting away, and Estee laughed as the door closed behind her, leaving her alone in the room once more. She set the flowers down, about to turn away, when she noticed a small white card sticking out from the side.

Curious, she reached for it and opened it. Something about the scrawly handwriting looked familiar to her, and her heart almost stopped when she read the words.

It can't be.

Estee walked backward in the small room, dropping into her chair and reading the note again, thinking she must be wrong, that she must be overtired or . . .

Dearest Estee, Didn't I always tell you that one day you'd be the most beautiful dancer La Scala has ever seen? I wasn't wrong.

Estee held the note in her shaking hand and looked up, staring at her reflection in the mirror. Eight years. It had been eight years since she'd seen him, since she'd left Piedmont as a naive teenager. Eight years that she'd held him in her heart, remembering him, wondering if his life had been claimed in the war or if he'd married the woman he'd been promised to. Eight years of never forgetting him despite trying so desperately hard to leave him, and her memories of him, behind. Eight years since he'd said those very words to her in person.

It took her a moment, a second of indecisiveness as she saw her own face staring back at her in the mirror, before leaping to her feet and flinging her door open, running out of her dressing room and to the back door. Gio, the older man who always remained there to ensure no unwanted or amorous patrons made their way to the dancers, singers or musicians, was sitting on a low chair. He'd been there before the war, and somehow he'd survived to resume the position after, too.

"Gio!" she called out. "How long ago did my flowers arrive?"

He looked up, his eyes sleepy, and she wondered just how effective he'd actually be at keeping anyone unwanted out. He shrugged.

"Five, ten minutes?" she asked.

The old man nodded.

Estee hurried past him, pushing the door open, the night air hitting her with a rush as she stared out into the dark. There was no one there.

She slowly turned, looking around for him, for any clue that it had actually been him and not her imagination, and just as she was about to return to the building, to her dressing room, clutching her flimsy robe around her body to stave off the cold, feeling a fool to be on her own out in the dark, a movement caught her eye.

It can't be. My eyes are playing tricks on me.

A man stepped out from the shadows, dressed in a tailored suit and with an overcoat draped over his shoulders. Her breath caught in her throat, her eyes misting with tears she hadn't even known she was capable of any longer, not after everything she'd been through, not after eight more years of perfecting the façade of her life.

She'd remembered a boy, but this was a man stepping toward her. He was nothing like she remembered and yet somehow exactly as she remembered, too.

"Hello, Estee," he said, his voice deeper than before, his hair cropped closer. But only one man could look at her like that, with such open, warm curiosity. Only one man could make her feel that way with his soft, gentle words.

"Felix?" she gasped, barely able to say his name for fear that he wasn't real, that he might disappear.

"I always knew we'd see one another again, but the principal dancer of La Scala?" He let out a whistle that made her laugh, that propelled her forward and sent her running into his open arms. "That performance was something else, although if I'm honest, I preferred you as Coppélia."

He held her so close that she could barely breathe, and she returned his embrace with just as much fervor, inhaling the scent of his cologne, which was entirely unfamiliar to her, as were the breadth of his shoulders, the height of his stature.

"You've changed," she said, stepping back in his arms, grateful when he caught her elbows to keep her trapped close to him. "And when did you see me as Coppélia? That must have been . . ." What year was it that she was understudy to Sophia, taking over as Coppélia when Sophia had fallen ill with stomach pains?

That had been the performance that changed the course of her career and made her the obvious choice to take over from her friend when she passed away.

"You've changed, too," he murmured, his gaze open as he appeared to admire her, shaking his head as if he couldn't quite believe it was her. "I saw you as the lead in Coppélia before the bombing, before . . ." Felix cleared his throat and she saw the flash of pain in his eyes. They'd all suffered over the past few years; there had been no way to avoid it, and they all had their scars. Looking at Felix, she wondered if he'd suffered even more than she had, although she'd never ask. They kept their secrets, their demons, like cards folded tightly to stop anyone else from seeing their hand, only to be revealed when absolutely necessary.

"Can we go somewhere?" he asked, looking around as if he didn't want anyone to see them together.

Sadness wrapped around her like a cloak, but she swallowed it away. Of course he couldn't be seen with her.

"Are you here with your fiancée?" she asked, trying to keep her voice light, jutting her chin slightly, her eyes meeting his as if the question didn't cut her right to the bone.

His silence told her she was right, and the silent acknowledgment shouldn't have hurt, but it did.

"Can I buy you a drink?" he asked, his hand falling away so he was just holding her by one elbow, as if he didn't want to let her go.

"Give me ten minutes," she said, staring into his eyes and seeing that the way he felt about her hadn't changed any more than her own feelings for him had dimmed. Only they weren't children now, they were grown adults, and he was a man soon to be married. Although a lick of anticipation did run through her as she considered that he wasn't yet married, which meant . . . *That's enough. He's promised to another, and nothing about that is ever going to change.*

"I'll wait here," he said, and before he moved back into the shadows, she reached for his hand and held it, their palms locked together for a moment as she stared at him.

"It's so good to see you, Felix. After all these years, I honestly never thought we'd ever cross paths again."

His eyes shone. "It's so good to see you, too, Estee."

With that, she darted away, holding her robe shut, her bare legs cold from being outside for so long. But nothing could stop the smile from warming her cheeks as she darted back past Gio, noting his surprised smile as she hurried to her dressing room. She nodded to the other girls she passed, some gathered in small groups outside the other, shared dressing rooms, knowing how curious they all were about her. She needed to make more of an effort with them, to show them leadership and embrace them as Sophia had embraced her so many years ago, but this season, she simply hadn't been able to muster the energy.

Estee sat, giving herself a few seconds to stare back at her reflection, her eyes so much brighter, her cheeks pinker than they'd been earlier. She quickly removed some of her stage makeup, touching up her lipstick with a softer color, looking at her tightly pinned hair and deciding to take them all out, leaving her curls to fall around her shoulders instead. She undressed and went more quickly through her usual routine of carefully hanging up her robe and ensemble before getting into her own clothes. She had a simple dress with her, and a coat, and she sighed as she looked at herself, hoping she didn't seem too bland. She toyed with the idea of asking the other girls if they had something she could borrow but decided against it. This was her, and if Felix didn't like her as she was, then a change of dress wasn't going to help that.

She gave herself one final glance in the mirror, pausing only to dab her new Chanel No 46 to her wrists and neck, a gift she'd treated herself to, to celebrate her first performance on the night La Scala reopened. Perfume had been her one luxury throughout the war, something she and Sophia had refused to give up, even if indulging in a fragrance had sometimes meant they couldn't afford to eat. But she'd had to change her fragrance, not able to use the scent she and Sophia had shared.

So long as you smell like heaven, the rest will work itself out.

With Sophia's words echoing in her mind, she stepped out and closed the door behind her.

Just one drink. Just one drink, and then I'll turn my back on him and say my last goodbye.

* * *

They walked to Bar Basso, a favorite meeting place of Milan's writers, designers, artists and dancers, in silence. The irony wasn't lost on her that they'd fallen straight into silence as they'd often done as young teenagers, only this time it wasn't an easy silence as it had been then. Previously, they hadn't needed to talk, but this time it felt as if there was so much unsaid hanging between them, neither of them brave enough to know where to start.

Felix stepped forward and opened the door for her, and they walked into the dim interior, her eyes taking a moment to adjust. Chandeliers hung above the bar, bottles and glasses lining the wall in front of them, before Felix's hand found her lower back and he guided her toward a low table tucked away in the corner.

He stared at the drinks menu for a moment.

"I don't even know what to order you," he said sadly. "What do you drink?"

"Pinot Noir," she said, settling back in her chair and studying him as thoroughly as he was inspecting the wine list. It only took minutes for him to decide and order for them, before discarding the menu and turning his attention to her.

"Well, you made it," he said. "I never doubted you for a moment, Estee. You were always so much more talented than you ever let yourself believe."

His words meant a lot to her. Flattery never failed to annoy her, but Felix had known her since she was a girl, and he'd first said those words to her at an age when they'd simply been the truth.

"And you?" she asked, grateful for the speed at which they were served their drinks. She wrapped her fingers around the long stem of her glass, glancing at the dark red liquid contained within it. "Are you in the family business now?"

She'd kept abreast of the Barbieri family business; knew how they'd prospered throughout the war in spite of the immense hardships felt by others. But she didn't want Felix to know that; didn't want him to know how often she'd thought of him.

"I am," he replied. "It seems my talents lie in developing new ideas. My brother is running the business side of things, and my brother-in-law is taking over some of my father's workload."

She nodded and held up her glass, touching it with the softest of clinks against his as they both raised them to their lips to sip. Estee felt the moment it hit her belly, and she immediately took another sip, hoping to calm her nerves. She thought she'd been anxious before her performance, but those nerves were nothing compared to how she felt now.

"I've imagined this day for so long, and thought of all the things I'd say to you, but now that we're here . . ."

She laughed. "You don't need to explain. I expect we're feeling the same."

"Do you ever return to Piedmont?" he asked. "I often passed your old house, but I wasn't sure about your family."

"My mother passed away some years ago, and my sisters live with my father still, here in Milan."

"Ahh, I see." He took another sip. "I'm sorry about your mother."

"Don't be."

That made them both laugh, although the feeling between them turned more solemn when he leaned in and took her hand.

"I still remember your bruises," he said, turning her palm over and running his thumb across the soft skin there, as if to tell her that he also remembered how she used to hurt herself. "I never knew what to say back then, but now . . ."

"You don't need to say anything, it was a long time ago," she murmured, letting him keep hold of her hand, remembering how her wrists had sometimes looked from her mother's discipline. She didn't want to go back there, not even for a moment.

"The only way I knew how to take care of you was to feed you. But I wish I'd been braver."

"Braver?" she laughed. "Felix, you risked your neck to bring me the most delicious food. My mother would have had your head if she'd known!"

"I just want you to know that if it were now, if I'd been older—"

She interlinked their fingers, breathing through the pain in her chest as she revisited memories she'd long ago let go of. "You were plenty brave enough for me, Felix. Only one other person in my life has ever been so kind to me as you were, so trust me when I say that I've never, ever forgotten what you did for me. Or what you meant to me."

"You have a, a—" His face registered his surprise, his shock, but she didn't let him flounder.

"The person I speak of is a friend," she said, wanting to shield him from the pain she felt at knowing he was attached to another. "A female friend. She passed away during the war."

"I'm sorry," he said.

They were silent again. There was so much left to say, but suddenly everything seemed to take them back in a circle, back to the reason why they could never be together.

"Tell me about her," Estee said, deciding she'd rather be with him and know about his life than let the pain and silence linger between them. *Are you happy with her? Do you love her?* They were the questions she truly wanted the answers to, but she'd never dare say them.

She sipped her wine in a bid to hold her tongue.

"Emilie?" he asked, clearing his throat as he prepared to answer her. He looked uncomfortable as he drained half his glass of wine. "She's, well, she's lovely. She's warm and kind, she loves children, and my sister already thinks of her as family."

Estee nodded, as if the information didn't break away a piece of her heart.

"I wish I could say she was ghastly and that I didn't like her, but it would be a lie." He paused, as if he had intended to say more but changed his mind.

"Then I'm happy for you," Estee said in a voice that sounded far braver than she felt. "All I ever wanted was for you to be happy."

"But she's not you," he murmured, closing his eyes for a moment as he nursed his wine. "She'll *never* be you."

Estee rose from her seat, taking her wine with her, following her instincts as she settled on the soft, cushioned seat beside Felix. Her thigh edged closer to his and their shoulders touched, and when Felix took the glass from her hand and set it on the table, her pulse started to race.

"Estee," he whispered, and she leaned back, letting him catch her eyes with his, before his hands followed, one falling to her thigh and the other cupping her cheek. "I always wondered if what I had was a boyhood infatuation all those years ago, but here I am, a man, and you're still every bit as captivating as you were then."

"I thought I'd never see you again," she said, her voice barely a whisper.

"Yet here we are," he said, his gaze falling to her lips.

She knew he was going to kiss her, but when his mouth met hers, it was still somehow completely unexpected. She'd thought nothing could surprise her any longer, feeling so much older than her twenty-one years, but in Felix's arms, it was as if the years had simply melted away. They were back by the river, bathed in youth and sunshine, only now their kiss was so much sweeter, the feelings pooling inside of her so much more complex.

And yet still he can't be mine, for nothing has changed.

When he finally broke away, she nestled against him, his chin resting on the top of her head, his arms warm around her.

"I won't be your mistress," she said.

His lips found her hair. "I'd never ask you to be."

They were back at their own personal crossroads; a crossroads that had remained the same despite the years that had passed, despite the fact that he was still to be married.

Estee reached for her glass and took a sip as emotion bubbled in her throat. This would be the last time she'd see Felix. It had to be.

His hand slid down her back as she nestled against him, her cheek pressing into his shoulder. *Just one more drink. One more hour. One more kiss.*

After that, she promised herself that she'd turn away and never look back into her past again.

18

PRESENT DAY

It was over. It had taken weeks of blood, sweat and tears, but harvest was officially over. There was no longer a grape left to be picked or pressed, no barrel left empty, and there was a strange feeling on the vineyard. It had been a hive of activity for so many weeks, day after day, with workers coming and going, often very early in the morning and carrying on until late into the day. Lily had worked as hard as anyone, determined to inspect all of the produce and oversee every part of the winemaking, as well as working as Roberto's righthand as barrels and vats were filled, throughout the fermentation process, and then bottling some of the varieties.

But now, it was done. For now, they could relax, before the second fermentation of the Franciacorta began.

"Lily!" Francesca called, waving her over. "Come! Sit with us!"

The end of harvest meant a post-harvest party, and from the looks of it, the Martinellis knew precisely how to make their workers, and everyone else involved on the property throughout the year, feel special. There were long tables set out beneath the canopy of huge, overhanging trees, with branches that swept low and wide to keep everyone out of the sun, and paper lanterns and fairy lights were strung to create something truly magical. She could only imagine how whimsical it would look when the lights came on at dusk, lighting the way as everyone partied well into the night.

"Francesca, you've outdone yourself," Lily said. "It looks incredible."

Francesca opened her arms and kissed Lily's cheeks, her face radiating happiness as she turned back to the setup.

"It's my favorite time of year," Francesca admitted as she swept her hand toward the trees. "The hardest work of the year is done, the weather is still warm, my husband and son are back to being best friends instead of adversaries." She laughed. "This is the time for us all to celebrate our hard work, and we're so pleased you're here with us."

Lily was pleased she was there, too. Of all the places she'd worked, she'd never felt like family so easily, and she knew it would be hard for anywhere else to ever compare. Leaving Italy wasn't something she was looking forward to, even though it was still a couple of months away.

"Ahh, there she is." Roberto appeared then with Antonio at his side, carrying a large crate of wine. Antonio gave Lily a wink, and she blushed when Francesca turned round, eyebrow raised, clearly realizing who her son was winking at. Thankfully she didn't say a word, instead giving her a telling smile, which made Lily blush all over again.

"Everyone will be arriving soon," Roberto said, touching her elbow and drawing her aside. "Before the celebrations begin, I want to ask if you'll consider staying on with us."

"Staying for—" she began.

"Staying here, as my assistant winemaker," Roberto said quietly. "You have your father's talent from what I can gather, perhaps even more so, and I'd like to make your job permanent, if you're interested. We can work out the details later, but I wanted to, how do you say? Put my hat in the ring and offer you the position."

Lily tried to compose herself, to say something intelligent, but he'd taken her completely by surprise. Spending longer on the vineyard would be incredible, there was no doubt about it. "I'm so flattered, Roberto, truly I am. This has been an amazing experience. In fact, it's probably my favorite harvest I've ever been part of."

"Think on it, then," he said, his smile wide and confident, as if he knew she'd have to say yes to him eventually. "Enjoy the next few weeks here and then give me your answer. I can be a patient man when I need to be."

"Thank you. I will," she said as guests started to arrive, the workers bringing their partners or families with them, the women all in dresses, their hair loose around their shoulders and looking so different to when they'd been working in the fields or in the production buildings with her.

Antonio came back over to her then, wiping his forehead with his shirtsleeve, hands on his hips as he stood. "What did Papà have to say?" he asked.

Lily opened her mouth and then shut it, not ready to say anything to Antonio just yet. Perhaps he already knew, or maybe he didn't, but for now she wanted to keep her job offer and her thoughts about it to herself. If she stayed, it had to be because it was the right decision for her career, not because she liked the winemaker's son and could see him romancing her beneath the Italian sun.

"It was just work," she said, smiling up at him.

His eyebrows formed a question, but he didn't press her further. "I'm going down to the house to change my shirt," he said.

Lily wanted to step into him, to clutch a handful of his linen shirt and tug him forward so she could kiss him. Ever since their embrace at La Scala, she'd gone to bed each night wishing she could have his lips on hers again. But instead she just smiled and watched him take a step back, his grin lighting up his face.

"Save a seat at the table for me," he said. "I want to sit with you tonight."

"Of course."

As he turned and disappeared, she let her breath go, only to be accosted by the younger Martinelli brother coming up behind her, brandishing a glass of wine.

"This is for our talented young winemaker," he said, holding it out to her. He was a slighter build than his brother, and his clothes were different, too, his chinos and shirt casual but more styled than Antonio. She imagined Marco would press his clothes each day, whereas Antonio couldn't have cared less, so long as they were clean.

"Thank you," she said, immediately raising the glass to her lips and sighing as she tasted it. "Your father's Chardonnay is exceptional."

"That's what I tell everyone when I'm selling it. The Martinellis' wine is world-famous in Italy."

"I'd say it's world-famous, full stop."

They stood for a moment, Marco watching her as she nervously took another sip, suddenly feeling as if she were being studied. Why was she so comfortable around Antonio, and a ball of nerves with Marco?

"My father and brother seem smitten with you," he said finally, folding his arms loosely across his chest as he smiled at her. "I can see why."

She laughed, but it seemed too high-pitched to belong to her. "I doubt very much that your brother is *smitten* with me."

"Ahh, but that's where you'd be wrong," he said with a conspiratorial grin as Vittoria came over to join them.

"Marco, leave the girl alone!" Vittoria scolded. "I'm sorry about my brother, this is the badly behaved one."

Marco just laughed and Vittoria pretended to smack him

around the back of the head, which made Lily smile, less anxious now that the attention had been diverted away from her.

"I was just telling Lily that Antonio—"

"No," Vittoria said, giving him a sharp glance.

"You don't even know what I was going to say!"

Lily watched the siblings as they switched languages and bickered in Italian, curious as to why Vittoria was suddenly so protective of Antonio. What had Marco been about to tell her?

"I was only telling her that our big brother seems rather smitten with her, that's all," he said, reverting back to English.

Now Vittoria looked like she was going to kill her little brother all over again, but instead she banished him, shooing him and muttering under her breath. He held up his hands and backed away, leaving Vittoria to groan. Lily took another sip of wine, not sure what to make of it all, but wishing she'd heard what he was going to say, nonetheless.

"I'm very protective of Antonio," Vittoria said, "but I'm sure that's obvious. My younger brother can take care of himself, but Ant, he's different and I don't like Marco teasing him."

"They're very different men." They both laughed. "But I can handle Marco, he's fine. And I would have thought Antonio was able to hold his own against his little brother."

"Antonio's had a hard year," his sister explained. "I wasn't always so protective."

"You mean with your father?"

Vittoria seemed to consider her a moment before answering. "Lily, Antonio was married," she said. "It's why he built the house on the property here, where he still lives."

"*Married?*" Lily immediately raised her glass again. She clung to the word *was* as she took a larger gulp this time.

"It's a long story, and his to tell, but, well, I just don't want to see him hurt again, that's all. He has a big heart, and I wondered for some time there if he'd ever find his smile again. He's been more serious since then, but over the past few months, well, it's been nice to see him happier, and I think perhaps you've had something to do with that."

"Me?" Lily shook her head. "I doubt that very much."

She wanted to know more, but Vittoria was smiling now and waving to more guests as they arrived.

"Just don't break his heart, okay?" Vittoria said, kissing Lily's cheek before slowly moving away. "He's a good man. One of the best."

Lily watched her go, standing away from the other guests as she caught her breath and gathered her thoughts, while music drifted in the air and children began to run between the vines, playing chase.

Vittoria has it all wrong. I'm definitely not the one at risk of breaking a heart here.

* * *

"I thought I'd never find you." The deep, silky baritone belonged to Antonio as he lowered himself to the grass beside her.

Lily had found a tree to sit beneath after her conversation with Vittoria, enjoying people-watching and listening to everyone speaking the kind of rapid-fire Italian that she hadn't a hope of understanding. But it didn't matter—she was happy on her own, lost in her thoughts and enjoying the sound of merry banter around her. Not to mention that she had a lot to think about, too. Some of the guests had begun to migrate to the enormous table that was now covered in plates of food, all brought over by waiters who'd taken over the serving earlier in the day, so the regular staff could enjoy the party, and it was a feast like she'd never seen before.

"Do you want to take a seat at the table, or shall we just sit here and watch a while longer?"

Lily leaned back against the tree, wishing she were brave enough to just ask him about his marriage and what had happened. Outwardly he seemed so warm and open; she couldn't imagine him having his heart broken by anyone, especially not so recently, not when he looked more like the heart*breaker*. And his smile; it seemed so easy, too, as if it didn't take any effort at all.

"I don't really want to move," she confessed.

"How about I get you a plate of food and we steal an entire bottle of wine then?" he teased. "We can hide here for at least an hour if we have enough supplies, just the two of us."

"Antonio! Lily!" Roberto called, his voice booming from the head of the table.

Antonio groaned. "And just like that, my plan is ruined."

She laughed when he jumped to his feet and gallantly held out his hand, offering her his palm and letting him pull her to her feet. But when she was up, he didn't let her go, slowly pulling her closer, their hands still intertwined as he gazed down at her. She was lost in those melted-chocolate eyes the moment she looked up into them, and no matter how much she'd been telling herself that she needed to keep her distance, that she couldn't let anything happen between them again, suddenly there was nowhere in the world she'd rather be.

"May I kiss you?" he whispered.

Lily forgot everything else as she stepped closer, her chest brushing his as she tilted her head back, lips parted. She stood on tiptoe as he dipped lower, and this time when he kissed her, she slid her hand around the back of his neck, savoring every moment of his mouth against hers.

"Antonio!" his father called again.

He sighed and stepped back, leaning down so his forehead was against hers for a moment before turning, her hand still pressed to his.

"Come," he murmured. "I think my father wants us both by his side, but especially his favorite little winemaker." He lifted and kissed the back of her hand before dropping his voice even lower. "We have all night to be together."

"Lily! Antonio!" Roberto leapt to his feet and opened his arms. "My winemaker and my viticulturist. What a fine pair."

She let go of Antonio then and beamed back at Roberto, who was holding out the chair beside him. Everyone clapped, and even the children joined in, as Roberto kissed her cheeks and she sat, thankful that Antonio was pulling out the chair on the other side of her. She suddenly wanted him close, all thoughts of keeping her distance having long since evaporated.

Roberto did a speech in Italian, and as Lily sat back, she felt Antonio's warm breath against her neck as he whispered in her ear, translating for her. A shiver ran through her that had nothing to do with the weather as she tried to concentrate on what he was saying, as his arm went around the back of her chair, fingers brushing her shoulder as he kept up the commentary.

And when his father finished and everyone lifted their glasses to toast the harvest, she held hers up and cried "Salute!" along with the other guests, before Roberto announced they were all to enjoy the feast. And for the next two hours, they all ate and talked and sipped wine, with Lily trying out new Italian words and doing her best to learn as everyone tried to teach her.

But it wasn't until later when the music started, the fairy lights creating a magical story around them as the sun went down, that she finally gave Antonio her full attention again. She'd been acutely aware of him, of every brush of their legs and bump of their elbows, her heart skipping a beat every time their eyes met. Now he stood, holding out his hand and raising an eyebrow in invitation.

"May I have this dance?" he asked.

She smiled and nodded, letting him lead her away from the table to where other couples were dancing, as if they were in another time, another place. She felt more like a character from a fairy tale; the setting, the people, the *man*, seeming as if they belonged to another life.

Antonio brushed her hair from her shoulders, boldly pressing a kiss to the soft skin of her neck, to the left of her collarbone, as he took her into his arms, and they danced across the grass. They were cheek to cheek, their bodies swaying, lost in their own little world.

"You know, I have a feeling you're Italian, Lily," he whispered, his mouth close to her ear. "I think your great-grandmother was Italian, and you're here, following in her footsteps. You're exactly where you're supposed to be."

She didn't disagree with him as she tilted her head back, gazing up at his face as he twirled her. When he moved closer again, his mouth was so close to hers, but this time he didn't kiss her.

Instead, he whispered in her ear.

"Why don't we go back to my place?"

Lily swallowed, her heart racing as he waited for her reply. Instead of saying anything, she just took his hand, and she almost melted into a puddle on the ground when he kissed her fingers and led her away.

19

"Good morning." Antonio's voice washed over her as she opened her eyes, stretching her arms out as the previous night came flooding back to her. She instinctively tugged the covers a little higher, but he artfully nudged them back down as he opened up an arm to her.

"Come closer. I promise I won't bite."

She laughed, knowing it was silly to be nervous after the night they'd just shared, but she'd never been one of those girls so comfortable with her own body that she could brazenly show herself in the bright morning light. And she also didn't have a huge amount of experience at waking up in a man's bed—especially one as bold and comfortable with nudity as Antonio.

"I can't believe I stayed the night," she mumbled against his chest, tucked beneath his arm and absently stroking his skin.

"Yesterday certainly exceeded my expectations," he teased. "Harvest has never been so good."

Lily smiled up at him, receiving a kiss on the top of the head in reply.

"I don't usually mix business with pleasure," she admitted.

"I've had this rule, my entire life, that nothing is more important than my job."

"Believe it or not, I don't usually mix business with pleasure either," he said. "But lately I've been wondering if that's where I've been going wrong. Perhaps I should have let my worlds collide instead of trying to keep them apart?"

"Meaning?" she asked as he started stroking her hair, his fingers tangling in her long locks as he made his way down to the tips, halfway down her back.

"I was married," he said, clearing his throat. "She wanted to move away from here, she couldn't understand why I was so connected to the land, and in the end, I had to choose between my family and my work, and my wife."

Lily swallowed, not sure what to say, and not wanting to give away that she already knew he'd been married. All this time she'd been wondering what had happened to him, what his sister had been talking about when she'd alluded to his having had a rough year. Now she knew, and it was almost like she could feel the pain radiating from him.

"I'm sorry," she said. "I honestly don't know what to say."

"It's fine, our marriage was over as soon as she asked me to choose." He sat up then and she pushed up to her elbows, the sheets pooled around her waist as she watched him. His eyes were so big and brown, and when they met hers, she knew just how easily she could become addicted to that gaze.

Antonio leaned forward, catching the back of her head in his hand as he brought his lips to hers. She didn't know whether he was kissing away his pain, but she was happy to be the recipient, whatever the reason might be.

When he pulled back, she saw that the sadness in his face had been replaced by a warm smile.

"What do you say to a road trip?" he asked.

"A road trip to . . ."

"Alba," he said, getting out of bed and walking into the bathroom, returning with an oversized robe that he threw onto the bed for her. He was dressed in his underpants and nothing else, and she had a hard time dragging her eyes from his body, wishing she had the confidence to ask him to come back to bed so she could explore his golden skin some more. "We can disappear for a few days and see what we can find out about the bakery Signora Rossi mentioned. I don't want you going home without at least trying to find answers to your clues."

Home.

She reached for the robe, inhaling the scent of his cologne that clung to the fabric as she wrapped herself in it and swung her legs off the side of the bed. "Antonio, I probably should have said something last night, before we, well . . ." She cleared her throat. "I want you to know that your father has asked me to stay on for the year, as assistant winemaker."

His smile didn't falter, but she could see a flicker in his eyes that told her he was surprised. "I see."

"So, well, I might be staying a lot longer than you expected, than *I* expected."

"So long as you're not looking for a husband, there's nothing to worry about," Antonio said as he stepped forward, leaning down and pressing another kiss to her lips. His voice was husky when he spoke again. "I didn't make love to you because I thought you were leaving, if that's what you're asking."

Lily hated the heat in her cheeks. She was in the man's bed, naked beneath his robe, and there was nothing to be embarrassed about! They were two adults who'd spent the night together, nothing more, but the way he looked at her had her insides tied in knots.

"Well, that's good then," she said. "And in answer to your question, I'm most definitely not in the market for a husband." What had happened between them was a summer fling, nothing more. The man had just left a marriage; she knew he wasn't looking for a relationship any more than she was.

"So, did you give him an answer?" Antonio asked, holding out a hand and pulling her up. "Or are you making him wait?"

She shook her head. "I haven't yet. I told him I'd consider his offer."

"You'll make the right decision, I'm sure of it. Now about that road trip, would you like to go?"

"Yes," she said, before she had time to overthink it. "I want to try to find out something, *anything*, so I can at least have a clear conscience. My grandmother isn't here to discover her own heritage, and I have a strong feeling it's a secret that's supposed to be uncovered."

"Is tomorrow too soon?"

"Tomorrow is perfect," she replied, tying the robe in a knot at her waist as she moved closer to the window, looking out at the spectacular view, the vines already bathed in sunshine.

"It's beautiful, isn't it?" Antonio said, coming up to stand behind her, his arms looping around her waist. "I can see by the way you look at the land that you love it just like I do, that making wine isn't just a job to you. If only I'd looked for that quality before getting married, I could have saved myself a lot of pain."

She blinked away tears, pleased he couldn't see her face as she leaned back into him. That was what her father used to say: "Winemaking isn't a job to me, it's a way of life." The fact that Antonio had said almost the same words to her, told her that she hadn't made a mistake in going to his bed, even if what they were having was simply a bit of fun.

"I don't understand how your wife could look out of this window and not fall in love," she whispered.

Antonio hugged her back into him, his cheek pressed to hers as they both stared out. "Trust me, neither could I."

He's just a summer romance. Don't go getting all sentimental thinking about anything more.

* * *

The next day, after tying up a few loose ends on the vineyard and double-checking Roberto wasn't going to need her over the coming days, Lily found herself passing Antonio her duffel bag and climbing into the passenger seat of his vehicle. But this wasn't going to be a quick drive like the other times she'd been in the car with him; this time they were traveling to the town of Alba, in Piedmont, which according to Antonio would take a few hours, and they were going to be staying.

She settled in, liking the way Antonio's fingers had brushed hers before he started the engine. But now that they were driving, she angled her body away from him so she could admire the view.

"Even if we don't find a connection to your family, I think you'll love it in Alba," Antonio said as they rumbled along the road. "They're famous for their wine, too, so we need to do some reconnaissance while we're there."

"Your father told me the very same thing," she said. "In fact, he specifically said I was to try their Sauvignon Blanc and bring my favorite bottle back for him."

"It's a wonder he didn't ask you to bring some of their famous white truffles, too!"

"Oh, he did." She smiled, glancing back at Antonio. "As well as some ripe peaches, if we manage to see any."

He muttered something under his breath that she didn't understand, but it still made her laugh, the comical way he shook his head as he spoke about his father.

"So, what's our plan when we get there?" he asked. "Do you want to find a bakery and start there? Show the recipe around?"

Lily wasn't sure what she wanted to do; she just had the most overwhelming feeling that when they got there, it would some-how all make sense.

"I think we ask some locals where the most famous bakery in town is, and start there," she said. "Hopefully someone will rec-ognize it."

"We have to check in to our accommodation by late afternoon, but we should have plenty of time for both."

"You've already booked somewhere?" She was impressed; she'd half thought they'd just find somewhere when they arrived.

"It's not every day I take a beautiful woman away for the weekend." She thought he was teasing her, but when she looked at him and saw the way he was staring at her, she realized he was being serious.

"I think you have the wrong woman," she tried to joke back.

"And I wish you could see what I see," he said, his face impossible to read as she turned in her seat to study him, to look at the man who'd somehow, so easily, made her drop her guard.

She glanced away, not sure how to respond.

"We're staying at the Villa del Borgo," he said. "I think you'll like it there. It's the perfect blend of modern and old-world charm."

"It sounds perfect," she said. And it did. But for some reason, they spent most of the rest of the journey in silence, with Antonio turning up the radio and singing along in a voice that almost made her want to join in, if only she'd known the lyrics.

* * *

Almost three hours later they arrived in Alba, and Lily was taking in the sights, eager to see what the picturesque Italian town was like. She was certain she'd heard of it before, or perhaps it was simply one of the many regions she'd studied during her postgrad years, but there was nothing she recognized—yet. She'd almost hoped to feel something when they got there, a connection perhaps, but she knew that was far-fetched. Why would she feel a connection to a place, just because her great-grandmother may have lived there?

"There are some beautiful buildings to visit if you're interested in ancient history," Antonio said. "Is that something you want to do while we're here?"

She shrugged. "Not really. What I'm interested in is wine and truffles, and how they're grown here." Lily laughed nervously. "Sorry if that makes me sound uncultured."

"No, it's kind of refreshing, actually," he told her, grinning as he pulled over and into a car park at the side of the road. "I'm just grateful I didn't try to impress you with a tour. I'd have been bored for no reason at all."

Once he'd parked the car, Lily got out the little box she'd brought with her, clutching it in her hand as if she might lose it forever if she weren't holding it. The papers in there were the final link to her grandmother's past, and she needed to pray that this afternoon she was going to have the answers she was searching for. If they didn't find anything, she was going to be facing a dead end.

"Hmm, that's strange."

"What's strange?" she asked, watching as he studied his phone.

"I have this address for the oldest family-owned bakery in town. I looked it up before we left, but . . ."

She stood, shoulder to shoulder with him, staring at the vacant shopfront. Whatever had been there certainly wasn't there any longer, and she felt her heart sink.

"I think we've come all this way for nothing," she said, wishing she hadn't become so invested in finding out what the second clue meant. Had it been stupid to come to Piedmont at all? To follow a trail that didn't even exist?

"Hey," Antonio said, giving her a nudge with his elbow. "We're not giving up so easily. Let's ask in there, it's just a place to start."

She followed him into a flower shop a few doors down, admiring an array of beautiful long stems and white bouquets as Antonio approached someone. The old man looked as if he might own the place, and he led them out onto the pavement at the front of the shop as he spoke to Antonio, pointing down the street.

"What did he say?" she asked the moment the man had turned away.

"That the bakery moved recently," Antonio said. "It's still run by the same family, but they moved to a larger building because this one was in need of repairs."

Lily nodded, chewing on her bottom lip. "So, what do you think?"

"I think we should start walking," he said. "He told me they were definitely the oldest bakery in town, and that it's passed through three generations of the Barbieri family."

The recipe felt like it was burning a hole through the box and into her hand. "Then that's where we go." *Perhaps it isn't going to be so difficult after all. Could we actually be getting closer to an answer?*

Ignoring the rattle of her nerves, she fell into step beside Antonio, following his lead as they tried to find the shop. She peered expectantly into every building they passed, until eventually he caught her hand and gave her a reassuring smile. Surely they were on the right track, especially if the business had been owned for generations? Although perhaps many of the successful Italian businesses were family-owned in the same way. Perhaps it didn't mean anything at all.

"This is the place," Antonio announced.

She looked in, happy to see that there weren't many customers inside. It didn't appear to be anything out of the ordinary, with a huge chalkboard inside detailing the drinks on offer, and a quaint set of cabinets filled with delicious-looking food. If nothing else, they could buy a nice lunch.

"Ready?" Antonio asked her.

Lily took a deep breath. "Ready," she replied, forcing herself toward the door and pulling it open.

But the moment she was inside, she was gripped with nerves. What was she actually going to do? Just thrust the recipe at the girl behind the counter and expect her to point her in the right direction? To tell her whether or not she recognized it? Should she ask to see the baker and show *them* the recipe? Now that they were actually there, standing inside a bakery, her plan seemed naive at best. How would someone there miraculously be able to solve the missing link between her clues? It suddenly felt stupid, and she wished Antonio hadn't indulged her quest.

"You look worried."

She groaned as he took her hand. "It's because I *am* worried. I'm starting to think this was a big mistake. What am I even going to say? We should never have come here."

His easy smile calmed her. "Worst-case scenario, we find nothing and have a relaxing two-day holiday at a five-star hotel. There are worse things in life than a failed plan, Lily. There's nothing to worry about." He shrugged. "We just ask if someone can help us, it's as simple as that, and then we see what happens. If you want to stop looking after that, then we stop."

He was right, but she knew that if she left with nothing, without being at least a step closer to finding out more, it would all feel like an incredible waste of time and energy. Both hers and Antonio's. Maybe she should just have left the clues at home and realized that something left to her grandmother over seventy-five years ago simply wasn't any of her business.

"Good afternoon," Lily said as she walked up to the counter, smiling to the woman who stood behind it. "Do you speak English?"

The woman smiled and moved her hand from side to side, as if to indicate she spoke a little, so Lily quickly turned to Antonio, who immediately stepped in and had a short exchange with her in Italian. It would be so much easier for him than her trying to explain why they were there. She looked between them as they spoke.

"What did you ask her?"

"Whether she was the owner," he replied. "She's not, but

she's going to get her as soon as she's served this customer. The owner is the baker."

The woman who eventually emerged from out of the back wiped her hands on an apron smeared with flour, but it was her bright blue eyes that made Lily pause. There was something familiar about them, something that made her wonder if she hadn't met this woman before. When she spoke, Lily was grateful they could converse directly in English, so she could ask the questions herself.

"I'm sorry to bother you, I know you must be busy," Lily said.

"It's fine. Is there a problem with the food? How can I help you?"

Lily smiled. "Oh no, there's no problem. We're actually looking for someone, that's all, and we thought that perhaps you might be able to help."

The woman looked over her shoulder, and Lily spoke quickly, worried she was going to lose her. She was clearly busy and didn't need the interruption, especially from a stranger.

"Antonio, could you order coffee and food for us?" Lily asked quickly, hoping she might at least keep the woman's attention if they were paying customers.

Thankfully he did as she asked and moved toward the counter to order. Lily reached into her bag and pulled out her little box, speaking as she reached for the right piece of paper.

"I'm searching for a connection to my grandmother or great-grandmother," she explained. "I was left this recipe as one of the only clues about her past, and I was told to come here, to Alba. Would you take a look at it and see if you recognize it? If it means anything to you? I know it sounds strange, asking to show you a recipe, but coming here is the only lead we have."

The woman looked at her as if she were deranged, but to her credit she took the recipe Lily was holding out. She gave Lily a long, considered look before giving the paper her attention, with

Lily certain she was wasting both their time. She was about to say as much, opening her mouth and framing an apology, when the woman slowly looked up at her, eyes narrowing and her nostrils flaring slightly as if she were annoyed.

"Where did you get this?" the woman demanded. "This doesn't belong to you."

She recognizes it.

Lily gulped, her heart starting to race. "This belonged to my grandmother," she said, holding out her hand for it to be returned to her. "We believe it was left to her by her birth mother, and as I said, I'm trying to find out what it means."

The woman clutched the recipe to her chest, as if she had no intention of ever giving it back. "I don't believe you. Tell me how you got this." She backed away a few steps, as if she were suddenly holding national secrets, the anger on her face palpable. "Where did it come from?"

"I'm sorry, I didn't mean to upset you," Lily said. "But I need you to give it back to me, please."

"You recognize this, don't you?" Antonio was suddenly at her side. "Tell us what this means to you, why you're so protective of it. Why do you not think it belongs to Lily?"

"This belongs to *my* family," the woman said, her eyes flashing with anger. "I don't know how you got this, or why you've come here, but it mustn't be shown to anyone else. It contains . . ." Her face had gone ashen white now. "Who sent you? Please, tell me who else has a copy of this?"

"What does it contain that's so important?" Lily asked, struggling to comprehend how a faded recipe on an old piece of paper could have elicited such a reaction from a stranger. "I've come all this way. If you could just tell me—"

"It's a recipe that has remained a secret for generations," the woman said, calling something in Italian over her shoulder. Lily thought she was calling for coffee, but she couldn't be sure. She shifted uncertainly, but Antonio's hand on her arm steadied her. Perhaps this woman was wanting her employee to call the police, but for what? An old piece of paper that she thought was somehow stolen?

"You haven't done anything wrong," Antonio whispered in her ear. "Just stay calm."

"Have you shown this to anyone else?" the woman demanded. "How many other people have seen this?"

"No one," Lily said. "No one has seen it, and there are no other copies that I know of." She wasn't entirely telling the truth; she had shown it to a few trusted people, but she wasn't about to admit that now.

"This is commercially sensitive, am I right?" Antonio asked, interrupting them. "Tell us, why does it mean so much to you? Let us understand why you're so angry."

The woman's wide eyes told Lily that he was right; she was most definitely angry, and she *was* worried they'd shown it to another baker.

"You're the first bakery we've come to," Lily assured her. "I showed it to a director at the La Scala Theatre, that's all, and she was the one—"

"La Scala?" the woman repeated, her voice dropping an octave. "You have a connection to La Scala?"

Lily nodded. "Yes, but..." She sighed. "Look, I don't know what my connection to La Scala is any more than I know what my connection is to this recipe. It's why I'm here, so if you could just tell me the importance of this recipe, then perhaps..."

"I can trust you?"

Lily touched her palm to her heart, sensing the change in the other woman. "Yes, you can trust me. I just want to know what all this has to do with my grandmother. I lost my father many years ago, and I owe it to him and to my grandmother to find out what this all means. To find out what our connection is and why these things are in my possession."

The woman folded the recipe and, after looking like she was doubting herself, finally passed it back to Lily with a trembling hand. "You need to speak to my uncle," she said, her gaze flitting between her and Antonio, before she disappeared behind the counter and wrote something on a piece of paper.

"Come to this address, tonight after work. Maybe six?" The woman still looked unsure, but Lily was inclined to trust her now that her anger was at a low simmer. "I'll call ahead and tell him to expect you. If you are who I think you are, he'll be able to explain why you're here."

"Thank you so much, we'll be there," Lily said, tucking the recipe back into the box.

"Just promise me that you won't show this to anyone else, other than my uncle," she said, stepping forward and reaching for Lily. "That recipe can't get into the wrong hands, not after being kept secret all these years until now."

Lily had no idea what could be so special about such an old recipe, but she quickly agreed. "Of course."

"I'm Sienna, by the way," the woman said, holding out her hand to shake Lily's.

"Lily," she told her. "And thank you again. It means a lot to me. I'm sorry we just turned up unannounced like this at your place of work, and that I upset you."

The woman turned and left them, but the way she looked back over her shoulder, her eyes still wide, did unsettle Lily. It was almost like she knew exactly who Lily was, although she knew that was impossible—that had to be her imagination. Didn't it? Or did the clue she had mean something more to this woman?

If you are who I think you are. Her words were playing over and over through Lily's head. Who did she think she was, exactly?

"Coffee?" Antonio asked, pulling her from her thoughts.

"I've never needed one so badly," she admitted, thankful he'd ordered their drinks and food to go. "Let's get out of here."

They left the bakery and started to wander down the street, leaving his car behind as they strolled and sipped. Lily took a pastry from the bag he proffered, biting into something that tasted of hazelnuts and chocolate.

"Oh my God, this is amazing," she said. "Have you tried it?"

He took one out and made a face that told her they were in complete agreement.

"Didn't that recipe have hazelnuts in it?" he asked.

She licked her fingers clean before taking the piece of paper out again and holding it so he could read it. He leaned forward and pointed.

"Hazelnuts," he said. "And chocolate."

"You think this is the recipe for what we're eating?" she asked. "Is that why she was so touchy about me having it? Perhaps it's been passed down for generations and they've never shared it?"

"I had no idea what to order, so I asked for their most popular pastry, which happened to be their special version of *saccottini al cioccolato*. So maybe you're right. She was certainly very upset when she saw it."

"But how am I connected to it?" she asked. "Why would this recipe have been left for my grandmother? What connection could a baby from London have to a recipe from a town in Italy? Or to the La Scala Theatre, for that matter?"

"Honestly, I don't know," Antonio said. "But you're getting close. I think she knows a lot more than she's letting on. In fact, I wouldn't be surprised if she's already called the rest of her family and they're all gossiping about it right now. It might be a secret they've held for years, because I have a feeling that she suddenly knew exactly who you were when you mentioned La Scala. Her face changed the moment you said it."

Lily dropped her head to Antonio's shoulder as they walked. "Thank you," she said. "For being here with me. I'm so pleased I'm not doing it alone."

He put his arm around her, squeezing her gently as they strolled through the town, as she wondered whether everything was suddenly about to make sense, or whether perhaps she was only going to end up with more clues and still no answers to her quest.

20

MILAN, 1946

Estee stood on the street corner, a cigarette between her lips as she took a long, slow inhale. It was a habit she'd once deplored, but when food had been scarce, it had helped stave off the hunger pains, and she'd struggled to stop ever since. It was also helping to pass the time while she waited.

So much for not seeing him again.

They'd both promised it would be the last and only time, that meeting that night had been a one-time thing, a chance to reminisce before they moved on with their lives again; but it turned out that neither of them was very good at keeping promises. Not when it involved staying away from one another.

She saw him coming, the street lights illuminating him as he walked toward her, her eyes drinking him in for the few seconds before he saw her. He was handsome, but then so had many of the men been who flirted with her before the war and sent her flowers, their dark eyes full of longing, their smiles promising a good time. She'd even been proposed to, by men assuring her of a comfortable life as they'd flashed diamond rings from velvet boxes. But none of them had so much as caught her interest; why would she give up her career as a successful ballerina to become a housewife? She'd worked hard for everything in her life, and her independence wasn't something she was prepared to sacrifice, not while she was still young enough to dance.

Until Felix had walked back into her life, and suddenly she could imagine sacrificing everything.

"Estee," he called as he neared her, reaching for her elbows as he drew her closer, kissing each of her cheeks.

She breathed in the scent of him as it wrapped around her, her palms finding their way to press against his chest as she lifted her face up to him. And suddenly, as she looked up at Felix, his lips met hers. Estee kissed him back, her fingers twisting into his shirt, holding him in place for a moment until they both pulled back, breathless.

"How long do we have?" she asked, glancing around as if someone could be watching them. Which was ridiculous; she knew no one passing them would have any idea that what they were doing was forbidden, but still. Felix was forbidden to her, or at least he should be, and that fact alone made her nervous. But her guilt at hurting his fiancée wasn't enough to stop her from tucking her hand into his and dropping her head to his shoulder, her other hand scooping around his arm as they walked. It should have felt like an affair, she *should* have felt a deeper sense of shame or guilt or both, but nothing about being with Felix felt wrong. How could it?

"We have all night," he replied, and she didn't miss the catch in his throat, the way he glanced down at her as he said it.

They kept walking, and although they'd planned on having something to eat, they didn't stop, their feet beating a slow, constant rhythm on the pavement. She should have been exhausted from a night of performing, of being on stage, and her muscles were sore, but she had the most ominous feeling that as soon as they stopped moving, the moment between them, the bubble, would burst.

"Estee, there's something I've been wanting to ask you." Felix took her hand then, squeezing it as he slowed their pace.

She squeezed back, not sure what to expect from the hesitant lilt of his voice.

"Would you come with me, to Lake Como?" he asked. "I'm going there with my family for two nights." He sighed. "I want them to meet you, to understand that there's another life waiting for me."

"But your fiancée?" Estee said, even as her heart almost beat from her chest with excitement. "You're already promised. You'll break her heart."

"What about my heart?" he asked, his voice husky. "What about yours?"

She looked down at their fingers intertwined, not wanting to think about him holding hands with another woman, lying in bed with a woman who wasn't her.

"What if your family says no? What if they shun me the moment we arrive?"

"Then at least I know I've tried," he said. "From the day I saw you on stage, I knew I couldn't go through with the wedding. A broken promise is better than a broken marriage, isn't it? And even if we could continue seeing one another, if—"

"I won't see you once you're married," Estee interrupted. "I can't go on like this, knowing you have a wife at home waiting for you. That will be the end for me."

He nodded, and as he stopped walking, their little bubble burst, just like she knew it would.

"What will your family think? Of me? Of you changing your mind?"

His smile was sad. "I've never changed my mind. They just weren't prepared to listen to me before."

She doubted anything would change, that his family would miraculously decide to let him choose his own path forward when promises had already been made, and so many years earlier. She knew well how these arrangements worked, two families negotiating a union without any thought for the lives caught in the middle.

"So we go to Como," she said, forcing the words out, not even sure she was brave enough to go through with his audacious plan.

"You'll come?" he asked. "You think you'll be able to take two nights off?"

She smiled. "Of course I'll come." *If it means one more weekend with you, a few more stolen moments, of course I'll come.* "If it's earlier in the week, I'll only have rehearsals."

"It's not going to be easy, even if they're open to the idea," Felix said, running his fingers through his hair, tearing at it as if he were already worried about his plan. "For one, they've always insisted on marriage within our religion. They may ask you to convert to Catholicism."

She didn't answer, but then she wasn't entirely sure it was even a question.

"Will I have separate lodgings?" she asked.

"Of course. We'll conduct everything properly," Felix said, his eyes lighting up as he spoke. "I'll organize everything. All you have to do is be ready when I come to collect you."

Estee knew it was a bad idea; she knew there was no possible way they were going to accept her or let Felix break off his engagement, but she also knew that she couldn't say no to him. Perhaps she needed to stop being a pessimist and believe that good things could happen to good people. Perhaps she was the one who was wrong.

"Come on," he said, tucking her under his arm as they started to walk again, as they found their steady beat. "I don't want to waste a moment of our time together."

His lips found the top of her head and she nestled closer, wondering why, in a city full of eligible men, she had to be in love with the one man she couldn't have. The mirror in her dressing room was covered in cards and notes from her admirers, and she often smiled and let her eyes run over them as they increased in volume throughout the season, flattered but never tempted.

But there was only one card in the drawer, hidden away safely with her most precious things, and that was from the man beside her.

"Would you like to come back to my hotel room for the night?" Felix asked, suddenly turning to her and taking her completely by surprise.

When she opened her mouth and nothing came out, not sure what to say, his face fell.

"That came out all wrong. I meant not that we'd, well—"

She laughed. "You don't have to apologize."

"What I should have said was that I want to be with you for as many hours as I can, and I'd happily give up my bed and sleep on the chair if it meant being in your company all night."

The warmth in her cheeks surprised her. "I'd love that. Can we stop at my apartment on the way, though, for me to pack a bag?"

He nodded, and they strolled back the way they'd come.

"Where are you staying?" she asked.

"Principe di Savoia," he said.

A shudder ran through her as she thought of the Germans who'd made it their headquarters throughout the war, the sight of them strolling in and out of the grand hotel almost too much to bear at the time. It had hardly been touched during the war, unlike her beautiful La Scala Theatre, which was situated close by.

But a night in any hotel would be a luxury, and she was only too happy to be ensconced there, now that they were living in peacetime again. Her apartment was comfortable; it had been home for years now, but it wasn't quite the residence she'd dreamed of when she'd been a young girl fantasizing about the life she might one day lead in Milan.

"Should we order food up to the room?" he asked. "If it's not too late? Perhaps spaghetti and champagne?"

Estee laughed. "You've always liked fattening me up. I suppose some things never change."

She left him on the street for a moment as she dashed up to pack her bag, thankful she lived alone so she didn't have to face questions about where she was going so late at night. Her reputation would be in tatters if she was seen with a man who wasn't her husband, escorting him to his hotel room and not emerging until morning. But then again, who was she trying to impress?

A tremor of excitement ran through her as she quickly packed her nightwear and a silk robe, as well as a change of clothes for the morning and her cosmetics. She clutched the duffel bag, took a long look at herself in the mirror, barely recognizing the young, flushed-faced woman staring back at her, before closing the door behind her and returning to Felix.

If she'd thought about it any longer, she'd have lost her nerve.

* * *

They lay together, she beneath the covers and with the pillows plumped up behind her, and Felix lying on top of the linen, his head bracketed by his arm. It had been the perfect evening, relaxing in the room, kicking her shoes off and eating spaghetti in bed while Felix made her laugh like she hadn't in so long.

She wiggled her toes beneath the covers, the softness of the sheets a luxury against her skin. She could certainly get used to spending time in five-star hotel suites.

"Tell me about your work," she said, turning the conversation back to him, no longer wanting to talk about dancing. She still loved it, but it was work, after all, and she sought to picture Felix in her mind as he went about his day, knowing where he was and what he did. "I want to know more about this hazelnut recipe you mentioned."

His smile was easy, the way he looked at her making her feel as if she was truly the most beautiful woman he'd ever seen. Other men might say the right words, but all Felix had to do was catch her in his gaze.

"My family did well throughout the war," he said with a sigh. "It wasn't easy, especially with rationing, but we grew famous in Piedmont and then farther afield when chocolate became almost impossible to procure. The high tax on cocoa beans meant we couldn't make our chocolate-based pastries, and my father was worried we'd have to close our doors."

"So he came up with something else?"

Felix cleared his throat, looking down before meeting her gaze again.

"*You* came up with something else, didn't you?"

His nod was slight, and she smiled at his modesty. "We worked together, but my father was getting so despondent with the pressures of trying to keep the business afloat, not to mention what was happening all around us."

"So, what exactly did you create?" she asked, dancing her fingers over his on the white bedsheet.

"Hazelnuts were plentiful, and we had so many of them being grown locally, so I experimented by mixing a hazelnut paste with about 20 percent chocolate. It was enough to taste good while still conserving our chocolate supplies and allowing us to continue."

"Your customers loved it?"

He grinned. "They certainly did. I started making replacement chocolate bars, and then a sweet pastry with the paste inside. When the war ended, we were ready to expand when most businesses were barely able to stay afloat. It changed everything for us."

Estee lay back, imagining him tasting the experiments until he had the paste just right. She wished she'd been there with him when he was working, to have seen the excited glint in his eye when he realized how clever his idea was.

"I was fortunate to come home from war with my life and a business to step into," he said, more softly now. "But even knowing how lucky I was, I still wasn't happy. It still felt like something was missing."

He didn't need to say what was missing, because she felt the same. She had the job of her dreams, performing at one of the most renowned, most beautiful theaters in all of Europe, but it wasn't until Felix had stepped back into her life that she'd understood what she'd been longing for all this time. *The missing piece of my happiness.*

"Tell me more about this hazelnut concoction," she said, not wanting their conversation to circle back to what could have been between them.

He pushed up and swung his legs off the bed, going over to his bag and returning with something in a wrapper. She studied him curiously as he tore it open and then passed it to her.

"You can try it for yourself and tell me what you think."

Estee knew she should have declined; after all that spaghetti, not to mention a glass of champagne, she was full to bursting, and she had her figure to watch. But she could tell how much he wanted her to taste it, so she brought it to her lips and nibbled the edge. The flavor danced on her tongue, sending a ripple of longing through her. It had been so long since she'd indulged in a sweet treat, and it took her straight back to her girlhood bedroom, eating the pastries that he'd left her.

"It's delicious," she said, taking another nibble, unable to stop herself. "Felix, it's absolutely delicious."

His smile shone with relief, and he resumed his position beside her, stretching out on his side, propped up on one elbow again.

"I'd like to create more," he told her. "If I'm honest, that's what I love, but my father has had a renewed interest in the company of late, and he sees my brother as the brains in the family."

"So you've been pushed aside?" she asked, her eyes widening at the sadness in his gaze.

"Not so much pushed to the side as put into a new role. But my heart's not in it."

He didn't have to elaborate; she knew what he was trying to tell her, that it was just one more aspect of his life that his heart wasn't in.

"What would you do, if you were in charge? Or if you could choose the role you could fill?" she asked him, lifting her hand and running her fingertips down his arm. "We can be honest with each other here, can't we?"

She watched him swallow, his throat bobbing as he slowly looked back up at her, his dark brows creased. "I want to develop this recipe further, and then create more flavors, open more bakeries throughout the country. I even talked to him about making things that people can keep for longer at home, something with a longer shelf life."

"And your father doesn't agree with your ideas?"

"I don't think he wants to step aside. Or perhaps he just doesn't believe in my ability."

She had no answer for him, but that wasn't what he was searching for. "We can't let anyone take our dreams away from us," Estee murmured. "Sometimes we have to make our own choices in life, even if it isn't the choice others would make for us."

They sat in silence, staring at one another, so much unsaid between them.

"Is it wrong to say that I'm already looking forward to Como?" he teased, leaving the heaviness of their conversation behind as he leaned forward and caught her mouth with his.

Estee let him, sighing into his mouth as their lips moved. She was exhausted and energized at the same time, her body aching from her punishing training and performance schedule, while at the same time coming alive beneath Felix's touch.

His hands ran down her back, settling on her hip, their lips parting and then finding their way back together again.

"You can't keep feeding me," she warned as he gently pressed his forehead to hers, their breathing unsteady. "My seamstress will be furious if she has to make adjustments for my stomach."

Felix laughed at her, cupping her face, the heel of his hand soft beneath her chin. "I love you, Estee," he whispered. "I've loved you since I was just a boy. I hope you know that."

Tears pooled in her eyes, but she bravely fought them, trying to enjoy the moment instead of wondering how many more times they could even be together.

I love you, too. The words were there, but she couldn't say them, even as they played frantically through her mind. But Felix didn't seem concerned. His mouth found hers again, his kiss slower this time, as if he'd remembered they had all night instead of one stolen moment by the river.

* * *

"Good morning, beautiful."

Estee slowly opened her eyes, snuggled beneath the covers, her head feather-light on the pillow. She turned and came face to face with Felix, who was also lying on the big hotel bed, only he was still above the covers, and in clothes that looked decidedly more rumpled than they had the night before.

I never thought I'd have the privilege of waking up beside you.

"What's the time?" she asked, yawning as she snuggled deeper into the covers. They'd stayed awake talking until after two a.m., and she could easily have fallen back to sleep.

"Almost nine," he replied, squinting at his wristwatch.

"Nine?" she gasped, throwing back the covers, not caring about her modesty as she ran toward the bathroom. "I have to go. I'm late!"

She heard a rustle behind her before she closed the door,

catching a glimpse of her mussed hair as she went to the toilet and then washed her hands and splashed her face with water. It wasn't a pretty face looking back at her, and she needed to hurry if she was going to make rehearsal on time. She'd never been late before, and she wasn't about to start now.

When she emerged, rummaging through her bag for her clothes, she heard a lazy chuckle and looked up.

"You're beautiful when you're flustered," Felix said.

"I'm grumpy when I'm flustered," she retorted, but she caught his smile before taking out her clothes. "Turn your back."

He followed her order and turned, facing the wall and leaving her to stare at his back as she changed, hurriedly throwing yesterday's clothes back into the bag and zipping it up, before dashing over to him.

Felix rolled over and she perched on the edge of the bed, one hand holding her bag, the other resting on his arm.

"I wish we had longer," she murmured, leaning down and pressing a kiss to his cheek.

He turned, cupping the back of her head and bringing her face down, but this time to his lips. His kiss was warm and slow, unhurried despite her urgency.

"I'll send word," he whispered. "But I'm already looking forward to Como."

"Me too," she whispered against his lips, pausing before indulging in one final kiss.

Felix caught her hand as she rose, pressing his lips to her wrist. "Can't I walk you to the theater?"

She shook her head, grinning back down at him as he stared up at her. "You certainly cannot!"

Estee turned, not able to look down at him any longer, knowing how easily her resolve could shatter. And then what would she have? A career in tatters, and nothing to show for it. Because no matter how much Felix thought he could change his parents' minds, she was a realist. It wasn't her he was going to be marrying, and unless she was prepared to be his mistress in the city, visited when he was bored or there on business and then discarded when he was with his wife and family, they simply didn't have a future.

She left the palatial hotel, glancing back as her shoe touched the cobbled street. *Go.* Estee forced one foot in front of the other, but every time she blinked, when she shut her eyes for just a second, all she could see was Felix, as rumpled as the sheets, his hair tousled, as those beautiful chocolate-colored eyes of his had followed her around the room.

I love you, too.

If only she'd been brave enough to say the words back to him at the time. But if she had, it would have been the first time in her life she had ever said them. Her mother certainly hadn't told her how loved she was, which meant she'd never uttered them in return, and her father had rarely spoken to her unless it was to scold her behavior or wish her "good morning" or "good night."

The theater loomed ahead of her, and she squared her shoulders, holding her chin high, transforming herself into the ballerina she was.

It was time to dance, and nothing was going to distract her from her performance, not even Felix.

21

PRESENT DAY

"This place is beautiful," Lily said as she turned around in the middle of the hotel room and took it all in. Antonio had been right; it was the perfect blend of modern and old, like two worlds merging.

She flopped down onto the enormous bed, her head sinking into the feather pillow as she kicked off her shoes. Antonio shrugged off his shirt and her eyes widened, but to her disappointment he rummaged through his bag and pulled out a fresh, lightweight white shirt and put it on. He looked devastatingly handsome, his skin appearing even more golden against the white fabric.

"We'll need to leave here in about fifteen minutes to get there on time," he said, turning as his fingers worked the buttons.

Lily silently groaned to herself, wondering what to wear. A dress? Jeans? She had no idea, and she was starting to get nervous.

"The pretty blue dress," he said. "The one you wore to the harvest party."

She pushed up onto her elbows. "You can read my mind now?"

"It seems I can." He sat down beside her, reaching for her hand. "Are you nervous?"

"I'd be lying if I said no."

"Don't be." He lifted her hand to his lips and murmured against her skin. "Wear the dress, you look beautiful in it. I have a good feeling about tonight."

"You do?" She sighed into his lips as he kissed her, his mouth moving gently back and forth across hers in a series of slow kisses that made her forget all about her nerves.

"I do," he said, stroking her cheek. "Now come on, we don't want to be late."

She sighed again before finally rolling to her side and getting off the bed. "Ten minutes?"

"Ten minutes," he repeated.

Lily found the dress, happy she'd packed it and deciding to take his advice, before disappearing into the bathroom with her makeup bag, the tiles cool against her feet as she padded over to the sink. She stared at herself a moment, before stripping down to her underwear and slipping into the dress. Antonio was right, it was perfect—it made her feel beautiful, especially knowing how much he liked her in it, and feeling good was one less thing to worry about.

She took out her foundation and a liquid blush, touching up her face until her skin glowed, following with a little mascara. She fluffed up her hair, deciding to leave it loose around her shoulders, and finished off with her favorite red lipstick instead of leaving her lips nude. It wasn't lost on her that it was the first time in her life she'd let a man tell her what to wear, other than when as a tomboy she'd acquiesced, at all of ten or eleven years old, and worn a dress for her father. She smiled at the memory, remembering him promising her the world if she would please don the dress her mother had bought her. Nobody else could have convinced her, but her father was receiving a prestigious award for his work, and she'd taken one look at his face, at the hope and excitement there, and decided that just once, she would do it. She would wear the flouncy dress that her mother had bought her, to make him happy.

She looked at the pretty, floaty fabric of the dress she was wearing now. *My, how I've changed.*

A knock sounded on the door, and she spritzed some perfume into her hair and on her wrists, before giving her reflection one last quick smile in the mirror.

"You ready?" Antonio called out.

"As I'll ever be," she replied.

When she walked out, he let out a low whistle and she gave him a twirl.

"Bellissima," he murmured, holding out his hand to her and tugging her close, but she quickly placed a hand to his chest to keep him at bay.

"Ruin this lipstick and you die," she teased, reaching past him for her bag. "Let's go."

Antonio groaned, but she tugged him along. For the first time since arriving in Italy, she truly believed she was close to finding out the truth about her grandmother's past, and even the most handsome of men couldn't make her late.

* * *

"Is this definitely the place?" She held out the slip of paper to Antonio as he drove slowly up the driveway.

"We're definitely at the right place," he replied. "This is it."

"I didn't expect it to be so grand," she mused. "Do you think Sienna will be here, too?"

Antonio shrugged. "I don't know. Perhaps. Or perhaps it'll just be her uncle."

The property was unexpected. She'd thought they'd be going to a small house in the town, but this one appeared to comprise acres, much of which were covered in trees.

"It's beautiful." She leaned forward as the house came into view, a two-story house cloaked in some sort of leafy green vine that crept all the way to the upper floor. But she didn't have long to admire it, because the moment Antonio stopped the car, the heavy-looking front door swung open.

Lily took a deep breath and smiled across at Antonio.

"Remember," he said. "Whatever happens, you're getting close. And I promise you, if they're who you're looking for, then they're going to love you. You have nothing to worry about."

"Thanks," she whispered, bravely stepping out and making her way toward the man. He was older than she'd expected, with a head of mostly gray hair and dark eyes framed by black glasses. She didn't see Sienna, and her stomach did a nervous dance as she approached him. Not for the first time that day, she wondered if she'd done the right thing in even coming to Alba at all.

"Signore, I'm Lily," she said. "I met your niece, Sienna, earlier today? I hope you're expecting me."

She had a sinking feeling that they had the wrong house, that this man would have no idea who she was or why she'd turned up at his home, but that feeling disappeared the moment he stepped forward and kissed both of her cheeks in greeting.

"I'm Matthew," he said, after shaking hands with Antonio. "It's so lovely to meet you. Please, come inside."

She glanced quickly at Antonio, who smiled at her and gestured for her to go first, and within moments they were standing in the foyer of the stunning country house, before walking through and into a large kitchen. It reminded her of the Martinellis' in size, although it was more modern, with the smell of tomatoes and garlic sizzling, creating a welcome that was unmistakably Italian.

"Lily, Antonio, this is my wife, Rafaella," Matthew said in English as a beautiful woman turned toward them, an apron tied at her waist covering a pretty red dress. She wiped her hands, her smile infectious as she gave them her attention.

"It's so lovely to have you here with us," she said, her English more stilted than her husband's, but impressive all the same. Lily was thankful she could converse with them at all. "My husband has been very impatient all afternoon, waiting to meet you. I haven't seen him this excited about anything in a long time."

Lily's eyebrows lifted in surprise. "Excited?" she asked. "About meeting me?" Her curiosity was piqued, and her pulse started to race.

Matthew smiled but didn't give anything away as he walked over to the counter, taking an already opened bottle of red wine and holding it up. "Pinot?"

She nodded. "Yes. Please."

He poured a small amount each into four large glasses, passing one to her and then Antonio, and they all sat, sipping their wine in an oddly comfortable silence, before Matthew finally spoke.

"Lily, I've been told that you have something that might belong to my family," he said. "Would you mind showing it to me so that I can verify it?"

"Of course." She set her wine down and produced the recipe from her bag. "Sienna asked me not to show it to anyone else, and I want you to know it's been hidden for many years, decades, in fact, in London. I've barely shown it to anyone, and certainly not to anyone of interest."

He took it from her and read it, while his wife excused herself and went back to the stove, stirring something that sent out the most heavenly aromatic notes into the air. She noticed Matthew's hand begin to shake, but he never looked up from the recipe, seeming to read it over and over.

"Is it what you think it is?" Lily eventually asked, impatient to know more. "Are you connected to this recipe in some way? To me?"

Matthew's eyes were full of tears when he finally looked up, letting the paper flutter to the table as he reached for both her hands, taking them in his. She let him, seeing how the recipe had affected him, the pain or perhaps it was happiness shining in his eyes as he clasped her fingers. She couldn't put an age to him, but she guessed he was maybe sixty; he appeared much older than his wife.

"This was left for your grandmother?" Matthew asked. "Is that how you have this recipe in your possession?"

"Yes. We believe it was left to her by her birth mother, before she was adopted. I've only very recently come into possession of it, as well as part of a program from the La Scala Theatre, which we understand was from a performance in 1946." Lily cleared her throat. "I don't know how my grandmother was connected to either piece of paper, or how they're connected to one another, for that matter. All I know is they were left to her, and I want to know why."

A tear slid down Matthew's cheek then, but he didn't let go of her hands to wipe it away. Instead, he looked into her eyes. "Would I be able to see it? Would you share it with me, this program?"

She nodded, and her fingers slowly left his as she reached into the box and took it out, unfolding the second piece of paper and passing it to him. Lily left the box on the table, wanting him to see it, to understand where the two clues had been hidden all this time.

"As I've said, I don't know why I've been left these things, or should I say, why they were left to my grandmother, but if there's anything you can tell me, if you truly think you might know who my great-grandmother was . . ."

"Lily, I believe your grandmother was adopted in 1947?"

She swallowed as he took her hands in his again, and she knew then that she'd misread the look in his eyes. It wasn't pain or happiness; it was hope.

"I don't have any adoption records," she whispered. "But that was the year she was born."

"*Santa Maria*," he murmured at the same time that his wife

dropped something with a clatter in the kitchen, and he rose from the table.

"Please, if there's something you can tell me, if there's something you know that will help me—" *Did* he know who she was? Who her grandmother was? Did he have the missing links to the puzzle she was trying to put together?

Tears welled in his eyes as he stared down at her as if he'd seen a ghost, and at the same time her body began to tremble.

"You know the link, don't you?" Lily asked, unsure why he'd suddenly stood. "Do you know who my grandmother was?" she turned to Antonio, but his lips were pursed, his confusion as evident as her own.

Within seconds Matthew returned, holding two frames that he placed carefully on the table in front of her.

It can't be. The woman looked the spitting image of her grandmother, with luxuriant black hair, her red-painted, full lips turned up in a smile. Only, this woman had a sadness in her eyes that she'd never seen in her grandmother's, as if her smile were hiding something. And the second photo was of the same woman, but with her hair pulled back into a severe bun, looking at the camera from a stage.

She was a ballerina.

The La Scala ballet company. That was the link. His mother had been a ballerina at the theater!

"Lily, I believe your grandmother was my mother's eldest child," he said. "Born out of wedlock in 1947."

"It's her," Lily gasped. "I just, I can't believe it." She reached for the first frame, bringing it closer to her as she studied the woman's face, before looking up at Matthew. "This looks the spitting image of my grandmother. It's such a strong likeness, it could actually be her."

She looked up, unable to believe what she was hearing; what she was seeing.

"This is her mother? My grandmother's mother?"

"Yes. I believe it is," Matthew said.

"And the recipe?" she heard Antonio ask from beside her.

"Belonged to my father," Matthew said. "And my mother, well, she was one of the only people in the world who had a copy of it, because he'd entrusted her with it. As soon as Sienna told me what you had in your possession, I knew. He wouldn't have shared it with anyone else other than the woman he loved, to ensure the recipe wasn't lost. I fear he was afraid he could be killed and wanted to make sure no one else other than her held his secrets."

Lily's hand started to shake as she pulled it away from the frame. Rafaella had come to stand behind her, her warm hand covering Lily's shoulder as Matthew sat down in the chair beside her. Her touch was comforting; the touch of a mother who could see what another, younger woman was going through.

"Your grandmother was my sister, Lily. I am her youngest brother," Matthew said, leaning forward and placing a gentle kiss first to her right cheek and then her left. "Which makes you, beautiful girl, my great-niece."

22

ITALY, 1946

Four weeks after she'd last seen him, Estee half expected that Felix wouldn't arrive to collect her. It wasn't that she didn't trust his intentions; she simply knew how difficult the entire weekend would be to orchestrate. The idea of meeting his parents made her want to be physically sick; the anticipation of the moment they set eyes upon her more terrifying than her first performance on the stage at La Scala. But she owed it to Felix, and herself, to at least try.

She shifted from foot to foot outside her apartment, not sure why she'd chosen to wait outside, but not bothering to climb the stairs and go back inside again, either. The days had become warmer and warmer lately, and now as the sun rose high in a blue sky, the humidity curled around her neck and left her skin damp. Or perhaps it was just that she was getting herself in a state of anxiety, the weather taking the blame when it wasn't at fault at all.

Honk, honk!

Estee dropped her bag, her mouth opening when she saw the car pull up. The shiny, burgundy-red convertible appeared to be brand-new. Felix opened the door and got out, a smile on his face that she was certain matched hers. He was wearing a shirt with the sleeves rolled up, one button too many undone, and she found herself itching to undo another, to show off the sprinkling of hairs on his chest.

"When you said business was going well . . ." she murmured.

His shrug didn't fool her; she knew the cabriolet was out of reach of all but the wealthiest of families in Milan, which also told her that their hazelnut experiment was much more of a success than he'd admitted.

"Ready for our journey?" he asked.

She nodded, forgetting all about the car when he bent to collect her bags, loading them into the car as she took a tentative step forward.

"You look nervous," he said.

She laughed, and she barely recognized the sound as belonging to her. "That's because I *am* nervous."

His smile caught her unawares, his arm slipping around her waist as he stared down at her. "You're beautiful enough to catch the eye of any man, and you're one of the most renowned ballet dancers in all of Italy. The world is at your feet, Estee," he murmured. "If my parents don't love you, there's something wrong with *them*, not you."

His words washed over her, and as much as they meant to her, she still wasn't inclined to believe him. Not to mention the fact that if his plan was a success, she'd be ruining the life of another woman. His fiancée certainly didn't deserve to be caught in the middle of what was happening between her and Felix.

"I wish it were enough for *you* to love me," she whispered in reply.

He pressed a kiss to her forehead before opening her door for her. Usually so discreet about her private life, not liking prying eyes or wanting anyone to be talking about her for anything other than her dancing, she hadn't exactly hidden the fact that she was going away with a man. She could already imagine the gossip spreading amongst the older ladies in the neighborhood as they watched from their windows. But Estee decided she didn't care, not today.

She took her seat, running her fingers over the immaculate cream leather interior. It was easily the most beautiful motor car she'd ever had the privilege of riding in.

But the car didn't keep her attention for long. As soon as Felix sat behind the wheel, starting up the engine and pulling out into the quiet street, he was all she cared about. His hand settled over hers, the weight of his fingers almost immediately calming her nerves.

He winked, making her laugh, and she nestled closer to him, keeping hold of his hand as she stared at the road ahead, wishing their drive were much longer than an hour.

* * *

When they arrived at Lake Como, the butterflies in Estee's stomach started to beat their wings again with fervor, and she stared out of the window, grateful for the air whipping around them from the top being folded down. She should have tied a scarf around her head, because when she looked in the vanity mirror, she could see that her tight bun was no longer immaculate, wisps escaping from all over her hair.

"Are your parents already here?" she asked as they turned onto a road that took them away from the lake.

"Actually, that was part of my surprise," Felix said, glancing over at her. "They don't arrive until tomorrow."

"Tomorrow?" her nerves almost immediately faded.

He grinned, although this time he didn't take his eyes off the road. "We have the rest of the day and all night to ourselves."

Estee leaned against the window on her side and smiled to herself, indulging in the idea of being alone with Felix. "We'll have to be careful," she cautioned. "I don't want the hotel staff telling your mother we were acting improperly. I want her to think I'm a respectable young woman."

He stopped the car and turned to her, his brow furrowed, even though he didn't manage to hide his smile. "Are you telling me you're *not* a respectable young woman?"

"Would a respectable woman have spent the night in a hotel room with you last month?" she replied.

Felix leaned forward and touched her lips with his, catching her off guard. She went to kiss him back before quickly pushing him away when she realized they could be seen.

"What did I just say about respectability?" she demanded, keeping her hand between them in case he tried to kiss her again.

Felix sighed. "Perhaps I should have checked us into a different hotel for the first night."

It was then that she turned and looked at where they were, taking in the stunning hotel. She could tell from the outside how special it was going to be.

"Welcome to Villa d'Este," Felix said, opening his door before moving around to hers. "I think you're going to love it here."

She was almost entirely certain she would, but just as she was gazing at the picturesque surroundings, a man dressed in a suit was welcoming them and offering to take the car. He promised to bring up their luggage, and when Felix held out his arm to her, she happily took it, following him up the steps and through the doors of the most elegant hotel she'd ever seen. Ornate chandeliers hung from the ridiculously high ceilings, and a sweeping staircase beckoned from the rear of the opulent foyer.

Estee sat down on a plush velvet chair as Felix checked them in and took care of all the details, and she rose when he returned to her, his hand finding the small of her back as they walked toward the stairs.

"We have separate rooms," he murmured, "but they're side by side. And I've ensured my parents are on a different floor."

She shook her head. "You've really thought of everything, haven't you?"

"We're going to get settled, then take a boat ride on the lake before lunch. I want this to be a day you'll never forget, Estee."

She didn't tell him that even without all the extravagance, it would have been impossible to forget a day with him. And for a moment, she wondered if she'd been wrong to be so pessimistic. Why would his parents not like her? She was from a respectable family, albeit not a wealthy one, but she was admired by people throughout Italy and beyond for her talents as a ballerina. She'd worked hard her entire life, providing for herself and her family, and there were no scandals to hide, either.

"Are you happy?" Felix asked, frowning as he studied her.

She smiled up at him. "Of course I'm happy. How could I not be?"

Estee saw their luggage then, and Felix temporarily left her side to speak to the concierge. But it was what she saw when he bent to unzip his bag that left her breathless, the velvet box impossible to miss as he slipped it from his jacket pocket and into the bag.

Her heart started to pound as he turned back to her, a wide smile on his face. *This weekend isn't just about meeting his parents. He's going to propose.*

She fought to settle her expression as he strode back toward her, and she must have fooled him because he didn't question her as they traveled the rest of the way up to their rooms. She let herself into hers, leaving the door slightly ajar for her bags to arrive, as she crossed the room and went to look out of the window, admiring the trees and rows of grapevines farther into the distance.

He wants me to be his wife. She'd vehemently told him she wouldn't be his mistress, but never in a million years had she expected him to propose to her, to ask her to be his wife. Had he already ended his engagement? Was he even free to ask for her hand if he was still promised to another?

In that moment, she wished she had a mother to turn to for counsel, although even if her mother had been alive, she'd never have spoken to her about such things.

There was a light knock at the door, and Estee turned, half expecting Felix, but seeing it was simply her bags being delivered. She quickly gave the man a tip, closing the door behind him as she turned to her things.

She glanced down at the dress she was wearing and immediately decided it was too plain if they were to spend the day gallivanting around Lake Como, not to mention her hair needed restyling. And so, to take her mind off what might or might not be happening that day, she hung up her clothes and chose her favorite pink sundress, pairing it with bright pink lipstick and brushing her long hair out around her shoulders, knowing how much Felix liked to see it loose.

The trouble was, she couldn't stop looking at the big, plush bed with its plumped-up pillows and wondering if she would be spending the night sprawled in it alone, or whether Felix might be wanting to join her.

23

Nothing had ever tasted better than gelato with Felix. The chocolate exploded on Estee's tongue as they strolled side by side, the sun warming their shoulders as they walked back in the direction of the restaurant where they'd had lunch. First, they'd drunk wine and eaten the best seafood she'd ever tasted, twirling spaghetti as they laughed and talked. They had so much to catch up on, so much of their lives to share with one another, as if they'd held back all of that until now, believing they could never have a future together. But the glint in Felix's eye, the way he was speaking to her—she'd never witnessed such true optimism, and it seemed to be rubbing off on her.

The ring.

Every few minutes she'd think of it, wondering where it was, whether he had it with him or if it was still in his room. And then she'd get nervous all over again, wondering how everything could possibly work out in their favor.

Something as simple as her religion, or lack of it, could stop his parents from ever giving Felix their blessing, but as huge an obstacle as her not being Catholic might be, it was bound to be nothing compared to asking his family to end an engagement that had been agreed upon when he was a child.

"You're thinking about tomorrow, aren't you?" Felix asked, his shoulder gently bumping into hers. "Is that why you're so quiet?"

She licked her spoon and considered him, the kind way he gazed down at her. There was still something different about Felix: the way he looked at her, the way he made her feel seen. No one else in her life, other than Sophia, had ever made her feel that way before. The years between leaving Piedmont and the La Scala Theatre being bombed had been filled with Sophia, her closest and only friend, the only true confidante she'd ever had other than Felix. But it was as if she were only allowed one of them in her life, one taken away before the other was permitted to come back. What she wouldn't have done to have them both!

"I just . . ." Her words failed her.

Felix stopped and touched his fingers to her hair, gently stroking it. "You need to trust me," he said, his voice soft and making it almost impossible not to believe him. "I've thought this through. I have an answer for every hesitation they might have."

Gelato started to drip between her fingers. Estee nodded, because she didn't know what else to do.

"Trust me," Felix said with a wink, catching her hand and kissing away the errant chocolate.

Estee laughed and snatched her hand back, glancing around them as if expecting to see his parents watching them, or someone else who might report back on their antics. But, of course, no one was there, apart from the other tourists and locals immersed in their own lives and caring little about whatever she might or might not be doing.

They started to walk again now, slower even than before, both of them eager to stretch their day out as long as possible. But only minutes later they were in a taxi and heading back to their hotel, standing at the foot of the palatial building that was waiting to welcome them back to their rooms.

"Shall we walk just a little longer?" Felix asked, holding out his arm.

Estee nodded. "I've never walked so much in my life, but yes," she said. "Let's walk."

The grounds were as magnificent as the hotel itself; the grass was green and expansive, and as immaculately trimmed as the hedges gracing the perimeter of the hotel's alfresco area, and beyond that were trees.

"I want a property like this one day," Felix said. "Not quite as huge, but with land as far as the eye can see and covered in hazelnut trees. I want to produce what I need for my hazelnut paste without having to rely on other growers. I want to say I can produce it every step of the way myself."

She glanced up at him. The way he'd said *my* surprised her. "You're thinking of moving away from the family business? Or are you just speaking figuratively?"

"Honestly, I don't know what I'm saying," he said, staring out at the land as she studied his profile. "I suppose I want to be prepared for whatever happens."

She swallowed, moving closer to him and looking in the same direction he was, seeing what he was seeing. *He's preparing for his family to say no. He's planning for the worst already.*

"I'm a little tired," she said, even though her mind had never been more alert. "I think I'm ready for bed."

He took her hand and they walked back to the hotel, the silence between them feeling heavier than it ever had before. When they reached her room, she stopped and turned to him, cradling his face as she kissed him gently on the lips.

"Thank you for today," she said. "I will never forget it."

His hands found her shoulders and then ran slowly down her arms until he caught her fingertips. "I'll bring you back here every year," he whispered. "It can be our special place."

Estee opened her mouth to say something, half expecting

him to propose to her right then and there, but instead he pressed a kiss to her forehead and took a step back.

"Sweet dreams, beautiful," he said. "I'll see you in the morning. Be ready for a late breakfast."

Estee nodded and opened her door, smiling at him one last time before shutting it behind her. She pressed her back to the wood, closing her eyes as she sank slowly to the floor, dropping her purse beside her. *What am I doing here?* She was going to end up with her heart broken, both her and Felix's fantasies crushed the moment his family was told of his dreams.

Yet here I am, going along with a plan that is destined to fail.

She forced herself to stand then, pushing up from the floor and kicking off her shoes. Estee took a deep breath, straightening her shoulders as she lifted her arms, tightening her stomach as she prepared to rehearse. She was thankful the room was large, because the only way she could distract herself from the impending disaster that was tomorrow, was to dance.

Suddenly, she would have done anything to be back in Milan, on stage, in the one place in the world she belonged.

The one place in the world she was supposed to be.

* * *

The next morning, there was a soft knock at Estee's door, and she rose, bleary-eyed from sleep. Eventually she'd curled into a tight ball on the bed, her pillow hugged to her chest, thinking slumber would never find her, but eventually it had—and she only wished she'd been able to rest for longer.

She glanced at her wristwatch and saw that it was after nine, and she hurried to the door, praying it wasn't Felix having already arrived for her. But instead she saw a silver tray, and she pushed the door open properly to retrieve it. She guessed he'd had breakfast sent up to her, and when she took it into the room, placing the tray carefully on the bed and lifting the lid, she discovered a fresh bread roll, jam and a delicious-looking pastry. She smiled, imagining him perusing the breakfast menu before deciding what to select for her, as she reached for an envelope that was tucked beneath the plate.

Estee slid her fingernail under the seal and pulled out a crisp sheet of paper.

ESTEE, ENJOY BREAKFAST AND MEET ME DOWNSTAIRS AT NOON FOR LUNCH xx

She placed the note back on the tray and reached for the pastry, unable to resist. Usually, she'd be more mindful about how much she was consuming, determined not to gain a pound, but meeting his parents seemed deserving of a treat. She eyed the still-warm bread and sighed, hoping she would be full after eating the pastry, because the bread was going to be almost impossible to resist, too.

After a leisurely bath that did little to quell her nerves, and an anxious back-and-forth over what to wear, Estee was finally ready to go downstairs. She'd decided on a pretty lavender dress that nipped in at the waist, pinning her hair back loosely from her face, so unlike her severe hairstyles for the stage. She wanted to look elegant yet soft, her lips painted a warmer pink than her usual favorite red, and she took one last look at herself before flashing herself a smile. *I can do this. They're going to love me.*

Just as she was reaching to collect her bag, sliding her lipstick and powder inside, there was a gentle knock at the door. Estee laughed to herself, crossing the room and reaching for the door handle. Trust Felix—he'd obviously decided he couldn't wait to see her, and she couldn't be more pleased that he'd decided to come for her. It would be much nicer to walk down on his arm than on her own, especially given how nervous she was.

Estee swung open the door, smiling as she said, "You couldn't stay away, could—"

"*Estee,* is it?"

Her words sank in her throat. *Not Felix, then.* She tried to stop her mouth from falling open in surprise, her poise difficult to muster despite her years of experience.

"I'd ask if I had the correct room, but then that would be pretending I didn't know exactly who you are."

"Mrs. Barbieri," she said, her voice barely more than a whisper. "I didn't expect us to meet this way."

"I thought we could get acquainted on the way down to lunch," she said, her words so cool they sent a distinct chill through Estee.

"Of course," she said, trying not to stutter over the words. "Just, uh, let me get my room key."

Estee turned, not hearing the door shut behind her and wondering if Felix's mother had perhaps stuck out her foot to stop it from closing. She fumbled for her key, dropping it before quickly scooping it up again and placing it in her purse. Her hands were shaking, and she quickly made fists of them, not wanting anyone to notice how rattled she was, her childhood habit of pressing her fingernails into her palms quickly coming back to her.

When she caught sight of his mother waiting, she was smiling, but there was no warmth in her expression, no kindness. Instead, she saw something far colder and calculating.

"Estee, there's someone I'd like you to meet," his mother said, her pointed eyebrows rising even higher as her lips curled into a smile.

Estee stepped out into the hallway and her heart sank all the way to her toes. *No, it can't be.* She'd never seen her before, but somehow she knew exactly who the other young woman was, and her cheeks flamed with embarrassment.

"This is Emilie. I'm sure my son has mentioned his fiancée?"

Estee's mouth moved, but no words came out. She was unable to utter a sound.

Emilie, the woman she'd tried to imagine in her mind a hundred times over ever since she'd known Felix was promised to another, or perhaps who she'd tried so hard *not* to think about, looked as embarrassed as she felt.

"Of course, how—how lovely to meet you, Emilie," Estee said, composing herself, miraculously transforming herself into the woman she was on stage, the ballerina that made crowds fall in love with her every night throughout the season. *The consummate performer.*

She cleared her throat and met the gaze of Mrs. Barbieri, refusing to feel small in front of her, as she straightened her shoulders and lifted her chin.

"As lovely as this is, I think I'll return to my room," Estee said as the other young woman looked like she wished the ground would open and swallow her.

"Nonsense," Felix's mother said. "And ruin this little surprise I have for my son?" She took hold of Estee's arm, her nails digging painfully into her skin. "It's time my son learned the consequences of his actions, although I do admit it's unusual for the wife-to-be to meet the mistress."

Mistress? Hot tears burned Estee's eyes. Is that what she'd been reduced to? The mistress? The one thing she'd always said she'd never be.

She should have stood her ground and refused, should have immediately rebuffed her for using that word, but it had come as such a shock, her hopes and expectations dashed the moment she'd opened the door and found his mother there. There didn't seem to be any use in fighting, and besides, they may as well get it all over with. She owed it to Felix to give him a chance, to let him see the way his mother was treating the woman he loved.

A little voice whispering in her head made her look across at the other woman in his life, the fiancée who wasn't being treated any better than she was. *Does he love her, too? Has he been fooling me all this time with his words of love? Has he been whispering the same thing to this young woman? Or is it all simply a cruel trick of his mother's?*

They descended the stairs and she searched frantically for Felix. But when she saw him, her heart broke. He was standing talking to another man, laughing, his face stretched into a wide smile, and that smile held when his eyes met hers, just for a second, until his face drained of all its color. Estee watched as he excused himself and took a few slow steps forward, the anguish in his expression telling her everything. His eyes barely traced over his mother and fiancée; his gaze instead locked on hers.

"Felix," his mother announced, finally letting go of her as she waved him over. "Please, come and introduce me properly to your lady friend. Or should I say *mistress?*"

His step was quick, and he came protectively to her side.

"Emilie, it's lovely to see you, as always," Felix said quickly to his fiancée, giving her a brief smile. She nodded in reply, and Estee could see how deeply uncomfortable she was, although thankfully she appeared more embarrassed than heartbroken. "Mother, may we have a word in private?"

There was a coldness about his mother as she studied her son, and Estee found herself wondering how she'd managed to raise such a kind, warm man. But then perhaps she hadn't always been like this; she'd seen firsthand how a change in fortunes also changed a person.

Before anyone could say anything else, Felix's father appeared, along with another young man who she guessed was Felix's brother. She only recognized his father because she'd seen him that first time they'd met, after her ballet recital when she'd been twelve years old, and again outside the bakery.

"I think we can all take a walk. This is no place to discuss family affairs," Felix's father suggested, touching his wife's arm. It seemed to work, as she immediately nodded, and they all turned to walk outside into the bright sunshine.

"I'm so sorry," Felix whispered, reaching for her hand, but Estee pulled it away, folding her arms instead. It wasn't that she was angry with him, but she couldn't see how their holding hands was going to help the situation.

She also felt for the other young woman caught in the middle of their relationship and had no interest in disrespecting her.

"Go to your fiancée," Estee murmured. "This isn't fair to her, and she deserves better."

Felix gave her a long stare, before crossing behind her and going to Emilie. She watched the way he talked to her, his hand brushing the small of Emilie's back, as he so often did her own, and a stab of jealousy rippled through her.

"Son, you have some explaining to do," his father said when they eventually stopped walking, far enough away from the hotel that they couldn't be overheard.

Felix stepped forward, and Estee stood and stared at him, committing him to memory, wishing she'd left the night before so her memories of their time together could have been fresh and beautiful and not tainted by his mother.

"It's my mother who has the explaining to do," Felix said, turning his back to his mother as he spoke. "This weekend was supposed to be for us, for our family, so I could—"

"Emilie *is* family," his mother interrupted. "Aren't you, darling? You've been family to us since you were a child."

"Papà, I asked Estee here this weekend so I could introduce her to you properly," Felix continued, and his mother looked as if she were about to have a heart attack at being disregarded by her son. "Emilie and I have been promised to one another for a very long time, it's true, but I've been in love with Estee for years, and I can't walk away from her simply because of a promise you and Mamma made on my behalf when I was a child. A promise I had no say in, and that I am certainly not bound by."

"Son, you're walking a dangerous path here," his father said, smoothing his fingers over his closely clipped beard. "Our families are united in business. This is more than just a marriage between two people, it's about family and honor."

"I have made up my mind, Papà," Felix said, before turning to Emilie. "I'm so sorry, you should never have been manipulated like this. We both know this has never been a love match, and I've been honest with you about my feelings all along."

"You mean to end your engagement to Emilie for a little ballerina? A pretty bauble you've taken as your mistress after seeing her on stage? Is she even Catholic?"

Felix shook his head. "No, Mamma, she's not Catholic. But Estee is one of the most talented ballet dancers in all of Italy. It would be an honor for her to be my wife."

"Did I mention Emilie's *family* is here? Do you know what this will do to our relationship with them?" his mother continued. "What the repercussions will be? We're here to shop for her wedding dress, not to call off the wedding!"

"I remember you," his father suddenly said to Estee, folding his arms across his protruding stomach. "You're from Piedmont, aren't you? You left Piedmont to dance for La Scala?"

Estee nodded. "Yes, that's me."

"And you've been in love with her since then? Since Piedmont, when you were just a boy?"

"I have," Felix replied to his father.

"I'm sorry, son, but as much as I wish I could understand, you cannot walk away from your union to Emilie. It would affect our entire family. However, if you and your fiancée can come to an agreement within your marriage, as is often the case—"

"I will not be anyone's mistress, Mr. Barbieri," Estee said, her anger flaring up as she cut him off, unable to stay quiet any longer.

"Today was supposed to be about you getting to know Estee, for me to explain to you how—" Felix was abruptly interrupted.

"Nothing will change the situation before us, son," his father said. "You must decide whether you want to continue with this,

this *relationship,* or whether you will continue to be part of this family."

Felix froze, his father's ultimatum sending a look across his face that pained Estee. She'd expected as much, but the weight of the words was heavy to bear. If he chose her, he'd be giving up so much.

"If you're going to give me an ultimatum, then I have no choice," Felix said. "I shall exit the family business and leave it all behind. I *will* be marrying Estee, there is no discussion to be had on the matter."

"How about we give you some time to consider your decision," his father said, shaking his head, as if it were finally dawning on him that he might lose his son, that pushing him into a corner wasn't going to scare him into acquiescing. "There's no need to rush these things. We can simply advise Emilie's parents that you're unwell. These things need to be discussed. You need to consider what you'd be giving up if you chose to walk away from this union."

"You would really cut me off, ask me to walk away from our family?" Felix asked. "After all I've done for our business?"

"Felix," his mother said. "You'd turn your back on your own family? You're actually considering this? For this, this, *dancer?* This *puttana?*"

Estee balked at the way she said the word, and decided to turn on her heel, not needing to be part of the vitriol before her. She'd had enough, and it wasn't fair on Felix to have her standing there, to know that she was hearing such hatred spouting from his mother's mouth.

"Would you like to come with me?" Estee asked Emilie, keeping her voice soft as she addressed the woman she should despise, even though she couldn't see her as anything more than a victim. In a way she felt guilty for her part in what was unfolding before them.

The other woman shook her head, and Estee nodded, understanding, even though she was disappointed that Emilie felt she couldn't walk away with her. "I'm sorry for any hurt I've caused you," she said in a low voice, so only Emilie could hear.

And with that, Estee left Felix behind, hoping with all her heart that he would follow.

She expected tears, but they never came. His mother might think she was better than her, by right of her perceived status and her religion, but Estee knew she could hold her head high. She'd worked hard for everything she had in her life; she was kind to everyone she encountered and held so much love in her heart, despite how cruel her own mother had been to her; and there was nothing Felix's mother could say that would make her feel as if she wasn't good enough.

* * *

Estee had decided to take herself out for lunch to pass the time, not returning to her room after leaving Felix and his family, and it wasn't until an hour later that she eventually made her way back upstairs, her key hanging from her finger.

When she looked up, walking down the hall to her own room, she saw a man sitting, leaning against the wall beside her door, his head back and his eyes closed, knees drawn up slightly so as not to block anyone from walking past.

Felix.

She slowed her pace, absorbing the sight of him, until she was finally standing in front of him. His eyes still didn't open, and she carefully slid down the wall beside him until they were sitting together, not quite touching. Estee reached for his hand, her fingers interlinking with his.

"I thought you'd gone," he said.

"I would never leave you," she replied, not daring to look at him as they sat together.

"I'm so sorry for what they said, for my mother—"

"You don't need to apologize for them," she said, finally turning to him and looking into his eyes, melting the moment she was caught in his gaze. The pain there was palpable, and she hated that she might have contributed to his heartache. Estee lifted her hand, stroking his cheek and down his jawline.

"Emilie deserved better than that. I hate that she was caught up in it all," he said, leaning into her hand. "She's a wonderful girl, and I wanted to tell her about us in my own way, in private. Instead, my mother took that away from me. I can't believe she even knew about you, that you were here. So much for surprising them at lunch."

There was nothing Estee could say. It didn't matter how she'd known; all that mattered was that she had.

"I'm not scared of walking away, Estee," he whispered. "I would, I *will*, give it all up for you."

"I would never ask you to walk away from your family, Felix," she said. "I need you to know that I will always love you, but you don't have to do this for me."

He reached into his jacket then, and her breath caught in her throat.

"Estee, I bought this ring the day after I saw you on stage at La Scala, all those years ago," Felix said, holding the little velvet box. "I knew that I couldn't marry Emilie, even then. You're the only woman I've ever loved."

She wanted to see it so badly, wanted to drink in the sight of the diamond he'd chosen for her, having thought about it since the day before, but instead she reached for his hand and closed it over the box.

"No," she whispered. "It's not the right time. I want you to propose to me when you're free to do so, once you've had time to think through your decision."

He stared at her, anger flaring, or perhaps disappointment, but within seconds he was sliding the box back into his jacket.

"Can I ask you one thing?"

She nodded. "Of course."

"If I'd asked you, would you have said yes?"

The tears that had been missing earlier suddenly filled her eyes. "Yes, Felix. A thousand times over, *yes*. You're the only man I've ever wanted."

He leaned over then and claimed her mouth, kissing her with more passion, more urgency, than he'd ever seemed to possess before.

"Stop," she said, sliding her hand between them to push him back a little. "Not here."

Felix stood and reached for her, pulling her up to stand beside him as she fumbled with the key and turned it in the lock. She waited a moment, taking a long, shuddering breath before pushing the door open, his body brushing hers from behind, making her feel safe.

She turned, looking up into his eyes. She was going to ask him if he was certain it was what he wanted, if he really wanted to take this step, but his gaze told her everything she needed to know.

They faced each other, neither of them moving, until eventually Felix stepped forward, closing the distance between them, his arms encircling her and drawing her in. She went willingly, forgetting everything they'd been through earlier in the day, surrendering to his lips on hers, his hands covering her skin.

"Estee," Felix said, but she didn't let him continue, slipping her arms around his neck to keep him close, to stop him from pulling away from her.

Felix walked her backward and suddenly they were tumbling down onto the bed, a tangle of limbs on the soft coverlet as she undid the buttons of his shirt.

"You're certain about this, Estee?" he whispered.

She cupped the back of his head, staring into his eyes, before nodding. "Yes."

It seemed Felix didn't need to be told twice.

24

PRESENT DAY

The night had been nothing short of perfect, with Lily telling Matthew and his family all about her father and their shared love of winemaking, but now she felt it was finally time to ask some questions of her own. They'd already told her so much, but she had a lifetime of questions to discover answers to.

"Did my great-grandmother continue dancing?" she asked as Matthew leaned forward and topped up everyone's wine glasses. "After she gave birth to my grandmother?" She had so many questions, including how her great-grandparents had managed to be together despite all the obstacles in their way. Had Felix walked away from his family as he'd threatened to?

"She did. But that's a story for another night," Matthew said. "Tonight, I want to tell you more about our family, and what that recipe means to us. Why my father never shared it with anyone else, until he had a family of his own."

"And why I was so upset seeing it today," Sienna added. She'd arrived in time to have dinner with them, stating she was far too curious to stay away. "Because I was one of those people entrusted with it, who committed it to memory so no one could ever steal it from us."

Lily waited, glancing at the recipe where it sat on the table. She could never have imagined a piece of paper with an old recipe on it could have meant so much, but to this family, it clearly did.

"Our family was divided many years ago because of my father, your great-great-grandfather," Matthew said. "His family went on to form one of the most successful businesses in the world, but no matter how hard they tried, they were never able to replicate my father's recipe, the one that had made them famous here in Piedmont."

Lily's eyes widened. "So I truly have one of the only records?"

"You have the only *written* record, Lily," Sienna said. "It has been passed down through the generations orally to ensure it never fell into the wrong hands. It's why I was so surprised seeing it in writing like that."

"And we have made our own fortune from this recipe," Matthew said. "Not the empire to rival the other Barbieris' but enough to be a thorn in their side, and to provide well for our entire family."

So Felix must have turned his back on his family after all. Or had something else happened to divide the family?

"You can keep it," Lily said, pushing the paper forward, suddenly feeling like it wasn't hers to hold. "I have no intention of doing anything with it, or—"

"Thank you," Sienna said. "We have no right to ask you for it, but—"

"All I ever wanted was to find out the connection," she said, nudging the recipe even closer to Sienna. "It's yours. Please. It was only ever supposed to be a clue to bring me to you, I'm sure of it."

"So, this recipe," Antonio asked, leaning forward in his seat. "How did it become such a secret? Or more important, *why?*"

"It was never intended to be a secret," Matthew said. "My father created something amazing, something that was very difficult to replicate, and he refused to share it with his father or brother after what happened between them."

"And this was his creation? This recipe here?" Lily asked.

"Exactly. And his hazelnut paste had just enough chocolate in it to make it sweet, especially the way he baked it into the flaky pastry. It was a phenomenon then, and it's still incredibly popular to this day in Italy."

"Once he walked away from the family business, he turned his hazelnut chocolate paste into something more, something people could have at home in a jar, just like he'd dreamed of," Sienna said. "It's what our family empire was founded on. For many years, it was a paste found in every Italian family's cupboard, and it was the one thing he and his father had disagreed on when it came to business."

Lily could almost see Felix and his family in her mind as she listened to Matthew speak.

"My family is one of the biggest consumers of hazelnuts in the world, but the other branch of our family uses even more," Matthew said. "They make very famous chocolates, with an entire hazelnut in the middle.

"At one point, they tried to stop my father from securing the produce he needed, so what did he do?" Matthew gestured to the window, and she looked out. "He started to grow his own hazelnut trees, here on this property, and he slowly purchased more and more land to convert so that he could guarantee at least most of his supply. There was no stopping him once he set his mind to something, and he also created the perfect environment for truffles as well."

"He was passionate about truffles, too?" Lily asked.

"Ahh, no, the truffles are all me," Matthew said. "My passion is white truffles, producing them for restaurants throughout Italy and abroad, which means I'm able to honor my father at the same time as doing what I love."

Lily let his words sink in. He may as well have been talking about her, only he'd found a way to both honor his father and create his own dreams, his own destiny. Tears welled in her eyes as she wondered if that's where she'd gone wrong. *But I love the wine industry, don't I? Or have I simply been single-minded in my desire to follow in my father's footsteps?*

She quickly blinked her tears away before anyone could see them.

"Lily, why don't you come back tomorrow so we can talk more?" Rafaella suggested. "It's been a long night for everyone, but perhaps we could invite the rest of the family over to meet you?"

"That would be incredible, thank you so much." She looked at each of them. "For everything. It's been a very special evening."

Antonio's hand found hers under the table, reassuring her.

"Until tomorrow night, then," Rafaella said.

"Before you go, let me give you something," Matthew said, disappearing from the room for a few minutes as they readied themselves to leave.

Lily was hugging Rafaella and Sienna goodbye when he returned, an album of some kind tucked under his arm.

"Bring this back tomorrow," he said. "I think you'll enjoy looking through it."

She took it from him and then kissed him on each cheek. "Thank you. It means so much to me that you've been so welcoming."

Moments later they were settled in Antonio's car and driving away from Matthew's house, and suddenly Lily couldn't stop her tears as they started to slide down her cheeks. She tried to remain silent, not wanting Antonio to see, but within seconds he'd pulled over to the side of the road, his fingers beneath her chin as he tilted her face up toward him. And when he saw her tears, he opened his arms, holding her as she cried.

"It's a lot for one night, Lily," he said, stroking her hair as he held her. "It's okay."

She wanted to tell him that it was because of her dad, that all she wanted was to have him with her, seated at the table beside Matthew, his eyes meeting hers as they discovered the past together. But instead, she just let Antonio hold her, until she finally took a deep, shuddering breath and managed to stop her tears.

When he finally let her go, he brushed her knuckles with a kiss before pulling back out onto the road to take them back to the hotel.

* * *

The next day, Lily strolled with Antonio, holding hands as they walked along the quaint cobbled footpath. Alba was beautiful in a way that only Italy could be; old houses with terra-cotta roofs and shuttered windows surrounded the village, sitting alongside buildings that housed bars and businesses, which looked as if they'd been there for hundreds of years. Wrought-iron balconies protruded from the upper levels of many of the buildings, perhaps apartments above the cafés, and the streets were littered with pretty tables and chairs, half covered by awnings.

"Shall we find somewhere to eat?" Antonio asked.

"Yes, please," she said, smiling up at him.

He looked at her as if he wasn't sure what to say, but he kept holding her hand as he moved them to the left, glancing over the menus displayed on the street.

"Coffee or wine?" he asked.

She glanced at her watch, surprised to see it was already eleven o'clock. How had it got so late? "Coffee," she replied. "I think I need it."

He kept moving and then stopped. "This will do."

They sat down and she looked over the menu, but no matter how many times she ran her eyes over it, she couldn't seem to see anything, the words a blur, her mind too preoccupied.

"Let me," Antonio said, reaching over and taking her menu from her hands.

"Thanks."

"Frittata, or something lighter?" he asked.

"Frittata," she replied. It had been hours since she'd eaten, and she was ravenous.

A waiter appeared and Antonio ordered them ristrettos and frittatas, before leaning back in his chair and studying her face.

"How are you feeling today?"

"I'm fine."

She cringed at the look on his face, the one that told her he didn't believe her.

"How are you really?"

"In shock," she admitted. "Never in my wildest dreams did I think I'd actually find anything from those clues. And all I can keep thinking is that I wish my dad were here, or that my grandmother could have met her birth siblings."

"But *you're* here, Lily," he said softly. "That little box, it could have been destroyed and the contents never discovered. But they weren't. Sometimes we have to believe in destiny."

"You think it was my destiny to come here and discover all this?" she asked.

Antonio shrugged. "Perhaps. My point is, don't overthink it, just take pleasure in the fact that you're here," he said. "Give yourself permission to enjoy being here, in Italy, sitting outside at a beautiful restaurant."

She grinned. "You forgot the *with a handsome man* part," she teased.

He just laughed back at her, seeming so at ease in his own skin, so relaxed as he sat there and gave her his worldly advice.

"So, what are we going to do today?" she asked him. "I need to keep my mind off meeting everyone later on."

Their coffees arrived then, and she inhaled the strong aroma of caffeine as she lifted her cup, eager for her first sip.

"We eat, we explore the town, we go back to the hotel to make love and rest," he said, grinning at her flushed cheeks as he reached for her. "We live today without worrying about tomorrow."

"How can you be so relaxed about life?" she asked.

"I'm not," he replied. "You've seen me pacing the rows of grapes at harvest time. But there's nothing we can control here. Here, we just have to live in the moment and enjoy ourselves."

Her phone buzzed in her bag then, but she didn't reach for it. Whoever it was, she'd call them back later. Antonio was right; she needed to live in the moment and enjoy the new people she was meeting, the different ways in which her family's history was being rewritten.

She sat back as her food was placed in front of her, eagerly picking up her knife and fork. She'd loved the sweet Italian breakfasts until now, but having a frittata almost made up for being deprived of her favorite scrambled eggs and mushrooms all these mornings since she'd been in Italy.

An hour later, as Antonio chatted with an old friend he'd bumped into on the street, Lily wandered past shops and took out her phone, seeing it was her mum she'd missed earlier. She immediately called her back, needing to hear her voice and realizing she'd be back in London by now. It felt like a lifetime ago that they'd sat and eaten lunch in Como, and she suddenly missed her.

"Lily!" her mother answered.

Tears sprang into her eyes the moment she heard her voice. "Hey, Mum," she managed, trying to disguise her emotion. "How are you?"

"Darling, what's wrong?"

"I just..." She took a deep breath. She'd wanted to call her the night before, as soon as she'd met Matthew, but for some reason she just hadn't been able to.

"What's happened? Tell me everything. Have you had any luck with the clues?"

She could almost see her mum at home, settling on the sofa and tucking her legs up beneath her. It made her homesick in a way she wasn't used to after so long living abroad.

"I don't even know where to start," she confessed. "I still can't believe it myself."

"You've found something, haven't you? Or some*one*?" her mother asked.

"There's a whole family here that we've never known about," she finally said, clearing her throat and swallowing away the emotion. "All these years they knew Grandma was out there somewhere, but they had no idea how to find her. It's just so surreal, and I wish . . ."

Her voice trailed off; the words impossible to say out loud to the one person she knew would understand how she felt.

"You wish your father were there with you," she said for her. "Now that you've found them, you wish your dad were there, too."

She nodded, even though she knew her mum couldn't see her.

"I miss him, too, sweetheart. Every time something big happens, every time you do something I'm so proud of, he's the first person I want to tell. I don't think that feeling will ever go away."

"But you've got Alan now, you've moved on," Lily whispered as her voice cracked.

"He was the love of my life, Lily," her mum said. "He will *always* be the love of my life. All I've tried to do is not let losing him stop me from living. It's not because I don't still love him."

Lily's breath audibly shuddered out of her as she pressed her phone to her ear, forcing herself to keep walking, not wanting to stand still.

"I needed to hear that," she said. "I think I've needed to hear that for a really long time, Mum."

"And I wish I'd told you sooner, so you understood how I

felt." Her mother was silent for a moment. "Now, tell me everything. I don't want you to leave anything out."

Lily smiled. "Well, actually, there's a man."

"A man?" She could almost see her mother's smile.

"Yes, a man. A very handsome, very charming man," she confessed. "I have no idea if it could ever be more than just a fling, but he's just . . ."

"Delicious?" her mother asked.

Lily turned to start walking back the way she'd come and spied Antonio coming toward her. She couldn't mistake his long stride, the confident way he held himself, even though he looked so casual with one hand slipped into his pocket.

"Yes, *delicious*," she agreed. "In fact, if it weren't for him, I would never have ended up here." Lily paused, waving to him. "Grandma has siblings who are still alive, would you believe? And nieces and nephews, blood relatives to me and Dad. It's almost impossible to comprehend that there's this big, entire family here that we knew nothing about. Antonio helped me to make sense of the clues, and we just stumbled upon the right bakery and the rest, well, it all just fell into place."

"So, what are you going to do? Will you stay in Italy for a while? Do you want me to come and be there with you?"

It would have been so easy to say yes and ask her mother to book a plane ticket, but she knew this was something she needed to do on her own.

"Yes, I think I might stay, but I'll let you know," she said. "I miss you so much, Mum, but I feel like I need to do this alone. Is that okay?"

"I completely understand," her mother replied. "But promise me one thing, would you?"

She smiled to herself, remembering the last promise her mum had got her to make. "What is it?"

"If you fall in love with this man, promise that you'll let me meet him," she said. "Something tells me this one is different."

"He is," she said, as Antonio fell into step beside her. She glanced over at him, studying him, breathing him in. "Or perhaps it's me who's different this time. Honestly, I don't know, it's all happened so quickly. But I think it's too complicated to ever be something more."

"Make sure you call me every day now that I'm home," her mum said. "I want daily updates on all the relatives you're meeting, okay? And complicated doesn't mean something can't happen, you remember that."

"I promise I'll stay in touch."

"Oh, and Lily?"

She held the phone tightly to her ear.

"Your father would be so proud of the woman you've become. Sometimes I whisper in the dark to him, telling him what a beautiful, successful young woman you are. He'd love to know that you're there, although I'm sure he's looking down on you every day, keeping watch over you."

"I do hope so," Lily replied.

"Well, I know so. Goodbye, darling."

Lily ended the call and slipped the phone into her pocket, turning to Antonio and smiling as she thought of her father being there with her in spirit. Her mum was right; he would love to know that she was in Italy discovering their heritage, and she needed to stop feeling guilty about being the one there instead of him. Nothing she could do would bring him back, but she could get to know his extended family—that was the one thing she could control.

"How do you feel about gelato?" Antonio asked as she tucked her hand into the crook of his arm.

"I feel that there is only one answer to that question," she said.

"Good, because I just found out there's a little place around the corner that makes the best gelato you've ever tasted."

She leaned her head against his shoulder, hearing her mother's words as they walked. *He was the love of my life, and he still is.*

For some reason, just hearing her say those words, understanding that she wasn't the only one who still grieved the man she'd lost, had created a shift inside her. She hated it that her mum still felt that—the bone-deep ache of loss that she felt sometimes when she least expected it—but it also made her feel closer to her mother all over again. Perhaps the distance she'd felt between them had been simply because she hadn't understood how her mother truly felt all these years.

"Chocolate, salted caramel or pistachio?"

She'd been in such a dream, lost to her own thoughts, she hadn't even realized they were standing outside the gelato vendor.

"Salted caramel," she replied.

Antonio chatted jovially with the man scooping their gelato into little cups, before turning to her. "You have to promise to share," he said, raising one eyebrow and making her grin. "I just had to order chocolate, but that salted caramel . . ."

She dipped her tiny spoon in, tasted it and then swooned, dipping in again and holding it out for him to try.

He licked it off the spoon and then offered her some of his.

"What do you think?" he asked.

"That your friend was right—this *is* the best gelato I've ever tasted."

What she didn't tell him was that she had a hunch her mother was right about something, too. *This man is different, Mum.* Lily just didn't know what that meant to her yet, and whether Antonio's feelings for her could ever turn into something more permanent.

25

The number of cars parked outside Matthew's house sent a bolt of anxiety through Lily. Was she really ready to meet so many people? So many people who were strangers to her, but who somehow felt such a strong connection to her because of the sister they'd yearned for all these years?

"If you ask me to turn the car around, I will," Antonio teased. "You look like a scared little rabbit."

"I *feel* like a scared little rabbit!"

He stopped the car and gave her a long, reassuring look. "You're going to be fine. And if you want to leave, at any stage, you just say the word and we'll go. I'll pretend I have a sore stomach or something."

"You would do that?" she asked, finding it impossible not to laugh at him when he gave her his puppy dog eyes and held his middle.

"I would do that for you," he said. "Now come on. They're all desperate to meet you."

"How do you know?" she scoffed.

Antonio pointed at the house. "I'd say that's why there are so many noses pressed to the windows in there."

She followed his pointing finger, dread swirling through her as she realized that he was, in fact, right. He took hold of her elbow and forced her arm up, at which point she limply waved back.

"Come on, they're all going to love you."

She hoped he was right.

It turned out that Antonio *was* right. Lily had sensed some hesitation from a couple of family members, but the rest had embraced her with open arms, and within minutes of arriving she'd felt like she'd somehow always belonged.

There was also something familiar about the long lunch they were having, reminding her of Antonio's family and the way they'd so readily taken her in. She smiled over at him, thankful to have him there. He'd fitted in easily with the others, seemingly able to talk to anyone and happily discussing everything from wine to truffles and even hazelnut production.

"So tell us, Lily, what first brought you to Italy?" Matthew asked.

Lily took a moment to finish her mouthful, seeing the curious expressions of the other family members as they looked on. Matthew and Rafaella were seated across from her, and she had Matthew's sister Carla to her left, and his other sister, Magda, a little farther away. She'd found them slightly less talkative, although she wasn't sure if it was simply their inability to converse easily in English or an actual distrust of her. Matthew's brother, Silvio, was more like him, though, quick to smile, as his wife was, too.

"My father passed away at a young age, but I've followed in his footsteps as a winemaker," Lily told them, glancing from face to face as she realized the table had fallen almost completely silent. Only the children at the smaller, adjoining table were still chatting, oblivious to the adults and what was being discussed. "We had plans to establish our own wine label one day, and before he passed away, we spent hours planning my future, *our* future, and the places I should go to learn before we founded our label. He was insistent about me coming to Italy."

"So it was a coincidence you came here?" Rafaella asked.

"Well, yes and no, I suppose," Lily replied. "I was always going to come to Italy to make wine, to learn as much as I could about the production of Franciacorta, but it was a coincidence that the clues also led me here. I suppose I would have followed them here eventually, even without my work."

When she thought about it, everything about those two clues was coincidental. The fact that she'd even been in London when the meeting had been arranged, that she'd opened the letter herself . . . it was as if fate had played a helping hand, as much as she was loath to admit it.

"When you were telling me about your mother, I couldn't believe the coincidences," Lily continued. "To think that I stood in the same hotel in Como, the very same foyer, where she once stood with Felix, it's, well . . ." She sighed. "It's serendipitous in so many ways. Even eating gelato and strolling the streets with Antonio, it feels like it was all meant to be, I suppose."

Antonio smiled at her and she managed not to blush in reply. He still made her stomach clench, her heart flutter, whenever his eyes met hers.

"And you say there were other women looking for their grandmothers?" Carla asked. "Did you not find it all, how do you say, *strange?*"

Lily could feel the distrust in the other woman's tone, and she reached for her wine, taking a sip before answering. She could understand why she'd asked, it wasn't unreasonable, but it still made her uneasy.

"I want you to know that I want nothing from you," Lily said, trying to keep her voice even. "I'm simply here to honor my grandmother's memory."

"Of course you are," Matthew interrupted, giving his sister

a sharp look. "And we want you to know that you're always welcome here."

"Thank you," she said. "But you're right, everything about finding my way to you all has been unusual. I almost didn't go to the lawyer's office that day, but I'm so pleased that my curiosity got the better of me."

Conversations slowly started again around her, and Sienna's hand brushed hers as she leaned in, her smile warm.

"They'll come round. They just need some time to process it all," Sienna said. "It's a lot to take in."

"I know," Lily said, picking up her fork and pushing some of the salad around her plate. "I just wish there were a way to show them that I don't have an agenda here."

"The rift my grandfather caused in his family, it became a bitter feud that continued for decades and still exists to this day," Sienna explained. "The litigation continued until Felix and his brother had both passed away, and our extended families came to a truce of sorts. But given the large amounts of money involved on each side, I suppose it's made all of his descendants cautious. It's exactly why I was so taken aback that day when you approached me with the recipe."

Lily nodded. "I understand, of course I do."

"Our family doesn't have the exorbitant wealth that Felix's brother inherited, but it's substantial enough that we want to protect it."

Lily ate a forkful of salad, taking in Sienna's words along with her food. She understood that it would take time to gain their trust, but she also hoped that it wouldn't be long before they saw that she was successful in her own right, that she didn't expect or want anything material from them.

The conversation moved on to other things, and Lily was grateful for Antonio's arm as it moved around the back of her chair, and she lazily leaned into him, basking in the late-afternoon sun. The wine had been easy to drink but was now making her sleepy, and she could have easily shut her eyes as she rested against Antonio. She could certainly get used to the Italian way of life, enjoying beautiful food and wine at lunch and then taking a nap during the hottest hour of the day.

"Shall we stay and enjoy the rest of the afternoon, or is it time for me to clutch my stomach?" Antonio murmured, leaning close to her.

Lily nuzzled into him, sighing against his neck. "Thank you, but no. I think we'll stay awhile."

"Good, because I think I was right about them all liking you."

He kissed her cheek as she tipped her head back, looking up at the cloudless blue sky above. It was going to take time for them all to accept, but time was something she had plenty of; and if she accepted the offer to stay on as assistant winemaker with Roberto, then she could have months or even years to get to know the family, for them to slowly embrace her as one of their own.

"All these years searching for their daughter, and somehow their great-granddaughter found her way to us from London," Matthew said, moving around the table and placing his hands on her shoulders. "It's almost impossible to believe, isn't it? And yet here you are."

"I can't believe that you all knew about my grandmother, when so many families would have kept such things a secret," Lily said to him as he pulled out a chair beside her. "Did they truly continue to search for her? Their entire lives?"

The table fell silent again and it was Rafaella who leaned across, her eyes on her husband. "Tell them," she urged. "Tell them what you did each year. She needs to know how much this means to you all, how much it means for this search to finally come to an end."

26

Matthew wiped his eyes, leaning back in his chair, wine glass in hand, his breath shuddering out of him. "At the start of every Christmas season, we lit a candle for our missing sister," Matthew eventually said. "Our parents would pray that one day they'd be reunited, each year asking for forgiveness. As we grew, we joined them in praying, taking turns at lighting the candle. They were a beautiful couple, so in love despite the hardships they'd endured, and such dedicated parents to us all, but there was always a sadness during those first few days of Christmas that my mother was never able to hide. And we all felt the loss of their firstborn, the missing sister that we would never meet."

Lily listened to his words with a heavy heart. She could only imagine how torturous it must have been, to give up a child so obviously conceived in love, only to be somehow reunited after the fact. Had they felt as if they were being punished in some way? How did it all happen? From what they'd told her, Felix was prepared to give up everything for his lover.

She turned to watch the children playing, having long since left the table, running across the grass in what appeared to be an elaborate game of tag, their laughter making it impossible not to feel happy. It was a lot to take in—she suddenly had an extended family that no one in her life had known about, the kind of enormous, rambunctious family that couldn't have been more different to her own upbringing. She watched as Antonio rose, going to join the children and some of their parents. *The kind of family I always wished for.*

"The strangest part of all this is that you all grew up knowing my grandmother existed, but that she herself was most likely unaware she was even adopted. I truly believe she would have confided in my father if she'd known."

"There's been a missing piece of this family all my life, and it broke something inside my father even more so than my mother, I think," Matthew said. "I believe he blamed himself for not leaving his own family sooner, for not going after my mother more quickly. If he had, perhaps he would never have caused her so much pain, led her to make such a desperate decision."

"Do you mind me asking how they found their way back to one another?" Lily asked. "What happened?"

"I think, like you finding us, it was destiny," Matthew said. "It was never meant to be, and yet somehow, it was."

Lily looked around the table, at Matthew and Rafaella, and at Matthew's siblings, Carla, Magda and Silvio, still in awe that they were related to her, as she pondered his response. Matthew was by far the youngest, which meant he also had the youngest children, but the others had grown broods of their own and grandchildren, who were sprawled across the alfresco area and lawn. *All connected to me by blood.* But it was Antonio who caught her eye as she looked out, standing against a tree with his hands over his eyes as he counted loudly, a little girl with her hands on her hips watching him as if she expected to catch him cheating. Lily instantly liked the girl—the child's female cousins formed a sea of pink, but she was dressed in a black tutu with sturdy black boots.

"How long have you and Antonio been together?" Rafaella asked as she sat between Lily and Matthew. "He seems lovely."

"We're not so much together as..." Her words drifted. "I've been working with him these past few months as assistant winemaker on his family's vineyard, and we became close very quickly." She hadn't really answered the question, but she hoped that satisfied their curiosity.

"I've always been interested in the wine business," Matthew said. "But when we found this property, I was able to pursue my love of truffles. The hazelnut trees provide just the right nutrients and fungi for them, so we've had quite a bit of success, from our white truffles in particular."

They were silent a moment as Antonio leapt from his hiding space and started looking for the children, the game having moved on rapidly from tag to hide-and-seek.

"Lily, what do you know of our family business?" Matthew's sister Carla asked. "Did it all truly come as a surprise to you, or were you aware of who we were? Of what your great-grandfather was famous for?"

She thought of Sienna's advice before she answered. "I knew nothing before I came here and met your brother."

"Enough!" Matthew demanded, slamming his hand down on the table. "What would our mamma say? What would she think, you asking Lily a question like that when we've finally found her? This ends now."

Carla was much older than Matthew, by perhaps fifteen years, and she stood and ambled away, muttering to herself rather than answering his question.

"I'm sorry," Rafaella said, reaching for her hand and squeezing it. "Please excuse her behavior. I think this has all come as quite a shock to her."

"It's a shock to me, too," Lily said. "When I lost my father, it was just me and my mother, we had no one else. But to find out we have family, and in *Italy*." She shook her head. "I had no idea that being given that box that day, following those clues, could ever have meant so much to me."

Antonio was coming back toward them, his smile broad as his eyes settled on hers.

"Our family is your family, Lily," Matthew said solemnly. "You are always welcome here, in our home, for as long as you would like to stay. It would give me great pleasure to hear more about my eldest sister, and my nephew."

Antonio joined them then, and Lily poured him a glass of water, amused at how quickly he gulped it down.

"Those children are demanding," he muttered. "I think I'll have to find somewhere to hide for the rest of the afternoon."

She poured him more water when he set his glass down empty, her hand on his thigh as he took the vacant chair to her left. It was nice having him here; she couldn't imagine having done this alone. Carla's comment had rattled her, but she understood her hesitation; she'd appeared out of nowhere, they knew nothing about her. She'd have been suspicious, too, of course she would have.

"Let's open another bottle of wine," Matthew announced, standing and waving to one of his children, before calling out something in Italian. "That way I can keep you here another hour, and you can tell me all about your grandmother and your father. I want to know everything."

Antonio seemed relaxed as he settled into his chair, crossing his legs at the ankle, and Matthew's eyes were attentive as he leaned forward in anticipation. So Lily began with her grandmother, knowing that if she started talking about her father, she'd never be able to stop. And as the hours passed, she finally got Matthew to open up more about Estee, and exactly how her grandmother had been put up for adoption.

27

LAKE COMO, 1946

Estee woke to sun streaming in through the window of the hotel room, the smell of coffee making her lift her head from the pillow. She clutched the sheet to her chest as she sat up, not used to the feel of cotton against her bare skin; she always went to bed wearing her silk nightwear. Memories of the night before came back to her, filling her mind, and she was pleased to have a moment to gather her thoughts as she watched Felix, his back to her as he sat at the little desk in the room.

"Morning," he said, not lifting his head immediately.

"Morning," she replied, wishing the coffee weren't so far away. Estee wasn't sure what he was doing, and she sat and craned her neck.

Felix finally stood and came toward her, a folded sheet of paper in his hand.

"What are you doing up so early?" she asked.

He sat on the bed beside her and reached his arm out, pulling her toward him as he dropped a kiss into her hair. "I want you to have this."

"What is it?" Estee reached for the piece of paper, opening it and studying the words he'd carefully printed.

"It's the recipe to my hazelnut chocolate paste," he said. "I've been working to get the recipe just right, and I'm the only one who knows it. Until now, it's only existed in my head, but now I want to share it with you."

Estee refolded the paper. "What do you want me to do with it?"

"It's a promise," he said, taking her hand and holding it in his. "I'm trusting you with this, because this recipe is how I can succeed on my own. My father can continue making chocolates and pastry, but he'll never know my recipe for this paste. You are the only other person I will ever share this with. I've also written down the recipe for my version of *saccottini al cioccolato* filled with my hazelnut paste."

Estee nodded, understanding the enormity of what he was doing for her. "So you're really going to walk away from your family? From your engagement?"

He lifted her hand and pressed it to his lips. "Yes. I told you I would give up everything for you, and I meant it," Felix said. "I'm just going to need some time to arrange my affairs, so I need you to be patient, to wait for me."

Estee was speechless. After what had happened with his family, and then spending the night together, it was almost impossible to digest.

"Won't your family be looking for you this morning?" she asked. "Won't *Emilie*'s family expect to see you?"

Felix leaned forward and kissed her lips. "You let me worry about who's looking for me," he said. "Just promise me you'll keep that recipe safe. You'll be the only person other than me to have it, and if anything happens to me, you don't give it to anyone."

"I promise, of course," she replied.

"Will you wait for me?" he asked. "It could take a couple of months to disentangle myself from my engagement and my family's business, but I promise I'll come to Milan for you."

"I have rehearsals and the rest of the season to complete," Estee said. "I have plenty to keep me busy while we're parted."

"Can I ask you one more thing?"

She nodded. "Of course. Anything."

"Would you let me put this ring on your finger?"

The grin spreading across his face made her laugh as he produced the ring. She held her finger out and let him slip it on, admiring the brilliant solitaire diamond as it shone in the light.

"I can't wear it like this, not until you're free to propose to me. We can't disrespect poor Emilie any more than we already have," Estee said, sighing as she carefully slid it off. "But I will wear it around my neck until you return for me, as our promise to one another."

"I understand. And just so you know, I hate that I've hurt Emilie. She should never have been part of this. I should have ended things long ago."

Felix took the ring from her and undid the clasp of the necklace she was wearing, sliding it on and then gently putting it in place, before sweeping her hair away from her neck and whispering a kiss to her skin. She let him, stretching to the side as his kisses trailed lower.

"You should go," she whispered.

"I know, but I've barely drunk my coffee and I'm sure it won't matter if I'm missing for another hour."

Estee hated to think what they were saying about her, what his family would think if they came looking for him or if they saw him emerge from her room at this hour, in the same clothes as the day before. But the more he kissed her, tracing the skin across her décolletage so gently now, the harder she was finding it to resist.

"We'll marry in private, once all this is over," he murmured. "You will be the famous ballerina, and I'll be the famous baker. We'll be known all through Milan, maybe even Italy."

"I like the sound of that," she whispered as she lay back and pulled him with her, tumbling together against the sheets. "The baker and the ballerina."

"Just promise you'll wait for me," he said. "No matter how long it takes for me to get everything in order, I'll come for you. I promise."

"I promise, too," she whispered in reply.

The paper he'd carefully committed his recipe to touched her bare hip, and she reached for it, missing it as it fluttered to the ground.

Don't forget it before you go. She tried to think about the paper, but Felix's kisses were relentless, and despite her best intentions, she never did place it on the bedside table.

* * *

Estee had left Felix with a lingering kiss and her promise to wait for him, and when they'd parted in the hotel room, she'd felt lighter than she had in a long time. Spending the night with Felix had changed everything, and so had the ring hanging around her neck. She instinctively reached for it, the weight comforting, reminding her of the promises he'd made.

Sometimes she wondered if they'd always been destined to meet, their lives on a course that was set to collide. All these years of yearning for him, it seemed almost impossible that they'd somehow found their way back to one another.

It took over an hour to reach her apartment in Milan, and she spent most of the journey with her head against the window as the world passed by. Vineyards stretched across much of the landscape for part of the drive, and farmers had enormous baskets of peaches for sale at the side of the road that made her mouth water.

But it wasn't long before they'd left the lush landscape behind and were back in Milan, and when she stepped out of the taxi, thanking the driver, she immediately felt at home. The cobbled street beneath her feet, the smell of the city and the sounds of people going about their lives—it had been *her* life for so long now. She'd never returned to Piedmont, not even for a holiday, since she'd been accepted to join the La Scala academy, staying with her aunt and then moving out on her own with Sophia as soon as she was able to afford it.

She walked up to her apartment, pushing open the door and looking around. Everything was so familiar, but nothing had been the same since Sophia had passed away. She'd simply shut her friend's bedroom door, not wanting to deal with her personal items, to smell her perfume or see the bed where they'd so often lain together, sharing their dreams and plans for the future. Sophia had lost her family during the war, which meant Estee had had to deal with everything after she'd passed.

Since Felix had walked back into her life, she'd barely thought about Sophia, and she berated herself for pushing her friend from her mind. She'd meant everything to her for so many years, but sometimes it was easier not to remember, not to keep returning to the pain.

If only I could tell you about Felix. If only I could show you my ring!

Estee nudged open the door to Sophia's room, the lingering scent of her friend's perfume filling her nostrils as she sat on the bed and took the ring from around her neck, carefully placing it on her finger so she could look at it.

"He wants me to marry him, Sophia," she whispered, sighing as she stared at the diamond. "He wants me to be his wife."

It was surreal, even after the weekend they'd shared, and after sitting for a bit longer, she got up and went to her own room, opening her bedside drawer and taking out a small file that held important documents. She had her passport tucked in there, along with her original acceptance letter to the La Scala academy and the program from the reopening of the theater. Estee slipped the recipe in there that Felix had given her and shut the drawer, before looking down at her ring again. She had every intention of putting it back round her neck, but since no one was going to see her while she was in her apartment, she couldn't see the harm in leaving it on for the night.

She wondered what Felix was doing as she changed into more comfortable clothes, deciding to stretch her body before making something to eat. She would be back in the studio tomorrow, and after a couple of days away, the last thing she wanted was to feel tight and stiff.

Estee touched her hand to her stomach, regretting the copious amounts of food she'd eaten with Felix—although she didn't really regret it one bit.

28

EIGHT WEEKS LATER

Estee came off the stage and ran, even as her name was called. She'd managed to hold it together during the performance, refusing to be anything but the consummate professional, but all she could think about now was making it to her dressing room.

She didn't make it.

She doubled over, gripping the bin outside another room and being sick, emptying the entire contents of her stomach. She stood for a moment, still bent over at the waist, desperately trying to compose herself. She eventually straightened and took the small bin with her, only making it into her dressing room before vomiting again, the bile rising within her as her skin turned hot and clammy. She'd never been so unwell in her life, and each day it was getting worse. She hadn't managed to go one night without rushing off stage all week, and the week before hadn't been much better. It didn't seem to matter what she did, she could barely even keep water down.

"Estee, are you all right?" There was a soft knock at the door, followed by one of the other ballerinas appearing round it.

"I'm fine, I just need a moment," Estee responded.

"You're sure it's not something more serious?" the other girl asked. "You've been sick now for—"

"I'm fine," Estee snapped, not turning, gripping the bin until the door finally closed, her knuckles turning white. She doubled over then, retching again and again. When she was finally finished, convinced there was nothing left in her stomach, she set the bin down and walked on unsteady feet to her chair, reaching for the glass of water she'd left there earlier. Her hand was shaking as she took it, slowly drinking a little before settling into the chair.

She stared at herself in the mirror, barely recognizing the face looking back at her. The sheer act of holding it together and then being so unwell had left her strained, dark under the eyes and without the luster she was known for. She'd pushed herself harder than ever these past weeks, throwing herself into dance in an effort to *not* think about Felix and how long it might take him to return, but she knew that wasn't why she was sick.

There was another tap at her door, but it was softer, and she looked up into the mirror to see her makeup artist walking in. For years she'd done her own makeup, but now she and some of the other more senior dancers had the luxury of someone else to assist them, and she was particularly fond of Marta.

"You're sick again?" Marta asked, clearing the bin and putting it outside the door, before walking over to her, her hands landing on Estee's shoulders as she met her gaze in the mirror.

Estee nodded. "I'm fine now, I just need you to get me ready again and—"

"The other girls are talking," Marta said. "You know they can be like vultures sometimes."

Estee sat up taller, defying her body as her stomach started to churn again.

"No one is taking my place," she said. "I'll be fine, I'm always fine."

Marta nodded and moved around to face her, powdering her

face and applying fresh bright red lipstick for her, as well as doing something to her under-eye area to take away the dark circles. Estee just sat, back ramrod straight, mentally preparing for the next hour on stage.

"Estee, have you thought about whether you could be . . ." Marta stood back and glanced down at Estee's stomach. "Pregnant?"

"*Pregnant?*" Estee gasped the word and followed Marta's gaze. She dropped her hand there, horrified. Is that why she'd been putting on weight despite how sick she'd been? Why their dressmaker had muttered under her breath about having to let something out for her? She'd thought she had some sort of illness, had eaten something particularly bad, perhaps.

"My sister, she was sick like this when she had her babies, so I just wondered . . ."

Estee shut her eyes, gripping the sides of her chair. "No, I can't be," she said. "There's not, I mean, I can't be . . ."

Marta leaned forward and dabbed at Estee's eyes. "No crying. Nothing's going to keep you from that stage, remember? Not in your final week."

Estee nodded, swallowing, trying to force away the crushing feeling of what Marta had suggested. How could she have been so naive? How could she not have realized what was happening to her own body?

"Please, Marta, you can't say anything," she begged, catching her wrist as she finished her face. "I can trust you, can't I?"

"You can trust me with anything, Estee. I'll never share your secrets, they're safe with me."

Marta kissed the top of her head as a sharp call echoed down the hall outside Estee's dressing room door.

"It's showtime, come on," Marta said. "You look beautiful, as always."

Estee stood, keeping hold of the chair for a moment as the room threatened to spin around her, before collecting herself and settling her face back into the perfect mask she'd perfected for showtime.

I'm pregnant. The words kept echoing in her mind as she made her way out, ignoring the whispers of the other ballerinas as she passed them.

There was only so long before her secret was discovered, but nothing was going to stop her from finishing the season. This was her dream, her destiny, and not even a baby who needed to remain a secret from the world was going to change that. *For now.*

The only person she'd tell was Felix, but even then, she would only tell him in person. Her career would be over if anyone found out. She would write him a letter and ask him to meet her; they could both decide what to do together.

The crowd was quiet, the murmur turning to absolute silence as she prepared for the curtain to rise again. And the moment the orchestra began, she became Estee the ballerina, her mind filled only with surviving until the curtain fell once more.

* * *

Estee couldn't stand still. She'd started to pace inside her apartment, waiting for Felix to arrive, but he was already late.

She'd written and asked him to come before midday, and she'd given him a week's notice. But other than a letter she'd received from him the week after their time away, she hadn't heard a thing. Now, with her final show taking place that night, Estee was at a crossroads, and she had no idea what to do.

She placed her palm to her stomach, feeling the ever-so-slight curve there, which was becoming almost impossible to hide on her slight frame now that she was two-and-a-half months pregnant.

Where is he?

Estee sat down, staring out of her window at the street below, searching for him in every man who walked past. But there was no sign of him. Fear had started to bubble inside her, even though she knew it was unfounded. He'd asked her to wait, he'd told her he didn't know how long it would take to disentangle himself from his family and the business, and she wouldn't have been concerned if it hadn't been for the baby.

The baby.

She stood again and resumed her pacing, watching the large clock that hung on the wall as it slowly ticked its way through the afternoon. It was no use. He wasn't coming. She could feel it in her bones that something was wrong, that she wasn't going to be seeing Felix's handsome face that afternoon, that she wasn't going to witness his broad smile light up as he cradled her belly and discovered that they were expecting.

Estee walked into her kitchen and looked in the cupboard, knowing she should make herself something to eat, but she couldn't muster the energy, and she had also left it a little late to eat before going on stage. It was closing night, which meant she had one more evening before having to decide what to do. She was supposed to have a short break before resuming with the theater, looking ahead to the next season, but she was going to have to tell them something to explain her absence. By three or four months pregnant, there was no way she'd be able to hide her condition from any of the other dancers, who were used to seeing one another's bodies in barely any clothes each day.

Eventually Estee bundled herself into a warm coat and left her apartment, walking the familiar path to La Scala, holding her head high as tears stung her eyes. There was nothing she could do about Felix. Perhaps something had come up, or perhaps he wasn't coming back for her at all, although she couldn't bear to think the latter could be the case. Felix loved her, she knew that, but it was so unlike him not to show, especially when she'd emphasized how important it was that he come to see her.

At the theater, Estee made her way straight to her private dressing room, before warming up and moving into rehearsals, the evening passing by in a familiar blur until it was finally time to make her way back to her dressing room after the show. She was thankful the sickness had mostly stopped over the past few days, but the fatigue was wearing her down and she needed a minute to herself before going to celebrate the end of the season with the other girls. Sometimes she felt as if they were just waiting for her to fail or injure herself, all desperate to rise through the ranks and take over a better role within the ballet company, but at times like this, they were her family, and she needed to be there celebrating with them.

Her dressing room was full of flowers, more than usual given it was their final show, but one bunch in particular caught her eye. The roses were white, the stems long, and there was a large envelope attached to the bouquet. Estee crossed the room and opened it, admiring the flowers as she pulled out the letter. A wad of money fell out with the paper, covering the floor, and she bent to scoop it up, baffled as to why someone would have sent her cash.

But the moment she looked at the paper, her heart sank, fingers clutching around the money as a sob rose within her.

Dear Estee

I write to you with a heavy heart. Despite my promises to end my engagement, I've realized I must honor the promise I made to Emilie and to my family. Estee, I wish things could have been different, I wish I could have left my family behind and started a new life with you, but I cannot leave everything I've ever known. No matter how much I love you, it is simply not possible for us to be together.

I will never, ever forget you, and I cherish the time we spent together. Please accept the money I've enclosed as my way of showing how truly sorry I am.

Yours, Felix

"*No!*" she screamed, and screwed the letter into a ball, throwing it across the room, her legs buckling beneath her as she dropped to the ground, cradling her stomach as the money left her fingers and pooled around her.

Tears bubbled inside her, overwhelmed her as the words in his letter repeated over and over in her mind. How could he do this to her? How could he simply turn his back on her? How could he break the promise he'd made to *her*?

She heard laughter outside her door and forced herself back to her feet, not wanting anyone to see her at her lowest. Instead, she checked her appearance in the mirror, quickly wiping under her eyes and then slipping into her robe, tying it loosely around the waist so as not to draw any attention to her figure.

Felix isn't coming. He's left me.

Tonight, she would make an appearance at the last-night party and celebrate a successful season with the rest of the dancers. Then she would pack up her life and leave Milan, giving notice on her apartment and coming up with a reason not to stay with the theater throughout the coming months. She would need to invent an opportunity elsewhere—perhaps London—so as to make it seem worthy of leaving La Scala with the promise of returning for the following season.

London.

London was perfect. It was far enough away that she could disappear until she could work out what to do. She had her own savings, the money from the envelope, which she would have to accept in order to survive, no matter how much she wished to send it straight back to him, and the ring around her neck.

Her fingers found their way there as they had done every day since Felix had given it to her, but today there was no comfort to be found. Today, she wished to yank it from her neck and hurl it across the room, but she wouldn't, because she had no idea how much money she might need to stay afloat. She would also have to pretend she was married to avoid questions, which would mean wearing the ring he'd given her.

Felix would never know about their child, and neither would anyone else in Milan. Of that she would make certain.

Felix is gone, and he's never coming back for me.

29

PRESENT DAY

"I still can't believe it."

Lily lay in bed, nestled in the crook of Antonio's arm, as she replayed the events of the night over and over in her mind. *I have family we never even knew about.* She'd tried to call her mum but hadn't been able to reach her, and she couldn't wait to tell her all about the extended family she'd met. But as excited as she was, it would be different for her mother. This wasn't her past; it was something that connected Lily with her father's family, not her mother's. And as devoted as her mum had been to Lily's dad, during their marriage and in keeping his memory alive after he'd passed away, this connection to the past was hers alone.

Lily must have let out a sigh, because Antonio's lips brushed her hair.

"What's wrong?"

"Nothing," she said. "Actually, everything."

He chuckled. "I can imagine. You must have a lot going around in your head right now."

She nestled even closer into him, knowing she wasn't going to find sleep, no matter how long they lay in the dark. Antonio had left the lamp on beside the bed, and she stared at the shadows cast across the ceiling.

"I can't stop thinking about Matthew's mother, my *great-grandmother*," she said. "Imagine living your whole life wondering what had happened to your daughter? Thinking you'd made the wrong decision in giving her up for adoption? It must have almost broken her at times."

"I'm sure it did," he replied. "I'm curious to know more. It's quite a tale."

"Me too."

Lily sighed and wriggled, hoping to get comfortable, trying to relax and clear her head.

"You know we're supposed to be going home tomorrow, don't you?" Antonio asked. "Although perhaps you'd like to stay."

She pushed up a little so she could look down at his face. It was as if he'd read her mind.

"What would make you say that?"

"Tell me you haven't thought about it," he said, his words kind as he stroked her shoulder. "You have a family you didn't even know existed until this day, a family who can't get enough of you." Antonio's smile was kind. "And it's a connection to your father. That must mean a lot."

She took a deep breath, holding it before slowly letting it go. "It's so strange, how connected I feel to them all," she said. "I know they're lovely people and I probably would have liked them no matter how I met them, but there's something about the way I feel when I'm with them. I keep wondering if I'm imagining it, or if it's because somehow, on some level, they remind me of my father. Especially Matthew."

"Then I think you have your answer," Antonio said, reaching for her and pulling her closer so that she was nestled against him again. "My father will understand, in case that's what you're worried about. They know what you've come looking for here, and

I promise you that nothing is more important to the Martinellis than family."

I need to give his father an answer, though, about the job.

Antonio reached for the lamp and turned it out, taking her into his arms once the room was dark and pressing a quick kiss to her lips. "Sleep," he whispered. "There's plenty of time to think about it all in the morning."

She kissed him back, grateful for his embrace, to have someone with her as she discovered a past she'd never even known she was searching for.

It took only minutes for Antonio to start breathing heavily, a light snore telling her he was asleep, and she carefully extracted herself from his embrace and slid out of the bed. She walked barefoot to the writing desk in the corner of the room, just enough light coming in through the curtains to stop her from bumping into things, and quietly flicked on the little lamp. She glanced over her shoulder, pleased to see she hadn't disturbed Antonio, then sat down and reached for the elegant stack of writing paper and a pen.

She did want to stay—Antonio had read her mind—but she also wanted to write a letter to his father. She would give it to him before he left and ask him not to open it, to simply deliver it once he arrived home.

Her feelings about Antonio were complicated—she wasn't used to being so close to someone, to feeling so deeply about another human being that she could see herself by his side in the future. But the one thing she was certain about was her career. She always had been, and that meant she had to give the Martinelli family a formal response about the job offered to her.

A shiver ran across her skin as she sat barefoot in her pajamas, leaning forward, pen in hand, as Antonio slept.

* * *

"Good morning, beautiful."

"What time is it?" she asked. She was an early riser by nature, and her job had only made her more committed to getting up early each morning, which made her sleeping in all the more surprising.

"Almost ten," he said, passing her a coffee cup. "I thought you might need this."

She groaned and reached for it gratefully, sitting up in bed and taking a sip. "Thank you. I stayed up a little late." It had ended up taking a long time for her to get the words just right.

He gestured toward the desk, and the sealed envelope addressed to his father.

"I take it you want me to give that to him?"

She took another sip of coffee before meeting his gaze. "Yes. You were right. I need to stay. It just . . ."

"Feels like the right thing to do?"

She nodded, feeling so conflicted inside. On the one hand, she desperately wanted to go with him and stay by his side, soaking up the way Antonio made her feel, but on the other, she wanted to learn more about this new family of hers, to connect with them. Didn't she owe it to her grandmother to create memories with people who'd waited their entire lives hoping to meet her? And she didn't really even know whether Antonio wanted to spend more time with her once their trip was over.

"You have to listen to your heart, Lily," Antonio said, cupping her cheek as he sat beside her on the bed. "You know where I'll be if you want to find me again."

She hated that tears filled her eyes, or that they were saying goodbye. The time they'd spent together had meant so much to her, more so than any other relationship she'd ever had with a man.

"Antonio," she began.

He smiled as he looked into her eyes.

"Since my father died, I think I've spent every waking minute trying to make him proud, to live his life for him." She cleared her throat as emotion bubbled up inside her. "I don't think I've ever actually asked myself what *I* want, because I've been too scared of not achieving all the things we talked about together before he passed. But I was only a teenager then. I didn't even know what I truly wanted. How could I have?"

"You don't need to explain yourself to me," Antonio said. "You don't owe me anything, Lily."

But she did, she owed him an explanation.

"I just, I think staying here will be good for me. Perhaps it will even help me find closure about my own father's death, reconnecting with blood relatives of his. But I want you to know that I'll be forever grateful for everything you've done for me. I couldn't have done this alone."

"I think you underestimate yourself," he murmured, his hand dropping from her skin. "You would have been just fine on your own."

"But I'm pleased I wasn't," she whispered as more tears threatened to fall. "I've never felt like this before, which is why I'm finding it so hard to make this decision."

He nodded, and if she wasn't mistaken, his eyes were brimming with unshed tears, too.

"I'm going to leave after lunch, but you don't have to check out until tomorrow morning," he said, glancing at their intertwined hands before looking up at her again. "For what it's worth, I'm going to miss you, Lily."

"I'm going to miss you, too."

They kissed; a warm, gentle kiss that made her ache for more.

"Was this truly just a holiday romance?" she asked. "Were we ever destined to be anything more?"

"If I'd known there was a chance of you staying longer in Italy, I'd never have taken you to my bed," he admitted. "Does that give you your answer?"

So he'd lied to her when she'd asked him after their first night together. Not that she blamed him; she had put him on the spot when she'd asked, and he obviously hadn't wanted to hurt her feelings.

"And how do you feel now?" she asked. "After the time we've spent together?"

"How about we simply say goodbye for now?" he said. "I'd be lying again if I told you I didn't wish we could spend longer together."

"Then it's goodbye for now," she agreed. "If we're destined to cross paths again, we will."

He stood and pulled her up with him, holding her in his arms so that her cheek could press to his chest. She inhaled the scent of him, felt the strength of his arms around her, and knew how easily it would be to follow him home. But she needed to do this for her, to discover who she was, before deciding whether he could be something more to her.

I've fallen in love with him. She knew it, and she wondered if he knew it, too.

"I made a bad decision some years ago," he murmured into her hair, still holding her. "I asked a woman to marry me because I thought I loved her, but if I'd been true to myself, I would have known it wasn't right. We were different people wanting different things from life, and if I'd only seen that before we were married, I could have saved us both a lot of pain. I wouldn't be so broken now."

She didn't reply; she didn't need to. Her time with Antonio had changed everything for her, and she had no idea what might happen between them or if they'd simply shared a moment in time. But she did know where to find him, and for once she wasn't going to let fear stop her from feeling, from falling for someone whether it was for a moment or a lifetime.

Lily leaned back in his arms as his mouth found hers, more passionate than before, an urgency between them that hadn't existed until now. And she wondered if, in just a few short weeks, it really was possible to be hopelessly, madly in love.

30

Estee walked slowly to the front door of the elegant yet understated house. She'd walked past many times now, trying to summon the nerve to enter, but at almost eight months pregnant, she knew it was time.

The past four months had been pleasant enough, if not lonely, especially for someone used to being busy with rehearsals every day and surrounded by others. But she'd made a little life for herself in London, and it hadn't been all bad. But her stomach had swelled now, and her back was frequently sore, and she knew that it was time to make a difficult decision, no matter how much she wanted to avoid it.

As she did so often these days, Estee gently rubbed her stomach, her palm flat against the side of her dress. The idea of parting with her unborn child left her feeling empty inside, but the one thing she'd come to terms with during her months in London was how difficult it would be to raise a child alone.

And so she stepped inside the gate, passing a simple sign that read HOPE'S HOUSE, and walked toward the front door. Estee lifted her hand, lining her knuckles up to knock on the shiny red timber, but something stopped her. Her baby moved inside her, the flutter of her child making her question her decision all over again. But as much as she could imagine holding her baby, cradling her son or daughter and whispering to them as she rocked him or her to sleep, she also couldn't stop seeing an alternate image in her mind. London was a beautiful city and had treated her well, and she could even imagine building a life for herself there once she'd given birth, joining The Royal Ballet company, perhaps. But she'd also seen women on the streets begging for money, their ragged children hiding beneath their mother's filthy skirts, their hollow cheeks telling Estee just how tough life was for them as they held up their cups looking for spare change. Not to mention the women who came out at night, prepared to do anything to entertain a man just for a few extra pounds. She was certain the only reason they were selling their bodies was to feed their families.

She would rather die than let her child grow up with a hungry belly or see their mother reduced to begging or prostitution.

The door opened before she had the chance to knock, and a woman with dark hair threaded with gray stood before her. Estee took one look at her and almost burst into tears; the kindness shining from the woman's face was unmistakable, despite her no-fuss appearance with her hair pulled back into a bun, her cotton dress and apron a muted blue.

"I'm Hope," the woman said, holding out her hand.

Estee raised her hand in response and Hope clasped it, her other hand closing over it in a hold so warm it made her realize just how long it had been since she'd been touched by another person.

"I, I . . ." Estee began, falteringly.

"You don't need to explain anything," Hope said, stepping back and motioning her inside. "I can tell why you're here, just like I know why you were standing out there so long before you knocked."

Estee managed a smile. "It's a difficult decision to make."

Hope returned her smile. "I know. But coming into my home and taking a look around doesn't mean you're obliged to do anything. Even if you stay here a month or give birth here, no one will force you to do anything you don't want to do."

Estee studied the other woman's face and immediately felt inclined to trust her. She'd walked by so many times and not gone in, mainly because she wasn't certain still of what she wanted to do, but if she didn't have to make a decision yet . . .

"Come on, how about we have a cup of tea and you can tell me all about what brings you here," Hope said. "Every girl who walks through my door has a different story, but the one thing they all have in common is that they need my help."

Estee followed her through a hallway lined with paintings and into a kitchen filled with light. There was a large table in the middle, and pots and pans hung on the far wall. It had a homeliness about it that reassured Estee; it was the type of home she'd envisaged she might live in one day, albeit in Italy, not in England.

"Now, let me boil the kettle and you can settle yourself there," Hope said, smiling as she pulled out a chair for her and moved toward the stove. "I have a few girls here at the moment, and you're most welcome to introduce yourself if you want to. I have no problem with you asking questions, either, because I know you'll have plenty."

Estee sat and watched Hope, full of questions indeed but for some reason unable to formulate any.

"You have a strong accent. Where are you from?" Hope asked. "And I don't think you told me your name."

"Estee," she said, clearing her throat. "I'm from Italy, most recently Milan."

"Ahh, Milan. What a beautiful city to spend time in."

She was grateful when Hope didn't ask why she'd left, but then it was most likely obvious given her condition. She guessed every woman who passed through Hope's House was unmarried and in need of refuge, so the why wasn't important to a woman like her.

"Have you seen a doctor at all since you've been in London?" Hope asked as she carried two steaming mugs to the table, returning with milk and sugar, before settling across from her.

"Ahh, no, I haven't," Estee said, taking the mug and touching her fingers against the warmth. Before moving to London, she'd never drunk tea, used as she was to drinking coffee, but she'd become accustomed to it now.

"I've been a midwife for many years, I've dedicated my life to delivering babies and caring for women, but it pays to have a doctor check you over all the same," she said. "I can organize that for you—we have a kindly doctor who drops in to check on my girls from time to time. And I have everything here an expectant mother might need."

"Why?" Estee asked, not able to stop herself from asking the question. "Why are you so kind to all these women?"

Hope sighed, as if it were a question she'd been asked countless times. Estee imagined she probably had. "Because every woman deserves someone to care for her when she's with child, no matter what the circumstances. Just like no woman should ever be forced to give up her baby unless she wants to."

Estee nodded, taking a sip of tea and trying to swallow her emotion away as she did so.

Hope leaned across the table and touched her hand. "You're safe here, Estee. Whether you want to stay from tonight or come back when you're closer to having the baby, I'll always take you in. There's no judgment under my roof, and even if you give birth here and decide you can't go through with an adoption, I'll understand. I'll never force you to do anything you don't want to." Hope gave her a long, steady look. "I want you to know that you can trust me."

The words caught in her throat, making it nearly impossible to get them out. But Hope's kind gaze encouraged her.

"You organize the adoption?"

"I do," she said. "Most of the women I see here, they come because I'm different to most other places. They choose to come here, whereas at other places they're sent by family and told not to return home until they've given up their child."

"Not many people would be so kind to women pregnant out of wedlock."

"We all have our reasons for what we do," Hope said. "Let's just say that I've always had a desire to help others, and when my uncle left me his estate, I chose to do something charitable with his money."

Estee gathered she wasn't going to find out anything else about Hope just yet, but even without knowing her whole story, she liked her. And if she was being truthful about it all being her decision, then she couldn't see why she wouldn't return.

"Would you like to take a look around with me?" Hope asked. "Or if you'd like to tell me how you ended up here, in your condition, I'm always ready to lend an ear. Without judgment, of course."

"Let's just say that the man I loved chose his family over me," Estee said, trying to keep the bitterness from her voice. "I suppose I was fortunate because I wasn't in danger of being destitute— I've got enough money to tide me over. But the idea of raising this child on my own . . ." She affectionately smoothed her hand over her stomach, something she found herself doing constantly now that her belly was so obviously rounded. She caught sight of the ring on her finger then, a simple gold band that she'd purchased to stave off any questions when she'd rented her apartment. It was easier for people to think she was a widow, or perhaps waiting for her husband to return from somewhere, and she'd found she couldn't stand wearing the diamond ring Felix had given her.

"Come on," Hope said, standing and holding out a hand to her. She let Hope help her to her feet, her lower back twinging in pain as it had frequently for the past couple of weeks. "I'm going to show you around, and then you can decide whether or not you'd like to come back."

They walked slowly, Hope taking her through the house and then out into the garden, which created a wall of greenery that shielded the rear of the property from prying eyes. Flowers filled planter boxes, too, dotted all around, making it seem like the perfect place to spend an afternoon, sitting in the sun with a book and admiring the surroundings.

A young woman, much younger than Estee, looked down at them from an upper-story window, raising her hand in a wave, and she waved back at her. But Hope's hand gently brushing her arm stopped her from searching the other windows for more expectant mothers as she turned her attention back to her.

"How do you feel?" Hope asked.

"Like I want to stay," Estee replied without thinking, surprising herself.

"Well then, stay," Hope said. "It can be as simple as that."

"May I come back in a few days' time?" Estee asked. "It sounds silly, but I want to have a little longer on my own, seeing the sights, thinking about what I want to do once the baby is born."

"You come back whenever it feels right for you," Hope said. "Trust me when I say I'm not going anywhere, and there will always be a room for you."

Estee smiled, already drawn to the woman who'd been a complete stranger to her only an hour ago.

"When you come back, we'll arrange for you to see the doctor and talk some more about adoption," Hope said. "And there's one thing I'd like you to consider. I always bring it up early, so you can take your time thinking about it."

Estee's eyebrows lifted in question. "What is it?"

"If you choose to let me find a family for your baby, it can be nice to leave something behind, something that gives your child a connection to you."

"I'm not sure I know what you mean."

Hope walked inside, and Estee followed, curious about what she was referring to.

"I have these little boxes made," Hope said, taking something from the mantel above the fire and passing it to Estee. "You can choose to put something inside here, maybe more than one something, just in case your child ever comes looking for you. Some families will keep the adoption a secret, but some will tell their son or daughter one day. So, I ask you to consider leaving a clue, a link to your child's past, because who knows? One day your child might want to find you, and when I'm long gone, there might be no one left to help them in their quest. I label each one as soon as the child's birth certificate has been signed."

Estee passed the box back, already wondering what she could possibly leave for her child. She touched the diamond ring at her neck. She'd put it back there, hanging it on her necklace before she'd left Italy, more to keep it safe than for any sentimental reason, intending on selling it once she arrived in London. But for some reason, she'd never been able to do it.

It wasn't the right thing to leave; it offered no clue, but it did make her wonder what she could leave behind in the small box that might lead her child back to her one day. She thought of the recipe Felix had left her—she'd unintentionally brought it to London with her simply because it had been in an envelope with her other important documents—but she wasn't certain she wanted to leave anything that pointed to him, not after what he'd done to her.

"You have weeks to decide, Estee," Hope said to her. "Go and enjoy your next few days, and I'll have a bed made up and waiting for you on your return."

"Thank you," Estee said, giving Hope an impromptu hug, grateful to have met the kindly woman.

Tears shone from Hope's eyes, and she blinked away her own as they stood for a moment. She knew how fortunate she was to meet a woman like Hope, someone prepared to take her in for the birth of her child, but it didn't make her impending decision any easier.

31

SIX WEEKS LATER

"Goodbye, little girl," Estee whispered as her hair clung in damp tendrils to her forehead, her skin still wet with sweat from the exertion of labor.

The baby's face was scrunched up, her little fist pushing out of the soft pink blanket she'd wrapped her in, and Estee leaned even closer to kiss her tiny fingers, to drink in the sight of her, to inhale the scent of her. She'd decided days earlier that she wasn't going to cry, not until after. She was going to make the most of the precious time she had with her daughter, to give her a happy, positive start to life, rather than have her mother weeping over her before she was even gone.

The baby opened her eyes then, and Estee almost gave in, a sob choking her throat as her daughter stared up at her, but she stoically forced it down.

"My beautiful girl," Estee said softly. "Look at you. Look how strong you are."

Her baby moved, stretching her limbs, starting to make a hiccupping kind of cry, and Estee instinctively knew what she needed to do. Hope had left, promising to return within the hour, giving her some time to say goodbye, which is what they'd agreed on. Hope had told her that some mothers preferred not to see their baby at all; others wanted the chance to cradle them, and some couldn't stand to be parted and chose to keep their infant instead. But Estee knew what she needed to do; Hope had found a loving family for her baby, and she knew that was the best decision she could make, but it didn't mean she wasn't going to be her mother right now, when her daughter needed her. *When she's still in my arms.*

Estee slipped her nightdress off one shoulder and positioned her baby, and although it was a struggle, her daughter seemed to know what she was doing. She nestled her close as her baby's mouth found its way to her breast, but it took many more attempts before she was suckling.

A soft knock echoed from the door, and Estee looked up as Hope came in, closing the door behind her. Hope's face fell for a moment, perhaps from seeing the baby feeding, but it was quickly replaced with a smile.

"You're taking to mothering like a duck to water," Hope said, moving to stand beside her and adjusting the way she was holding the baby. "Does it hurt?"

"A little," Estee confessed.

"Well, it'll hurt even more when your milk comes in properly," Hope said. "I would have told you not to feed her at all, but I have a feeling you wouldn't have listened to me."

Estee gazed down at her daughter's little head. "She's so beautiful, I can't stop looking at her."

Hope sighed and sat down beside her, her eyes searching Estee's. "I know I've asked you many times, but seeing you like this . . ." Hope paused.

"I've made my decision," Estee said firmly, before Hope could ask her again. "I just want a moment. I just want my daughter to know that she was loved from the very moment she entered this world."

Hope nodded. "Shall I ask her parents to come back later?"

"They're here already?" Estee asked.

"They are. But it won't do them any harm to wait another few hours, or even a day." Hope shrugged. "You let me worry about them."

"A few more hours," Estee found herself saying. "I just want to hold her a little longer and feed her some more."

Hope stood, stroking Estee's hair for a moment before wordlessly leaving the room. Estee started to sing, softly under her breath. She sang to her little girl as she fought for her first meal, her hungry little baby who was so perfect it almost broke Estee's heart. For what could have been, for everything she'd lost.

Tears began to fall, catching in the baby's blanket, and this time she couldn't stop them. But she kept singing, kept forcing her smile as she gazed at her child, loving her more with every passing second.

Felix had given her the most precious gift of her life, but because of him, she was having to give that gift away.

She pushed thoughts of him away, exhausted from childbirth as she continued to cradle her baby, but she refused to shut her eyes for even a moment. She had only hours to absorb every little detail of her daughter, and she wasn't going to miss a moment.

Four hours later, Estee heard the door open again. She was still staring down at her baby, but she knew from the soft footfalls that Hope had returned.

When she looked up, she saw tears in Hope's eyes, but neither woman said a word as Estee pressed one final kiss to her daughter's head and Hope took her from her arms.

"I love you," Estee whispered as Hope paused, staring into her eyes, until Estee found the courage to nod and then turn away.

She buried her face into her pillow, sobbing as her daughter was taken from her, as the door shut with a gentle thud and

Hope's steps echoed away from her. She wanted so desperately to run after her, to scream and snatch her daughter back into her arms, to cry that she wasn't going to go through with it, but instead she reached for the ring around her neck and ripped it from the chain, hurling it across the room.

"Bastardo!" she screamed, reverting to her native language, sobbing as she clutched the damp sheets beneath her. "Fottuto bastardo!"

You did this to me, Felix. And I will never, ever forgive you.

Estee curled into a ball, her body sore as she clutched her pillow and cried; for the child she'd never hold again, for the man she'd once loved with all her heart, and for the dreams that were now lost to her forever.

First, she'd lost Sophia, her friend passing away during the war, then Felix, and now her daughter. She'd thought losing Sophia would break her, and then losing Felix? It had torn away a part of her heart that she knew would remain forever broken. But losing her daughter, that was something else entirely. That had taken a piece of her soul that could never be forgotten. Or forgiven.

She would mourn the loss of her forever.

32

PRESENT DAY

Without Antonio, Lily found herself feeling lonelier than she had in a long time. Up until recently, she'd been so comfortable in her own company, used to being on her own; a typical only child who'd grown up independent and happy to be alone. But that was before she'd met Antonio; the man had filled a space beside her that she hadn't even known was vacant. Somehow, when she'd arrived in Italy, the walls she'd built up around herself had unintentionally been lowered.

She stood in the middle of the little house, a cottage of sorts on Matthew's vast property, aware suddenly of how quiet it was. She felt alone, when she was, in fact, less alone than she'd been since her father died, and she had to keep reminding herself of that. Here, she had uncles and aunts, cousins and second cousins that she could never have dreamed of, not when she was a solitary child from London with only one parent. It was surreal, as if she were living someone else's life. Except she wasn't.

Lily walked to the window and stared out at the view. She was used to moving somewhere different for work and staring out at grapes, but here, it was hazelnut groves for as far as the eye could see. She put on her shoes and went outside, deciding to take a walk through them. From out of nowhere Matthew's dog appeared, and she bent to pat him. He was a spaniel of some sort, she wasn't sure what; all she knew was that it was nice to have the company. It had been years since she'd had a dog—their terrier had passed away when she'd been at university—but as she buried her face in the dog's soft fur for a cuddle, she realized just how much she'd missed being around animals.

"Hey, you," she said as the dog lapped up her attention and tried to lick her face. "What are you doing here? Are you allowed to go off on your own little adventure?"

The dog wagged his tail and trotted off, clearly on a mission to find something, and she walked along behind him, happy for the company and something to focus on. After a few minutes, she heard whistling and stopped, although the dog chose not to notice, even when the whistling turned to calling.

"He's over here!" Lily called back.

After a few more shouts back and forth, Matthew appeared from between the trees.

"I spend half my life looking for that damn dog," he growled, as if speaking to the dog as well as her, but once again it was only she who bothered to listen; the dog wasn't the least bit interested in his master.

"Is he looking for truffles?" Lily asked, amused at how riled her great-uncle was.

"Not today, it's not the season, but he has an excellent nose and finds almost all the truffles on the property," Matthew said. "Which means he's incredibly spoiled and thinks he's the master."

She laughed as the dog trotted past, oblivious to the fact that his actual master had been looking for him. Or perhaps he simply didn't care.

"We give him a little piece of fillet steak every time he finds one, and all the restaurateurs come throughout the season to see our harvest," he continued. "They make such a fuss of how clever he is, so it's given him a great sense of importance!"

They both laughed and then fell into a slow walk as they followed the dog, and Lily found her head suddenly full of questions; questions she hadn't wanted to ask in front of everyone the other day.

"Antonio left yesterday?" Matthew asked.

"He did. I never expected him to be returning to the vineyard without me, that's for sure."

Matthew seemed to be mulling something over and she waited for him to speak, finding it surprisingly easy to be in his company. She wanted to believe it was because he reminded her of her dad, but she knew that was a stretch; although she did believe that they had a connection that only family could. They didn't know one another, but they had shared blood, and a shared heritage, and that meant something.

"I'm pleased you stayed," he said. "We have a lifetime to catch up on, and there's so much I want to know about you, about your own family."

They walked close but not touching, talking about her parents, about his children, about the property that he was so passionate about. But it was his love for his land, for what he did, that she connected with the most.

"You talk about truffles like I talk about wine," Lily said as he smiled broadly after showing her through the hazelnut trees. "I've always said that my one true love is wine, and not just the end product. It's everything from the grapes through to harvest, to the people I work shoulder to shoulder with."

"You're right," he said as their walk took them closer to his house. "I'm the same. I love caring for the land throughout the year, the lead-up to our harvest beginning, everything about it. It's been my passion for so many years, but I still love it as much now as I did when I first started planting out these trees." He sighed and looked back at the grove of trees as they stepped out into the sunshine. "It was a labor of love then, but it's so much more now."

"I've started to question everything since coming here," she admitted, talking more openly to Matthew than she'd talked even to her mother over recent years. "Sometimes I wonder if I'm trying so hard to follow in my father's footsteps, to keep the memory of him alive and do the things we talked about, things I promised him . . ." She shook her head, not used to feeling so uncertain. "I'm the girl who left school knowing exactly who and what she wanted to be. I've had my entire life mapped out for me, ticking off this list of things I need to achieve."

"Do you still have the passion for your winemaking?" he asked. "Do you still feel the beat of your heart, the love for what you do?"

"Yes." The word exhaled from her as easily as her own breath. "Yes, I do."

"You can follow your own dreams and still honor your father, Lily," Matthew said, his considered gaze full of concern. "And if something changes, if your life takes you in another direction, then trust your instincts. As far as I can tell, you've made excellent choices until now."

She bent to stroke the dog when he came back, tail wagging and a big smile on his face as he looked up at her.

"Tell me what you're thinking, what choice you want to make that is going to stop you from ticking something off this list of yours," Matthew asked, crouching down beside her and patting his dog.

"I want to stay in Italy," she said, the words whooshing out of her so fast she could barely believe she'd said them. "I feel at home here, this pull toward the land that I've never felt before, and I want to stay."

There, you've said it out loud. You've finally admitted it.

"Then stay," he said. "Trust your instincts. You're an accomplished, intelligent woman, Lily. If you want to stay in Italy, then stay."

"I was only supposed to be here for a season, to learn as much as I could before returning home to England. Everything I've learned, the years I spent in New Zealand, they were to plan for growing our own grapes, to make our own sparkling wine back home."

Matthew's hand was soft, gentle as he reached for her, his palm against her arm.

"Your father is gone, Lily," he said softly. "Those were dreams you shared together, but your father would never hold you to those dreams, not when he's not here with you. He would want you to have your own dreams. Perhaps it's time for you to consider what *you* truly want."

She started to cry, and he took her hands, holding them as she let go of something she'd been holding on to for far too many years.

He's gone. No matter what I do, no matter how closely I hold to those dreams, nothing is going to bring him back.

"Lily, I know we've only just met, that we're barely more than strangers, but I know about being a father. I know about wanting my children to be happy, to live their own lives on their own terms, and being proud of every achievement," he said, his voice low and choking with his own emotion. "You need to give yourself permission to make mistakes, to fall in love, to let your life change direction sometimes and be okay with that. And to know that your father would accept whatever you decided if he were here."

She nodded, pulling one hand away from him so she could wipe her cheeks.

"And let me tell you, my love affair with my truffles? It would be nothing without my Rafaella," he told her. "We can achieve many things, but nothing brings true happiness like the love and companionship of another person. It can for a while, years even, but eventually we need someone in our lives."

She stared into his eyes, his words taking her by surprise. And she knew, by the way he was looking at her, that he'd sensed how she felt about Antonio, even if she hadn't truly admitted her feelings to herself yet. Or how much of an influence he'd had on the decisions she wanted to make.

"I've spent my life not only trying to stay true to my father and the dreams we shared but trying not to let my feelings for anyone else distract me," she admitted. "I didn't want anything or anyone to derail my life."

"My father almost lost the love of his life forever, Lily, but he found a way to combine what he loved and *who* he loved. There's no reason why you can't do the same." He patted her shoulder, in a fatherly kind of way. "But imagine what his life would have been like if he hadn't fought for her? If he hadn't followed his heart?"

"But what if this isn't love? What if it doesn't work out?" She closed her eyes. *What if Antonio doesn't want me in the same way I want him?*

His smile was kind. "Sometimes you just have to take the risk. And the worst thing that can happen?"

She found herself holding her breath.

"Is a broken heart. You will never lose your talent for wine-making, Lily. No one can ever take that away from you," he said softly. "But what's the point in a successful life if you don't have a partner by your side to enjoy it with you?"

"Some people would say that's old-fashioned."

"Old-fashioned? Well, maybe," he said with a shrug. "But I don't believe love and companionship ever go out of fashion."

He watched her for a long time before she finally nodded, acknowledging he was right. *Of course he was right.* Her great-grandparents had had to fight against everything, give *everything* up to be together. And here she was, too scared to give up anything.

"Do you think your parents ever regretted what they did?" she asked. "Do you wonder if your father ever wished he'd stayed with his family?" She still didn't know how they'd ended up back together after everything that had happened to keep them apart.

"I don't think he even considered it," Matthew answered without hesitation. "He created a life with my mother, a family of his own, and he always said that he'd give up everything, all of his success, for his wife and his family. He said it was worth more than anything to him."

The dog ran back to her then, jumping up on her and covering her with his dirty paws. But she didn't even have the heart to tell him off; she needed the hug.

"Stay here with us, Lily," Matthew said. "Relax a little, take the time to really think about what *you* want. A few weeks hiding away from the world might be just what you need."

In Italy. Soaking up the sun, enjoying meals with Matthew and his family, learning about truffles and eating Rafaella's cooking.

There are worse things I could be doing.

"I will, I promise," she said. "I'm going to give myself a month. If I still feel the same as I do now, then I'll make my decision. I'll be brave."

"Come, it's time for lunch, and Rafaella is looking forward to seeing you. With our daughter away, you're the best thing that's happened to her."

33

VENICE, 1948

Estee went through the motions on stage, but she no longer loved what she did. No one else seemed to notice; she always finished each performance to rapturous applause, although the crowds were nothing like La Scala. And afterward, she could barely stand to look at her reflection in the mirror, her dressing room used more for changing than working on her appearance. Her gaze was too sad to return, her eyes too haunted for her to ever want to stare into them.

She shuffled past the other girls, not acknowledging the way they parted for her, creating space for her to walk through. They were all talking and laughing, as energized by their dancing as she was drained.

"Estee!" one of them bravely called out.

She paused, turning her head slightly to listen without actually looking back.

"We're all going for drinks tonight. Do you want to join us?"

"Not tonight," she said, clearing her throat. "Perhaps next time." But next time would be no different; she always declined. She knew what they thought: that she thought they were somehow beneath her, and she didn't want to socialize with them, but it couldn't have been further from the truth.

After leaving Hope's House, Estee had eventually moved out and said goodbye to Hope, renting her own apartment again and slowly stretching and dancing, getting her body back into shape. It hadn't taken long for her to find a new home with The Royal Ballet, but after a season with them she'd decided to return to Italy, finally settling in Venice. It was close enough to Milan to feel somewhat like home, although she'd never been able to return to La Scala; it held memories she didn't want to stir up, and she was fearful still of seeing Felix's family if they ever came to the theater.

Estee walked into her dressing room and shut the door, pressing her back against it for a long moment as she caught her breath. She found herself holding it sometimes without even realizing that she was doing it, leaving her gasping to fill her lungs when she was finally alone.

Tonight, she undressed, hanging her costume and then putting on her own clothes. She daren't look at her body, hating how easily it had gone back to normal after giving birth to her daughter. She'd worked so hard to become fit and strong again, to get her lean body back so she could throw herself into her ballet, but in doing that, she'd lost all the soft curves that told the story of her child, of what her body had been through.

She didn't spend long alone in her dressing room, but she did wait until the noise from outside had died down, knowing most of the girls would have spilled into their joint dressing rooms by now. Estee finally emerged, head down, her bag over her shoulder as she walked quickly. She looked up and smiled at a couple of the ballerinas who appeared, wishing she had the energy or desire to stop and chat, to talk about trivial things and say yes to drinking with them and smoking cigarettes late into the night. Part of her wondered if that would actually help, if staying out late and drinking every night would help her to forget, but most of the time she felt as if there were a permanent rain cloud above her that she just couldn't step out from under.

"Estee?" a voice asked, a man stepping out of the shadows. "Estee, is that you?"

She recoiled, jumping back and clutching her bag to her side. Once again, she was used to men sending her flowers, admirers who wanted a date with her, but calling to her in the street was something else entirely.

"Estee!"

No. Surely not.

Felix?

She shook her head. It couldn't be Felix; her mind was just playing tricks on her again, in the same way she saw her daughter in the faces of other babies she passed in the street, staring into baby carriages as her heart broke.

"Leave me alone," she said firmly. "This entrance is only for performers."

"Estee," the voice said again, moving closer.

"Estee, is someone bothering you?" Mario, her male lead, appeared and she gratefully stepped back and let him take her arm. She couldn't look at the stranger, couldn't let her mind play tricks on her. This was just some man who'd taken a fancy to her and seen her name in the program, nothing more.

"I'll walk you home," Mario said, and she moved in close to him, trying to scurry away, still too afraid to look.

"Estee!" the man shouted, racing after them, the thud of his footfalls making her hold tighter to Mario's hand. Their pace quickened, walking briskly away from him. "Estee, it's me. It's Felix! Please, stop!"

Her feet slid on the cobblestones beneath her then, but Mario took a moment longer to slow, tugging her along with him. She shut her eyes, a loud roaring in her ears that sounded like the ocean but was more likely the sound of her own pulse beating in her ears.

Estee turned, her back to Mario as she faced the man, as she took in the dark rings under his eyes, the unkempt beard, the pain in his expression. It was him.

"Felix?" she whispered, not believing her eyes.

"Estee," he murmured, reaching for her, dropping to his knees, his eyes welling with tears as she stared down at him. "I've searched for you for months, this entire past year, I've . . ."

"You know this man?" Mario asked, still standing protectively at her side.

Estee nodded, exhaling as she shut her eyes, as she tried to accept the fact that the man who'd broken her heart was on his knees before her. "I do. I didn't think I did, but yes, it's someone from my past. You can leave me."

This is the man who gave me my daughter and ruined my life all at the same time.

"Are you sure you don't want me to stay?" Mario asked.

She shook her head and turned to him, finally able to tear her eyes from Felix. "Thank you," she said. "But I'll be fine. I'm not in any danger." *Although Felix might be. I could kill him with my bare hands for what he did to me.*

Mario left her, but not without a frown that told her he wasn't comfortable in doing so. He was the only other dancer who rarely partied with the others, preferring to leave as soon as each show was over, which is probably why they got along so well.

"Get up," Estee said, turning to Felix, who was still on his knees.

Felix stood, and when he reached for her, she snatched her hands away. "Estee, I—"

"I have nothing to say to you," she said, folding her arms across her chest, refusing to acknowledge the pain pulsing through her body at the sight of him. "Why are you here? There's nothing left between us."

"If you'd just let me explain—"

"Whatever you've come to say, I don't want to hear it," she said, her hands beginning to shake violently as her voice caught in her throat. "You'd be best to leave here, Felix, and never return."

"Estee, please—"

"Don't ever come near me again. Do you hear me, Felix? I don't ever want to see you as long as I live!"

She turned on her heel, her arms wrapped tightly around herself to keep from shaking; away from the man who'd ruined her life and consumed her thoughts for too many years to count.

* * *

Knock, knock, knock.

Estee held the cushion close to her chest as she curled around it on the sofa. Tears pricked her eyes, and she hated herself for them; she did not want to shed another tear over Felix Barbieri, and she certainly wasn't going to answer the door to him.

"Estee, please," he begged, knocking again.

There was silence for a moment, and she thought that perhaps he'd finally gone, before the knocking sounded again. This time it was followed by a yell from one of her neighbors, clearly unimpressed with the noise at such a late hour, which was the only reason she eventually dragged herself from the sofa and hauled open the door.

"I told you, I don't want to hear anything you have to say," she hissed. "You need to go."

Felix's face crumpled, but he stubbornly stuck his boot out when she tried to shut the door.

"Felix, leave me!" she cried.

"No," he said. "I'm not leaving until you hear what I have to say."

She glared at him. "Where's your wife? Or doesn't she know you're here?"

Felix shook his head, removing his boot from the door as he looked into her eyes.

"Estee, I don't have a wife. And before you go slamming the door on me, you need to know that I never sent you that letter," he said, speaking quickly as if he expected her to shut him out again. "I've spent every day, every week, every month, since then searching for you, but it was as if you'd vanished without a trace."

Her heart picked up its beat then. *He what?* "But you said, *it* said—"

"My mother sent you that letter, Estee," Felix said, raking his fingers through his hair as he stared down at her, as he edged a step closer. "I came for you, and you were gone, and that's when I discovered her duplicity. She expected me to return and marry Emilie, to accept that you'd disappeared, but when I still refused, the ugly truth finally came out."

Estee stared at him, digesting his words, feeling all the color drain from her skin as she went deathly cold, as a rage within her built with such fury she could barely stay upright.

All these long months, and the letter hadn't even been from Felix? What kind of fool was she that she hadn't questioned whether it was truly from him or not? How could she have accepted so blindly that he had written it with his own hand?

"You . . . you came for me?" she managed, her words barely a whisper.

"Of *course* I came for you, Estee. How could you believe I'd ever do anything else?" Tears filled his eyes. "I gave everything up for you, just like I told you I would, but by the time I came, you were gone."

She doubled over then, the pain inside of her too much to bear, the loss carving away a part of her that could never be replaced. She cried, a sob that sounded more animal than human, her body folded into half its usual size.

"Estee, I'm so sorry, I . . ." Felix's arms closed around her then, and she let him hold her, let him comfort her as her body seemed to splinter in half. "I'm here now, and I promise I'll never leave you. I will never, ever leave you again." He whispered into her hair, his lips against her, his arms holding her.

"But it's too late," she cried.

"It's not too late," he said, sounding so certain as he cradled her.

She started to tremble, her body shaking as she pushed back and looked up at him, as deep inside she broke all over again.

"You're not married, are you?" he asked, his eyes dropping to her hand. "Please tell me—"

"I was pregnant, Felix," she sobbed, staring up at him, violent stomach pains making her feel like she was going to be sick. "I had our baby, our *daughter*. I was alone, I didn't have a choice, I . . ."

"We have a daughter?" he asked, his eyes huge, a smile stretching his face so wide it made her feel as if a knife was twisting her heart.

How can this be happening to me!

"I'm so sorry, Felix," she cried. "I'm so, so sorry. If I'd known, if I'd—"

"Estee," he whispered, taking her face in his hands. "You have nothing to apologize for. Why are you crying? This is wonderful news. Why—"

"Because she's gone," Estee whispered, leaning into his palm as she slowly raised her eyes. "I had no other choice. There was nothing else I could do."

Felix went still, as if he was finally beginning to understand what she was trying to say. She went to press her cheek against his palm again, but his hands fell away, his eyes wide as he stared at her.

"Our daughter," he said slowly. "Where is she, Estee?"

"I need you to know that I had no other choice," Estee whispered. "She was the most perfect little girl, but I was alone, and . . ."

She looked away from him and then back again as he stood, unwavering, searching her face with his eyes.

"I gave birth in a home for unmarried mothers," she said, struggling to say the words. "They arranged the adoption for me, even though it broke my heart."

Felix dropped to his knees then, like a strong tree being felled, and she stood, watching as he crumpled, as she broke his heart just like hers had been broken so many months earlier. She could only see his pain for so long before the ache inside of her became unbearable, and she found herself reaching for him. She'd blamed Felix for so much, for *everything,* but seeing him now, it was obvious he was as broken as she was.

"Felix," she said, taking his hands and encouraging him up. "Please, come in."

He slowly rose and she kept hold of his hand as they turned. How long had it been since she'd touched someone like this, since she'd been this close to another, other than on stage? *Since Hope held me as I cried. Since she'd soothed my pain like a mother would a child in the days after the birth. Since I'd mourned the loss of my daughter.*

"Estee," Felix finally said, turning to her as they stood in the center of her apartment. "If you want me to leave, if you never want to see me again—"

"I don't want you to leave," she whispered, finding her strength, knowing that it was his turn to grieve now that she'd told him what they'd lost.

She reached for him, hugging him tightly before gesturing for him to sit on the sofa. She considered making them coffee but changed her mind, finding the one bottle of wine she'd been keeping for a special occasion and deciding to pour two glasses of the deep velvety red Pinot.

Estee took a deep breath before finally facing Felix and passing a glass to him. They gently touched their glasses together before they sat opposite one another, and she tucked her legs up beneath her on the chair, sipping nervously at her wine.

"You know, I've thought so many times what I'd say to you if I ever saw you again," she admitted. "But now that you're here, I find myself at a loss for words. I've blamed you all this time without even knowing the truth."

"Will you ever be able to forgive me?" Felix asked, and now that they were closer, in the light of her apartment, she could see how bloodshot his eyes were, noticed just how long his hair was, the lines feathering from his eyes not something she'd ever noticed when they'd been together.

"It seems we were both victims," she said, taking another sip of wine. "Your parents, they were never going to accept me. We should have known from that day in Como that it was never going to work. That no matter what we did, we were destined to fail. That your mother would do anything she could to ruin us."

Felix reached inside his jacket and produced a small velvet box, and her heart skipped a beat, remembering the last time she'd seen a box like that.

"I've carried this in my pocket since the day I came for you," he said, passing it to her without opening it. "When I left Piedmont, I had everything planned. I was going to ask you, properly, to marry me in Milan. I was going to tell you that nothing else mattered so long as we could be together."

Her eyes brimmed with tears as she opened the box and stared at the two simple gold bands, one fine and obviously made for her finger, the other thicker, stronger. She looked up at him.

"I searched Italy for you, Estee. I contacted every ballet academy, every theater, but it was like you'd disappeared. But I never gave up. I couldn't."

"When I received that letter, I knew I had to go. I couldn't stand the pain of knowing I might see you with Emilie, with children, of knowing what your family thought. And I knew that if I wanted to save my career, I couldn't let anyone see me pregnant," she told him.

They stared at one another as she held the rings in the palm of her hand, her wine glass in the other.

"Will you ever forgive me?" Felix asked. "*Can* you ever forgive me after everything? For the pain my family caused you?"

Estee didn't know what to say, but what she did know was that Felix was in as much pain as she was. She put down her glass and stood, looking down at him before settling into his lap and curling into him, her arms scooped around his neck as she laid her cheek to his heart. Felix's arms surrounded her, and she lay like that, listening to the steady beat of his heart, feeling the warmth of his embrace after so long being apart.

"My family is no longer part of my life, Estee," he whispered. "I walked away, and I took my recipe with me, the same recipe I entrusted you with that day. We can build a life together, we can . . ." He hesitated, as if he wasn't sure whether to continue. "We can become a family."

Her breath shuddered out of her, but she couldn't look up at him; she knew her emotions would only get the better of her if she met his gaze. *A family who would forever be missing their first-born daughter.*

"If you'll have me, we can get married here, in Venice. If you can ever find a way to forgive me for what you've been through."

She found herself nodding against him. "Yes," she whispered.

"You'll marry me?"

Estee forced herself to lift her head. "I'm broken, Felix. Something died inside of me when I gave our daughter up, and you need to understand that I'm not the same woman you parted ways with in Como. I'll never be the same again. Giving her up will haunt me for the rest of my life."

"We'll find her, Estee. I promise you," Felix said, his eyes like a pathway to his soul as he murmured to her. "I promise you, we'll find her. I will never, ever forgive myself for this. I'm to blame for what happened, for the situation you ended up in. You did nothing wrong. *My* family did this to you, and I will fight for you, for our daughter, until my last breath. I promise you that."

Estee kissed him then, her lips unexpectedly finding his as he held her. "I never stopped loving you, even when I blamed you for it all."

They stared at one another a long while, before Felix's lips settled on her forehead and she melted deeper into his arms. It was the truth; even when she'd cursed him and cried, blaming him for everything, somewhere deep inside she'd still loved him. She'd still wished for him to be part of her life.

"Tell me about her," he asked, stroking her back as he softly spoke. "Tell me everything."

"She was perfect," Estee said, surprising herself with how easily she said the words. "She had a dark head of hair, and her lips, they were the most beautiful shape. She was everything that's good in the world, so pure. When I held her, the love I felt for her, I've never felt anything like it before."

They sat like that for a long while, Felix's arms never faltering, holding her as they whispered about their daughter, as they cried, as the darkness outside lifted and morning greeted them with a warm, bright light.

"We'll find her, Estee," he whispered. "I promise you, we'll find her."

And if not, maybe she'll find us one day. Estee's lips parted, murmuring at the same time as her eyes closed, exhaustion finally catching up with her as sleep reached out and made it impossible to resist. She'd tell Felix about the little box she'd left behind in the morning. Because maybe one day their daughter would come to Italy looking for them, clutching a recipe and the 1946 La Scala program she'd left for her, and they'd be reunited after all.

34

PRESENT DAY

"You came back."

Lily stood and stared at Antonio, her breath catching in her throat. His dark eyes were trained on her, and for a moment she couldn't read them, didn't know what he was thinking or what to say.

"Did you come back for the job, or . . ."

She didn't hesitate when she recognized the hope in his gaze, the way his voice lifted. Lily ran the rest of the way to him as he opened his arms, his lips brushing against her hair as she hugged him fiercely.

"I came back for both," she told him, leaning back in his arms as she looked up at him. "I have no idea whether this, *us,* will work, if there even *is* an us, if you even want something more, but no one's ever looked at me the way you do. But if this is just a moment in time, then so be it." She laughed. "I don't even know if you're interested, if you even wanted to see me again . . ."

He laughed as he kissed her, his hands circling her waist.

"I'm interested," he murmured. "I promise you, I'm *very* interested."

"I've had a lot of time to think these past few weeks," she said, still leaning back to look at him. "I've spent my life so focused on the future, but I don't want to do that anymore. I just want to be open to what life has in store for me."

His voice was husky when he spoke again, his fingers soft against her cheek. "It's so good to see you again, Lily."

She smiled up at him, not bothering to hide how deeply happy she was to see him again. "It's good to see you again, too."

They stayed like that for a long moment, until Antonio cupped her cheek and pressed a kiss to her lips; a kiss that told her she'd made the right decision. Because when Antonio looked at her, he seemed to truly see her; and the way he touched her, it made her feel more alive, more beautiful, than she'd ever felt before.

"I don't expect anything from you, Antonio," she said, running her fingers across his broad shoulders and down his arms. "But I think this, whatever this is between us, it's worth giving it time, to see if it's something special."

"Ahh, Lily, but that's exactly what I'm good at," he teased. "Did you know that I grow grapes? I'm very good at nurturing special things slowly in very difficult conditions until they grow into something spectacular, even if in the beginning I'm not sure whether it will work."

They both laughed as she pressed herself to his side, her arm looped around his waist as she looked up at the house. It was as beautiful as she'd remembered, big yet not austere, grand yet understated.

"I owe your father a conversation," she said. "Is he home?"

"He's here," Antonio said. "I have a feeling he'll be pleased to see you. Everyone's missed you."

"Your family made it impossible to say no to coming back," she said. "I've worked all over the world, but the way they embraced me—"

"Wait," he said, laughing as he attempted to look horrified. "I thought *I* was the reason you couldn't say no?"

She pushed him away, but he was quick to catch her in his arms again, pulling her back against him. "You and your family feel like a package deal to me," she said.

"If only I'd been smart enough to understand that before I married," Antonio said wryly.

She dropped her head, nestling into the spot below his shoulder, but she didn't have long there. Within seconds his mother appeared at the door, her arms flung wide as she saw Lily. The smile on her face, the absolute joy in her expression, made tears fill Lily's eyes, and she hoped her own face reflected how happy she was to be back amongst the Martinellis.

"Lily!" Francesca called. "It's so good to have you home."

Home. She laughed, but it quickly turned to tears and she wiped them away as Francesca hurried over to her, embracing her in a hug so full of love and warmth. She truly, with all her heart, did feel as if she was home; as if part of Italy was inside her now, under her skin and impossible to remove. Something had been missing in her life for so many years, and she couldn't help but wonder if it had been her connection to her heritage, to her father.

You always knew Italy was the place I was supposed to be, Dad. You always told me to come here, and we never even knew why.

"It's so good to be back," Lily said to Francesca as the older woman held her at arm's length, gently wiping the tears from Lily's cheeks.

"You belong here with us, Lily," Francesca said earnestly. "I knew it when I saw you walking the vines with my husband, and I knew it when I saw you in the arms of my son."

"Thank you," Lily whispered, because she didn't trust her voice to utter anything else. Somehow, she'd ended up with two new families instead of just the one.

"Antonio, go and tell your father that Lily has returned." Francesca turned back and frowned. "You are staying, aren't you?"

"Yes," she replied. "Yes, I am. But Roberto already knew that. In my letter I told him that I'd take the job, I just didn't know if it would be . . ." She glanced at Antonio and felt the heat rise in her face.

"You just didn't know whether or not you were coming home to my son as well," Francesca finished for her.

"He knew all this time?" Antonio asked, throwing his hands into the air. "*Santa Maria*. All these weeks, and he could have told me? I was going out of my mind wondering if Lily would return!"

"Thank you for not opening the letter," Lily said.

"Enough of this, let's go and celebrate," Francesca said, threading her arm through Lily's on one side and Antonio's on the other. "Ant, I think we should open the vintage Franciacorta. Our new assistant winemaker has returned!"

* * *

"I've missed this," Lily said with a sigh. Everyone else had slowly left—friends of the family who'd called in for dinner, Roberto and Francesca, who'd retired for the night, followed eventually by Antonio's sister, who'd given her a kiss on the top of the head and a whisper of encouragement that had brought tears to Lily's eyes again.

There were reminders of the night that had been—candles still burning, chairs pushed out haphazardly after being vacated and empty wine bottles that had been discarded across the table. But the night was now quiet, the warm air starting to blow slightly cooler as midnight approached, and most important, it was just her and Antonio left.

"Come here," he said, pushing his chair back and beckoning.

She rose and went to him, curling into his lap. "I've missed this."

"I've missed this, too," he said.

He stroked her hair as they sat, her head tucked beneath his chin as she listened to the rise and fall of his breath.

"You're going to love it here, Lily," he whispered. "Every season, every year, this place—"

She sighed. "I know. I already can't imagine leaving. I can't imagine anywhere else in the world I'd rather be."

She leaned back a little to stare up at the sky, admiring the black blanket of midnight dotted with stars. Antonio kissed her cheek, and she turned to him, staring solemnly into his eyes.

"I forgot to tell you something."

He groaned. "Tell me."

"My mother wants to meet you. In fact, she's coming to visit next week."

"No problem." He laughed. "Mothers love me."

She softly punched his arm. "*Mothers?* Exactly how many *mothers* have there been?"

Antonio opened his mouth to answer her, and she quickly interrupted him.

"No, don't answer that!"

They both laughed, and she curled even tighter into his lap again.

"What did you tell her?" he asked. "About me?"

She smiled to herself. "I didn't have to tell her anything. The moment I said there was a man, she booked her ticket. She's been waiting years for me to call her and say those words."

"Bed?" Antonio asked with a knowing grin.

Lily stretched, catlike, in his lap. "Bed," she agreed as she rose.

Antonio took her hand and led her away with him, their fingers intertwined, and when he looked back at her, the butterflies in her stomach slowly started to settle.

No man has ever looked at me like that before. They were the words she'd told herself when they'd been apart, but she'd almost begun to wonder if she'd imagined the passionate, intense way he looked into her eyes.

Italy had changed her life; it had led her to family she'd never known existed, and a man who'd changed the way she felt about love. The only thing missing was her dad, but the Martinellis were giving her a way to stay close to him, and for that, she'd be forever grateful.

"Lily?" Antonio asked, lifting her hand and kissing her knuckles as he caught her attention again.

Lily smiled at Antonio, pushing her thoughts from her mind as she let him tug her forward. "To bed," she told him.

Antonio didn't need to be told twice, sweeping her off her feet and into his arms as he marched toward her room.

EPILOGUE

LONDON, 1955

Estee held her son's hand on one side and her husband's on the other as they strolled through London Zoo. Her heart was beating loudly, her breath ragged, as they hurried toward the monkeys. She'd barely noticed the animals on their way in, and it wasn't anything to do with the zoo—if her mind hadn't been so preoccupied, she'd no doubt have loved admiring the scenery.

Felix glanced down at her then, squeezing her hand as she hurried their little boy on, happy to see their daughter skipping ahead in front of them, eager to see the promised monkeys.

There she is.

Estee's heart started to pound then, and she thought she was going to collapse.

The memories came back in a wave, crashing through her, making her legs wobble. Holding her daughter in her arms, kissing the top of her damp little head, pressing a kiss to freshly parted, newborn lips; holding her to her breast to suckle.

Whispering goodbye.

Without Felix, she could never have done it. Could never have been brave enough to think they could secretly find her after all this time. But he'd been relentless in his inquiries, retaining a lawyer and private investigator in London who'd somehow managed to access their child's adoption papers and give them the information they needed.

He kept a tight hold on her hand as they walked closer, their children thankfully captivated by the little monkeys playing, jumping from branch to branch. But Estee couldn't even read the sign to see what type they were; she was transfixed by the little girl sitting atop her father's shoulders.

The woman, the *mother,* was laughing, looking up at the girl, her hair as blond as the child's was dark. And the moment Estee set eyes on her, she couldn't look away; taking in the polished shoes, the pretty pink ankle socks, the embroidered dress covered in tiny flowers that must have taken hours to sew.

"Your daughter seems to be liking this exhibition as much as our children are," Felix said, smiling at the couple beside them. Estee's own voice was trapped in her throat, amazed at how easily, how *calmly,* her husband was finding his words.

The man turned, his hands resting on the child's knees to hold her in place.

"We come here every month," he said. "It's Patricia's favorite place in the world to visit."

The woman smiled at Estee, and she forced herself to return it, summoning her manners so they didn't think her strange. The last thing she wanted was for them to walk away, even as the child's name lodged in her throat like a lump too big to ever swallow.

Patricia.

"Your daughter is very beautiful," Estee managed, quickly blinking away the moisture in her eyes when Felix tightened his grip on her hand, giving her the strength she needed to hold herself together. *Keep breathing, keep smiling, stay calm.*

The woman beamed at her, clearly so proud of her daughter. Estee almost choked on the word in her mind, the betrayal of even thinking that this little girl belonged to another woman, even though she knew how unfair that was. This mother had done nothing wrong; in fact, she'd done everything right.

"Well, we'd best be off," Felix said, letting go of Estee and holding out his hands to their children instead. "So many animals to see. Enjoy your visit."

The couple smiled, and the little girl looked down at Estee, catching her eye, staring straight at her. *It was almost as if she could somehow feel the connection.* Estee touched her fingers to her lips, blowing her a kiss, turning as the little girl leaned down and asked her father in a voice just loud enough for Estee to hear, who they were.

"Keep walking," Felix murmured, his palm finding the small of her back and forcing her forward.

Estee wrestled with every step, forcing herself to keep going, despite the desperate pull inside her to turn round. But they'd promised one another, sworn when the private investigator had passed them the file, that if she was happy, they wouldn't intervene. And everything about that little girl's life looked perfect, which meant that no matter how badly it hurt, she had to walk away. *She's not mine any longer, she has her own family, and they love her.*

When they were out of sight, when their children were absorbed in watching yet another animal, Estee let out a gasp, and Felix wrapped his arms protectively around her, holding her as she sobbed into his shoulder.

His lips were warm on her cheek, his tears mingling with hers as he touched his forehead to hers for a moment, as if they were alone and not standing in the middle of a zoo.

"She's beautiful," he whispered. "Our little girl, she's as beautiful as her mamma. I'm half surprised they didn't see the resemblance."

Estee's breath shuddered out of her, and she pressed her lips together, holding her head high as she fought a fresh wave of tears.

"We can't ever see her again," Estee whispered. "It's too painful."

"Will you ever truly forgive me?" Felix asked. "After all these years, now that you've finally seen her..."

Estee rose onto her tiptoes and scooped her arms around her husband's neck, cheek to cheek as she held him, whispering in his ear. "I forgive you, Felix. It's myself I'll never forgive."

His kiss brushed her lips this time, and she could see the pain in his eyes when he stepped away from her as their children collided with their legs, tugging at their hands to go and see yet another attraction, not even noticing their emotion.

She knew how Felix felt, that it was his fault she'd had to give up their baby. Just as she would forever feel the weight of her decision, he felt the weight of his family's betrayal and the loss that he'd endured without even knowing it at the time.

"We'll never forget her, Estee," he murmured as they walked, as their children squealed in delight, making it impossible not to smile back at them. "Never."

"I know," she said, leaning into him, their hands still intertwined.

Goodbye, baby girl. May you have a lifetime of laughter and happiness. I love you.

Estee turned, a shiver playing down her spine, the pull to look back over her shoulder impossible to resist.

The little girl still sat on her father's shoulders, but her gaze was fixed firmly on Estee. She held up her hand in a wave as her hair whispered around her in the breeze. Estee held up her hand in reply as the girl, as her daughter, blew her a kiss in return.

She knows.

Perhaps it was her imagination, although Estee would forever wonder if the child had felt the energy between them, somehow had a flicker of memory within her, even though she knew how impossible that sounded.

"Mamma, let's go."

The tug at her skirt pulled her back to her family as her son looked expectantly up at her, his face falling into a frown.

"Why are you crying, Mamma?" he asked, finally noticing that something was wrong.

"Because I'm so happy," she whispered, quickly wiping her cheeks as she smiled down at him. "Don't you love the zoo?"

He studied her a moment, as if trying to decide whether to believe her or not, before shrugging and running ahead again, his arms outstretched, pretending to be a plane.

And this time, when Felix's arm looped around her waist, the sadness finally lifted. She'd made the hardest decision of her life in giving up her firstborn, but after seeing her today, it was as if the cloud of pain that had followed her around these past eight years, shadowing even the happiest moments of her life, had finally lifted.

Felix was right; they'd never forget her, but they could live their lives now in the knowledge that she was content and well-cared-for, and they'd never tell another soul that they'd seen her.

Estee turned one more time, even though she knew before she did so that the little girl was gone. The space behind them was empty now, other families passing by in the distance with strollers and sticks of cotton candy, but there was no little girl astride her father's shoulders.

She's gone.

Her husband's hand brushed her stomach then, and she smiled down as his hand smoothed over the round curve of her belly.

She would never come back to London; it was too difficult to be in the city where she'd endured such pain.

It was time to go home to Italy and never look back. But on this day, every year just before Christmas, she would let herself remember the little girl with the raven-dark hair.

Patricia.

The daughter who would be forever in her heart.

READING GROUP GUIDE

DISCUSSION QUESTIONS

1. Lily already has plans to travel to Italy when she is given her box of clues. Do you think she still would have gone there to uncover her family secrets if she wasn't already intending to travel abroad? Why or why not?

2. If you were given clues about your family's heritage, to what lengths would you go to understand them? Would you disregard the clues, or search until you discovered your past?

3. The Martinelli family is so different from Lily's family, and also very different to Estee's. Which family do you identify with the most? Do you think the author was deliberate in her decision to show such different family dynamics?

4. This book is set in Italy, where family is such an important part of the culture. Do you think the book would have been such a powerful read if it were set in another country, or was Italy integral to the storyline? Why?

5. Estee and Felix's relationship begins as an innocent childhood attraction, but it's clear when they meet again some years later that they are still in love. Was Felix naive to believe his family would ever accept Estee? And how did you feel when Estee turned down his proposal because she wanted to wait until he was truly free to marry her? Did you respect her decision?

6. Estee's decision to give her baby up for adoption was a very emotional part of the storyline, but very authentic given the time period. And she held so much resentment toward Felix because of this. Did you think their relationship could

succeed, given the loss they shared? Did Estee's decision to forgive Felix surprise you?

7. Lily still misses her father terribly, despite losing him many years earlier. Do you think she was finally able to move past her grief after connecting with Matthew and discovering she had a wider family on her father's side?

8. At the end of the book, we see Lily return to the Martinelli property, and to Antonio. Did her decision surprise you? If so, what other decision did you expect her to make?

9. In the epilogue, Estee sees the child she gave up for adoption. Do you think this gave her the closure she needed, and how did the scene make you feel? Do you think Estee should have searched for her in this way?

AUTHOR Q&A

Q: Why was it so important for Lily to discover her grand-mother's heritage?

A: Lily has experienced great loss in her life, with the death of her father and grandmother, so I think that family is incredibly important to her. She is determined to keep the memories of her loved ones alive, especially the memory of her father, and I think she feels she is doing this for not only herself, but her father, too.

Q: Family is a key feature in the book, and the dynamics of Antonio's family are so different to Lily's own family, and also to Estee's. Did you make a conscious decision to explore different family dynamics?

A: Yes, I did. Because Lily is an only child and lost her father when she was only a teenager, I wanted Antonio's upbringing to be the complete opposite of hers. I'm an only child, and larger families have always fascinated me, so I wanted Lily to experience a very busy, loud traditional type of family. For me, it was important for Lily to feel welcomed by Antonio's parents and siblings, and I really enjoyed exploring this kind of traditional Italian family.

With Estee, I wanted to explore an entirely different dynamic again. Both Lily and Antonio are raised in very different, but very loving families. With Estee, I wanted to show a child having to live up to family expectations, and with a mother who showed her little love or affection. This was much harder for me to write, but I felt it was important to explore.

Q: Why is family important to you? If you were Lily, would you have traveled to Italy to discover your heritage?

A: Family is incredibly important to me, and I think that I, like many others, take for granted that we know our heritage. If I were Lily, I would definitely have traveled to Italy to discover the past. I think it's so important to understand the stories of past generations, and to listen to and remember the stories of our parents and grandparents.

Q: Do you prefer writing the passages that take place in the past or the ones that take place in the present? Which story do you feel most connected with?

A: I actually love both! I love the balance of going between past and present, although if I had to choose, I'd probably have to say the past. I love going back in time and I've written historical fiction for many years.

Q: This is the first book in a series. What can readers expect from the next book, and how is each story linked?

A: The stories are linked by the connection to Hope's House. Each main character in the present day receives a small wooden box that contains a clue to her grandmother's past, that was left behind at the home for unmarried mothers and babies. Each woman goes on a journey to discover her secret heritage, which will take my readers all around the world to beautiful destinations!

The next book is *The Cuban Daughter*, which is set between London and Cuba, in both the present day and the early 1950s.

Pre-revolution Havana was truly incredible; it was a time of absolute opulence amongst the wealthy, and it was such an amazing period to write about. Readers will fall in love with Claudia in the present day, and Esmeralda in the past.

Q: Do you have a favorite character in the series?

A: My favorite character is always the character I'm currently writing! I love all my heroines, so it would be impossible to choose only one, but I must say I very much fell in love with Antonio in *The Italian Daughter*, and even more in love with Mateo in *The Cuban Daughter*!

Q: What does your writing routine look like? Do you write full-time?

A: I am so fortunate to have been writing full-time for the past nine years. It's my absolute dream job! I have a daily writing goal when I'm working on a draft of 2,000 words per day, and I'm very disciplined about achieving that target. Generally, I work school hours, as I have two children, but I'm often back at my desk at night and on the weekends. I always have a half-finished cup of tea beside my laptop and a dog at my feet while I'm writing, and I find that chocolate always cures writer's block!

Q: Who are your favorite authors, and do you have an all-time favorite book?

A: I have so many favorite authors, but if I had to pick a few, they would be Kristin Hannah, Chanel Cleeton, Sally Hepworth, Elin Hilderbrand, and Taylor Jenkins Reid. I have two all-time favorite books—*The Bronze Horseman* by Paullina Simons and *The Seven Husbands of Evelyn Hugo* by Taylor Jenkins Reid.

Q: What advice would you give to aspiring authors?

A: Just write! I think of my pre-published years as my appren-ticeship, and I truly believe that the best way to learn, to develop your own voice, to become better as a writer, is simply to write. Writing is a creative muscle—you need to write as often as possi-ble, even if it's only for fifteen minutes each day. And never, ever give up. If your dream is to be a published author, then the only way you will achieve it is by continuing to write—finish one book, and then start the next! Also, read as widely as possible in the genre you want to be published in.

ESSAY: THE IMPORTANCE OF FAMILY

Where do I come from? It's a universal question that many people ask, and although some of us are fortunate to know the answer, others struggle to obtain information about their past. The rise of ancestry websites and other tools to allow people to discover their heritage and connect with relatives have become hugely popular worldwide, as more and more people seek to discover their heritage. But what is it about discovering who we're connected to by blood that is so important?

In writing this book, I wanted to explore the concept of family, and what it means to search for answers in the quest to understand one's heritage. What lengths might a person go to discover a history they never knew existed? To seek out their wider family, even if that family is unaware of the connection? The saying "you can't choose your family" is often quoted, but even if you can't choose them, there is more often than not a desire to at least know who that family is.

Lily is similar to me in the fact she is an only child, and in writing her character, I kept asking myself how I'd feel if I discovered my grandmother had been adopted. Would I accept the secrecy of her generation, or would I want to honor her memory and seek the answers that she never had the chance to search for? To questions that she didn't even know existed? To have the opportunity to discover a larger family, which is so different to the one I was raised within? On reflection, I do believe that I would have followed the same path as Lily, to at least try to understand where I came from, to put the pieces of the puzzle together in a way that showed respect toward a loved one, while also allowing me to understand a part of my own history. It's something that I personally take for granted, knowing the history of both of my families on each side, but I am acutely aware that others aren't so fortunate.

Today, the adoption process in many parts of the world is vastly different to the way it was in the 1940s, when Estee gave up her child. For those children adopted then, they very often didn't know they were adopted—it wasn't something that was spoken about—so it's unlikely Estee's daughter (Lily's grandmother) would have been aware. During the 1940s, adoption was common, with a large number of babies given up predominantly by mothers who couldn't raise their child after losing a husband to war. After this boom in adoptions, there was a shortage in the late '40s, with newspaper articles declaring the lack of available babies for adoption in many Western countries. My research showed me that adoption was clearly much more prevalent than I'd ever imagined during that time, and I'm certain this will come as a surprise to many of my readers.

But despite the number of families adopting children back then, it was still often kept a secret. Even if a child found out later in life they'd been adopted, it was usually extremely difficult for that child to ever obtain details about their birth parents, or any other meaningful information about their heritage. In the case of Lily's grandmother, we presume that she never found out that she was adopted; or if she did, perhaps she chose to keep it a secret from her children and grandchildren because she felt ashamed? Did she not want to admit that the couple who raised her weren't biologically her parents, and even if she'd found out much later in life, would she still have chosen to keep that secret from her own children, and her granddaughter, because of the generation she was raised in? We will never know the answer to that question, however what I was able to do in this novel was to show how opinions and knowledge around adoption have changed. Lily simply had a personal choice to make: did she want to discover her heritage, or did she not? Shame and embarrassment weren't even emotions that she considered, because adoption isn't something that needs to be hidden from society any longer. That, at the very least, was a heartening realization.

Now that adoption is widely discussed and accepted in Western society, it has become more straightforward to find out information that can connect a person with their birth family. For me as a writer, I'm always trying to put myself in the shoes of someone else—how would I feel if this were me? How would I react? To what lengths would I go to understand clues left behind? And most importantly, how would I respect a loved one, and decide how to best honor their memory and my love of them? Certainly, I feel that Lily managed to do all those things with grace and courage, and she became a character I not only came to love, but one I respected.

Family and heritage are the core themes of The Lost Daughters series. It gives seven granddaughters the opportunity to discover their heritage, through information left about their grandmothers. Will they go on the journey, or are they comfortable enough in their own lives not to want to find out more? Or will they eventually become curious and decide they *do* want to seek out that information? Ultimately, I think everyone wants to know where they come from; sometimes it might be an immediate desire, other times it might happen later in life, or when family medical history becomes important. At some point, we usually ask the question: where did I come from?

In this novel, the quest to find the answer to that very question gave my character clarity about her family history, and also introduced her to a wider family she would never have otherwise known existed. It expanded her life in ways that she hadn't even considered possible. Which tells me that it is always worth asking the question, and taking every opportunity to discover more about those who came before us, to find the people to whom we are biologically linked.

A LETTER FROM SORAYA

Thank you so much for choosing to read *The Italian Daughter*. If you enjoyed the book and want to keep up to date with all my latest releases (including the next books in the series!), just sign up at the following link. Your email address will never be shared, and you can unsubscribe at any time.

sorayalane.com

I do hope you loved reading *The Italian Daughter* as much as I loved writing it, and if you did, I would be very grateful if you could write a review. I can't wait to hear your thoughts on the story, and it makes such a difference in helping new readers to discover one of my books for the very first time.

This is the first book in my Lost Daughters series, and I can't wait to share more books with you, very soon. Next up will be *The Cuban Daughter,* which will take you on a journey from London to Cuba, moving between the present day and the 1950s.

One of my favorite things is hearing from readers—you can get in touch on my Facebook page, or by joining Soraya's Reader Group on Facebook, via Goodreads or my website.

Thank you so much,
Soraya x

KEEP IN TOUCH WITH SORAYA

www.sorayalane.com

www.facebook.com/groups/sorayalanereadergroup

facebook.com/SorayaLaneAuthor

ACKNOWLEDGMENTS

First of all, I need to say a huge thank-you to my editor on this series, Laura Deacon. I pitched my idea for The Lost Daughters series to Laura via a video call one night, and I knew from that moment that we were going to work together. Laura, thank you for believing in my writing and for sharing my vision for this series; I have absolutely loved working with you and love your ongoing enthusiasm for my work.

I'd been thinking about this series for such a long time, so it's a wonderful thing to have this first book out there in the world. I wanted to write a series that transported my readers to incredible places around the globe, moving between past and present, and I can promise you that if you loved this story, you're going to be excited to read the rest in the series. My next book, *The Cuban Daughter,* will move between London and Cuba, and future books in the series will take you to Greece and France!

If you've read my books before, you'll know that I always thank a small but amazing group of people. To my agent, Laura Bradford, thank you for all you do! To my amazing writer friends—Yvonne Lindsay, Natalie Anderson and Nicola Marsh—thank you for supporting me and being there at the other end of the phone or on email whenever I need you. I would hate to be on this writing journey without you!

To my Blue Sky Book Chat ladies, thank you for having me as part of the group, and for your ongoing support. I love that we are such champions of one another's work! I would also like to thank my wonderful readers who are part of Soraya's Reader Group on Facebook, which is a private group that all of my readers are welcome to join. There is nothing more rewarding for me than to connect with you all and talk books and writing, and I very much appreciate the support you give me throughout the year.

And finally, my family. Thank you to my husband, Hamish, who has to listen to me constantly talking about characters, asking obscure questions (that he never seems surprised by!) and listening to me as I fret about things like cover art, sales and publication day. Thank you to my boys, Mac and Hunter, just for being such great kids and for always understanding when I have to hide away in my office to reach my daily word target. And last but not least, to my parents, Maureen and Craig, who always receive the very first print copy of each and every book I write before anyone else! Thank you for your constant support of my career.